ABSALOM'S DAUGHTERS

ABSALOM'S DAUGHTERS

A Novel

SUZANNE FELDMAN

HENRY HOLT AND COMPANY

NEW YORK

Henry Holt and Company, LLC
Publishers since 1866
175 Fifth Avenue
New York, New York 10010
www.henryholt.com

Henry Holt® and ⊞® are registered trademarks of
Henry Holt and Company, LLC.

Library of Congress Cataloging-in-Publication Data

Feldman, Suzanne, 1958–
    Absalom's daughters : a novel / Suzanne Feldman.
        pages cm
    ISBN 978-1-62779-453-4 (hardcover)—ISBN 978-1-62779-454-1 (electronic book)
    1. African American girls—Fiction.   2. Sisters—Fiction.   3. Racially-mixed
people—Fiction.   4. Family life—Fiction.   I. Title.
    PS3606.E38685A38 2016
    813'.6—dc23   2015029160

Our books may be purchased in bulk for promotional, educational, or
business use. Please contact your local bookseller or the Macmillan Corporate
and Premium Sales Department at (800) 221-7945, extension 5442, or
by e-mail at MacmillanSpecialMarkets@macmillan.com.

First Edition 2016

Designed by Kelly S. Too

Printed in the United States of America
1 3 5 7 9 10 8 6 4 2

To my parents

The past is never dead. It's not even past.

—William Faulkner, *Requiem for a Nun*

ABSALOM'S DAUGHTERS

CHAPTER ✦ ONE

Cassie and Lil Ma and Grandmother lived in a house at the far end of Negro Street in two rooms over the laundry that they ran in Heron-Neck. Whoever had lived there before had papered the walls of the upstairs rooms, every inch of them, with newspapers, spread-out magazine pages, and letters. One crumbling page of newspaper showed a white man with a rifle standing over an animal, which Lil Ma said was a lion, which Grandmother said was a wild animal from Africa that would eat you in one bite. Below the lion a page torn from a magazine showed a rabbit eating a head of lettuce. Underneath the rabbit the words said, *Ridding your garden of pests.* Over by the back window were pictures of ladies in beautiful dresses, all tall and slender, like Lil Ma. There were no pictures that looked like Grandmother, who was short and round. None of the ladies on the walls were colored either.

Lil Ma taught Cassie to read by showing her the words on the walls and making her say them properly. Before bed, she and Cassie would find a patch of wall and sound out the letters. There was a picture of an elephant by one of the front windows with words underneath that said, *Tuska Lives on Coney Island.* Coney

Island was a long way from Heron-Neck, Mississippi, Lil Ma said. One summer when the circus came to town, Lil Ma took Cassie down to the other end of Negro Street and across the railroad tracks to see the animals, but said Grandmother wouldn't want them to spend the nickel to see the show. They watched an elephant sway in its chains and a lion pace in a cage. Clowns sang a funny song; a monkey in a little suit danced and caught peanuts in its mouth. Music started inside the tent, and the white people went in with their ice cream cones. Cassie and Lil Ma went home, across the tracks and back to the laundry, where Grandmother was waiting with a stack of linens to be pressed.

Negro Street had houses on one side and railroad siding on the other. Instead of trees there were electric poles that had been standing beside the tracks for years without wires. Beanie Simms, who lived in the house next to the laundry, had three shoeshine chairs in front of the barbershop on the white side of town and a falling-apart truck in front of his own place. In the spring, when everyone on Negro Street planted greens, melon, and tomatoes between the electric poles, Mister Simms was the only one who didn't put up a wire fence to keep the rabbits out. The rabbits got into the other gardens anyway, but Mister Simms said they left his alone. When Cassie asked him why, he showed her a stick carved to look like the head of an animal poking out from between perfect heads of lettuce.

"It's a fox," Cassie said.

"It only look like a fox," said Mister Simms. "But th' rabbit *think* it real."

When Cassie told Grandmother about Mister Simms's fox, Grandmother said that Beanie Simms worked his soil with chicken innards before he planted, and the smell of blood was what kept the rabbits away.

Beanie Simms was sought after on account of his advice and his magic. Sometimes people would come in from other towns and wait at his door all day for him to come home from the shoeshine so they could ask him for guidance when they'd been 'witched. Because she was only six, Cassie was allowed to sit unnoticed on her own front stoop and watch as Beanie Simms dispensed special charms. All his business was transacted in front of his house in a couple of lawn chairs; Beanie Simms never let anyone inside, and Cassie learned a lot from what she heard. For example, there was a special way black folks could turn white, but it required a long trip east of town, and once you went there, you could never come back. She was so captivated by this information that she asked Grandmother about it. Grandmother gave her a hard look.

"If that's true," Grandmother said, "then why doesn't he leave town and take his hoodoo with him?"

Lil Ma was neighborly enough with Beanie Simms, but after Cassie told her story about how black folks could turn white, Lil Ma told Cassie never to sit on the front stoop while Mister Simms was out there with his eager listeners. When Cassie knew Lil Ma wasn't watching, she sat out by Beanie Simms anyway.

As for schooling, when she was seven, Cassie went to school for one whole day. Since she already knew how to read and count, the teacher let her sit in the back of the classroom with a group of older boys, who ignored her, talking in low voices about girls and money. The way they talked sounded improper, but Cassie couldn't keep herself from listening. Finally, one of the boys noticed her and said, "Ain't you the laundry girl?" When she said yes, he said, "Ain't your mama Adelaine?" The other boys snickered. The first boy said with a knowledgeable air, "You know what we call your mama? '*I'da Lain*' down with any ol' white man.'" The other boys hooted with laughter, and the teacher looked at them. The first boy leaned closer to Cassie. "So how come you ain't any lighter than your ma?"

When Cassie got home that day, Grandmother asked what she'd learned, and Cassie said, "I ain't learned nuthin'." Grandmother decided it was the last of school for her.

That same year Cassie noticed the southern Mississippi heat for the first time. On dry days the dust rose in weightless puffs when Cassie stepped her feet in it, and stayed in the air around her, sticking to her sweaty legs and to the hem of her dress, to her hands, and to the white sheets when she took them down from the lines strung in the yard behind the laundry. Dust flavored the collards and sweet potatoes Lil Ma cooked. Dust lay on the walls and collected in the creases of the papers, letters, and spread-out pages of old magazines, drifting into a thin layer over everything. On wet days, when the air was too heavy even to rain, the heat turned the distance into a white haze, and the dust became a damp grit. On those days it was impossible to run; no one went out to play.

On summer evenings, the houses on Negro Street cast shade over their own front stoops, and the maids, the oil men, and Beanie Simms would come home and sit out front until after dark. Grandmother sometimes pulled a chair out in front of the laundry's plate-glass window to peel potatoes or snap beans. Men would walk by and nod to her. Lil Ma would come out from the storefront after doing the ironing, shiny with sweat, her blouse as wet as if she'd just washed it. Other colored women would stop and talk to Lil Ma and Grandmother. Every one of these women called Lil Ma *Lainey* instead of *Adelaine*, and every time they did, Grandmother would correct them. She was unfriendly about it, as though she was the only one who knew what was proper. Eventually, the only people who stopped by were the colored women who brought the laundry from the big houses across town. None of them stayed to talk, and after two or three weeks without conversation out front, Grandmother took her chair to a shady spot out back of the laundry and snapped beans and peeled potatoes there.

One afternoon while Lil Ma was cleaning collards and Grandmother was peeling potatoes, Cassie heard Grandmother tell Lil Ma that the Negroes in Heron-Neck were the most rude of any, anywhere they had ever lived. Cassie asked, "Where did we live before?" And Lil Ma told her that she and Grandmother had been in another part of Mississippi before Cassie was born. Cassie asked if that was where Lil Ma was born, and Lil Ma told her, no, she had grown up somewhere else, and Grandmother had been born and grown up in a place even farther away. Cassie asked where those places were, and Grandmother would only say that they were farther south in Mississippi and that it only mattered where they were right now. Other children on Negro Street had aunts, uncles, cousins, and grandfathers. "Where is the rest of our family?" Cassie asked. Lil Ma got down on her knees and hugged Cassie and said this was the only family Cassie would ever need. Grandmother sliced the skins off the potatoes with short, angry strokes, and the subject didn't come up again until well after Cassie discovered her father.

Cassie's father and his real family lived on the other side of town, but not in one of the big houses. She found out about him the same summer she noticed the heat and dust. She and Lil Ma and Grandmother were walking across the hot street between Saul's Grocery and the Mobil station. Lil Ma had been saying something about rain coming on when a fat, clean-shaven white man passed them, crossing the other way. He barely glanced at the three of them, but Lil Ma, holding Cassie's hand, tightened her grip and stopped talking. Cassie said, "Who is he?" and Grandmother said, "You've got everything you're ever going to get from him." From that, and from murmurs she heard on the rare Sundays when they went to church, Cassie knew the fat white man was her father and that his name was William Forrest, and that what had happened, in order for him to be her father, had happened before she was born, when Lil Ma had been doing laundry for the oil men south of town.

After that, Cassie noticed him more often. She noticed his family. His flushed wife, Miz Helen, came to pick up the wash for the wealthy white women in town whose colored maids were too busy to do it themselves. Miz Helen loaded the cloth sacks into two faded red children's wagons and took them, rattling along the street, all the way across town and up the hill to where the big houses idled under big trees. She earned pennies this way. Her children came with her, in patched hand-me-downs. One was a boy named Henry. The other was a girl, Judith, a year older than Cassie, who had the same look as her father—as Cassie's father—and who stared over the counter at Cassie as if she saw something she recognized while Cassie folded white handkerchiefs. There was a mirror upstairs, and when Cassie was nine, she was tall enough to see herself without having to stand on a chair and see only the top half of her face. She tried to see what Judith saw. Narrow jaw. Wide-set eyes. The color Lil Ma had said was cinnamon, when Cassie was little, and Lil Ma had given her the wonderful-smelling stuff on the tip of her tongue. Cassie grimaced, thinking of the spice's dry, sweetish taste, and in the sudden twist of her mouth saw William Forrest and also saw Judith. She stared at herself and understood why Judith stared.

On Mondays, Wednesdays, and Fridays, when Miz Helen came for the laundry, Cassie couldn't take her eyes off Judith. There was a week when Judith came in every day, and the two of them would study each other. It was all Cassie could do to keep from saying something. She was never sure what that something would be, but words were about to spring out of her mouth. One Friday when Judith came in, Lil Ma took Cassie's chin between

her fingers and, as Judith watched, pulled Cassie's face around so
Cassie could see the expression on Lil Ma's face. It was different
than any she'd ever seen before, or maybe it was the same look
she had been too little to understand when William Forrest had
walked by on the street two years ago or when she'd asked Grandmother about Beanie Simms's magical destination where colored
folks could turn white. Lil Ma let go, and Cassie concentrated on
her folding until Miz Helen and her children left.

William Forrest left his family the year Cassie turned ten.

One morning in August, Judith came to pick up the laundry
without her mother. Mrs. Duckett, who cleaned for the Clements,
was there with her big son, James. Mrs. Duckett, who was in a
gossipy mood and didn't seem to mind calling Lil Ma *Adelaine*,
said, "Watch if Miz Helen show up." Miz Helen didn't.

Judith was eleven and thin. She stood outside in the heat with
her hands at her sides while James Duckett, whose mind, at seventeen, had grown no older than five or six years old, took the
heavy bags of laundry down from the counter and out to the two
faded red wagons. Cassie and Lil Ma and Grandmother and
Mrs. Duckett watched through the plate-glass window

"How she gone haul all that up the hill?" said Mrs. Duckett.

"Maybe she thinks your James'll do it," said Grandmother.

"I ain't sending my boy no place with that girl," said
Mrs. Duckett. "Let the whole town talk about her daddy 'fore
she gets to makin' up stories about my James."

James patted the bags into place and smiled his big little-boy
smile and walked back into the laundry. The screen door slapped
behind him, and the hot breath of the day followed him in.

Outside, Judith picked up the handle of one of the wagons and
then the handle of the other. She turned and pulled like a plow

mule. The wagons barely budged. She pulled again, arms stretched out behind her, eyes on the hot white concrete sidewalk. She certainly knew the faces behind the plate-glass window were watching.

Cassie stood at the screen door, feeling the heat behind it. Judith moved away, slowly, down Negro Street.

"Don't you think about going out there," said Lil Ma. "She's doing just fine."

Cassie pushed the door open and stepped into the hot, humid morning. The words she felt finally formed and came out of her mouth. "She didn't know who her daddy was gone be!"

She ran and caught up to Judith at the corner, where she was waiting for a break in the scant traffic.

"Git away," said Judith. "I don't need no help."

"I ain't here to help you."

Judith kept both hands locked around the wagon handles. Sweat ran down her neck. There were purplish circles under her eyes. Her lank brown hair looked uncombed. Her dress was a grimy pink, falling just above her knees, like she'd grown out of it too fast for the next hand-me-down to catch up. Cassie wore hand-me-downs too, but hers were freshly laundered, and Lil Ma hemmed them properly.

Judith jerked the wagons over the wooden planks of the railroad crossing and across the next road. Cassie followed her into the shade of the trees lining the old neighborhood streets. The houses had been nice once; they were shabby now and broken up into apartments. The white men who worked in the oil fields lived here. Their wives and daughters did what they could for money, and those who couldn't find work watched what went on outside from their windows. The colored maids who kept the big houses on the hill walked through this neighborhood every day. Judith and her family lived around here somewhere.

Judith stopped and wiped her face on her sleeve and held one of the wagon handles out to Cassie. "Well, it don't look right, do it?" she said and angled her head at a clapboard house with peeling paint. In one of the upstairs windows, a flowered curtain fell back into place.

"I ain't here to help you."

"Why the hail *are* you here?"

All Cassie's life there had been a laundry counter between the two of them. This close, the family resemblance seemed less clear. Cassie knew she'd be punished when she got back to the laundry, which made her less in a rush to get back. She took a wagon handle and pulled.

Each wagon was heavy enough where the street was flat. Judith could not have managed both once the road angled upward. The two of them walked along, the wagons rumbling behind. It was so hot, even the birds were quiet, and the leaves of the old plane trees hung limp.

"You wanna know where my daddy went?" said Judith.

"I guess."

"He run off with 'nother woman." Judith changed hands on the wagon handle. "Rich woman, my momma said."

"What rich woman?" said Cassie.

"No one ever said her name."

"Why a rich woman wanna run off with a oil-field man?"

"My momma said she was a hoor."

"A rich hoor?" said Cassie. The rusty wagon handle felt gritty in her fist. "I never heard of a rich hoor."

"I seen 'em dressed real nice."

"I seen 'em wearin' the same clothes all the time."

Judith wiped a damp hand on her grubby dress. "You know any? I mean personally."

"One. But I only see her in church. My mama don't mix with her."

"We got three come to our church." She aimed a thumb over her shoulder, back toward town. "I hear the Catholics got half a dozen."

Cassie laughed and then stopped herself. "Jesus prob'ly didn't laugh at the hoors."

"Prob'ly not. Here's the hill, now. Pull!"

Cassie had never been up the hill or anywhere near the mansions. The first house sat well back from the curb at the end of a driveway lined with rosebushes and azaleas. The front yard was like a forest, filled with spreading maples. The front door, which Cassie could just see through the canopy of leaves, was framed by tall columns. Pots of flowers lined the front porch. Wisteria in full bloom hung from the eaves like bolts of purple bunting.

Judith flipped through the tags on the laundry sacks until she found the one she was looking for. "Leave that wagon," she said. "Come on."

Cassie followed Judith down the cobbled driveway. The wagon rattled between the trees, and Judith slowed, concentrating on noiselessly approaching the house. The driveway split as they came out from under the trees, one part leading to a side entrance where there was a low roof. Cassie came to a stop in the split while Judith labored on, dragging the wagon along the drive to where it disappeared around the back of the house. Cassie had seen pictures like this side entrance to the house on the walls at home. The side entrance was a place made for carriages and horses. Carriages and horses and white women in silks filled Cassie's mind until she noticed that the sound of wagon wheels had stopped. She saw the white face in the window of the side door, looking right at her. Was it a man or a woman or a tall child? The face vanished, and the door jerked open. Cassie turned and ran down the drive, to the other wagon, pushed up against the curb.

Judith clattered back while Cassie waited, pulling up her wilt-ing socks. Judith hauled her wagon into the street. She had some-thing clenched in her fist. Nickels.

"Why you run off?"

"There was someone at the window."

Judith put whatever she'd been paid into the pocket of her dress. There wasn't even the clink of two coins. "You supposed to be helpin' me."

"Then you should pay me."

"I ain't payin' you nuthin'."

Cassie eyed the road ahead. It was long and steep. "Guess I'll go home."

"Your momma sent you to help me."

"My mama said you doin' just fine. She gone whup me when I get back."

"I give you three—no, two cent."

"How much you get?"

"A nickle each house."

"You had nine bags."

"MacReedys' get two."

"Three cent."

Judith pushed her hands into her hair. "Cain't," she said, and Cassie thought Judith might start to cry. "Mah daddy ain't left us nuthin'."

The next house was well out of sight of the first one, though only partway up the hill. Judith took the wagon Cassie had been pulling. Cassie waited, sweating at the curb. Even the driveway went *up*, vanishing into a forest of lilacs, oak, and hydrangea. Cassie could barely see the house. Judith returned with money in her fist. She held her palm out to Cassie, and Cassie took the hot nickel.

The transaction felt strange. "Thanks," said Cassie.

"Don't tell nobody I'm payin' a nigger girl."

"You say that again, an' I'm tellin' everybody you my sister."

Judith worked her fist around the handle of the wagon. Her mouth tightened and made a little twist at the edge, not like a smile, not like a reflection of her father. The meaning in the look wasn't something Cassie could identify.

"All right," said Judith.

This felt strange, like Judith had been waiting for Cassie to say what they were.

"You swear," said Cassie.

"I swear." Judith looked at her. "You think people can tell?"

"Only if they want to."

Judith turned to plod up the rest of the hill.

Cassie came home late in the hottest part of the afternoon through the white part of town, past Tawney's Store, past Beanie Simms's three shoeshine chairs in front of the barber shop, past Saul's Grocery, where Mister Saul would wait on white folks in the front and coloreds in the back. She crossed the tracks and made her way to the end of Negro Street, where the front door of the laundry was propped open for whatever breeze there was. Inside, Cassie pushed through the swinging gate in the laundry counter and through a second door, which opened into the tiny kitchen in the back room. An old coal stove took up half the space in the kitchen and got hot enough to warm both rooms upstairs in the winter. There was room for a table with three chairs. Two shelves for dishes and cups fit into the space under the staircase that led up to the second floor.

The kitchen was blistering: The stove burned high, lined with half a dozen irons, which Cassie would be using after supper to press shirts and trousers. Cassie wiped sweat from under her lip. She opened the back screen door into the small dirt yard. Even the heat of the evening seemed cooler than being inside.

Grandmother was pinning up the day's wash—mostly sheets. Bleached and starched, the sheets hung in tight rows. Before Grandmother clipped each sheet to the clothesline, Cassie was supposed to dampen the small dirt yard with a watering can to keep the dust from rising up to grime the clean white seams. Dampening the ground had been Cassie's job even when she was too little to do much else. Today she had forgotten to do it, so Grandmother probably had. No doubt Cassie would hear about it. Once, when she was six or seven, Beanie Simms had told her that his father had owned the shoeshine chairs before him and had told Beanie Simms when he was a boy that the business would be his one day. The thought that something might be hers when she was grown had struck Cassie—the watering can, the newspaper pictures on the walls upstairs, even the laundry itself—all of it hers. She had asked Grandmother about it, and Grandmother had taken the clothespins out of her mouth and said, "When you have your own child, we'll go away and raise it in some other place." When Cassie thought about that conversation later, she was never sure she hadn't dreamed it, but the force of Grandmother's reaction had seemed real enough.

Grandmother shaded her eyes at Cassie and pointed to a pan of yams and a bowl of green beans sitting on the back steps. There was a knife to peel the yams. Cassie sat and took the pan of yams in her lap and slid the knife under the clay-colored skin.

Grandmother sat next to her. She took up the bowl of beans.

"You shouldn't have gone off with that white girl," said Grandmother. She began snapping the beans, pulling out the tough threads. "You made your mother and me very unhappy."

A window rattled open in its sash upstairs. Lil Ma, in the heat of the second floor.

"You went with her because you think she's your sister. Did she act like your sister?"

Cassie wasn't sure what the correct answer was, but she knew what to say. "Nome."

"She never will." Grandmother broke a bean neatly in half. "You want to know where you come from. I'll tell you where you come from. From Lil Ma's blood, and Lil Ma came from my blood, and my blood came down through your great-great-grandmother, who was a slave woman named Cassandra, just like we named you." Grandmother took up another handful of beans and snapped their ends off. "Cassandra's father was a white man. He seeded the land with cotton, and he seeded his slave women, and he got him a white woman for a wife, and he seeded her too. He had two children by her, a girl and a boy. The girl died of sickness, and the boy grew up into a murdering criminal. The boy had to run from the law, but while he was running, he took after his father and seeded his way all around the state. His descendants are all around here. I'm one of them. You're one of them. That white girl is too, I'd bet, which would make her your half sister and your cousin. But no matter how twice-related you are, she's no kin to you. Kin has a feeling for how far back the blood goes." She rifled the beans, looking with her fingertips for any that had escaped with their ends on. "She'll never have that feeling for you."

Later that summer, Lil Ma sent Cassie up to the Wivells' to give Mrs. Hill a package of table linens, which had been specially pressed. At the Wivells' big fancy house, Mrs. Hill's daughter Bethel opened the kitchen door. Bethel was eleven, a year older than Cassie, and was allowed to play the organ in church. She wore black-and-white saddle shoes, which were always spotless no matter how dusty or damp the ground.

"Them the linens?" said Bethel.

Cassie handed them up. Bethel examined the package, wrapped with paper and string, but didn't open it. "My mama have to check 'em," she said.

"Check 'em for what?"

"Wait here." Bethel disappeared inside. The screen door slammed behind her.

The late August air was hot and thick. Bethel's shoes clumped away and then returned. She opened the door and came outside. "Mama's busy," she announced. "She be here presently."

They stood together on the threshold of the kitchen in the heat. Cassie's eyes wandered downward to Bethel's shoes again. "Where'd you git those?" she said.

"Mama brought 'em home."

Which meant they were castoffs from one of the little white Wivell girls.

"You like 'em?" said Bethel. She cocked her hip so one shoe stuck out farther than the other. "Mebbe you should ask your daddy t'git you a pair."

"I ain't got no daddy," said Cassie.

"You know who your daddy is."

Cassie looked past Bethel at the gleaming kitchen to show that even if she did know, she didn't care.

"My daddy got a wood shop," said Bethel. "He fix stuff for folks."

Cassie had once overheard Beanie Simms tell Lil Ma that Bethel's daddy couldn't put a broken-down, two-dollar chair back together proper.

Bethel shifted and stuck out the other shoe. "Wanna hear who I'm a'gonna marry?"

This shoe had a dent in the toe, but the dent was mostly hidden with white polish. "Who?" said Cassie.

"You know Tommy Main?"

"No."

"His daddy got ten acres o' good lumber. You know what lumber is?"

"No."

"Trees. Tommy's daddy make wagons and such. He sell 'em to the white folks. Tommy gonna take over the business one day. I'll be his wife, an' we gonna have some money. Money and ten acres of good lumber."

What would happen when all the trees were cut down? Bethel would probably consider that a stupid question. Any eleven-year-old who already knew who her husband was going to be would probably have thought that far ahead.

"I'll be Bethel Main," said Bethel.

"That sound nice," said Cassie.

Bethel pulled her dented saddle shoe back. "Who you gonna marry?"

She said it in such a mean-sounding way, Cassie had to look up from the fascinating shoes.

Bethel gave Cassie a nasty little smile. "You ain't gonna git married. Your granny gonna find you a white man an' make you have a baby with him." She waited for Cassie to say something, but Cassie was too surprised to say a word. "She made your mama do it. She gonna make you do it. She gonna find the whitest boy in town for you—ghost-white if she can. Ever'body in town know it." She took a step closer. "You think it gonna be one o' the Wivells? Or maybe Joey MacReedy—that blond-headed boy plays football?"

Cassie reached for Bethel's arm, meaning to grab her wrist, to squeeze it hard enough to hurt. Bethel yanked back, tried to turn, and fell in the dirt outside the kitchen door instead. She kicked at Cassie with the hard saddle shoes, missed, and jumped up to let fly with both fists. Cassie hit her first, in the shoulder. Bethel staggered. Cassie swung again and caught the girl's mouth with the edge of her hand, and Bethel fell hard with a split lip. Bethel touched her mouth, saw the blood, and screamed. The screen door opened, and Mrs. Hill came down on the two of them like a thundercloud. She jerked Cassie up by the yoke of her dress and shook her hard. "What's the matter with you, crazy gal? What is the *matter* with you?"

Cassie opened her mouth to say what Bethel had said, but what came out in a hot rush was *"What she said!"*

Bethel, on her feet and quivering, hand over her mouth, said, "I tol' her the truth, Mama."

Mrs. Hill let go, and Cassie jerked away. Her head felt like it was boiling and light and ready to float off into the trees. She ran down the long drive and out into the street. A breathless wind was rising from below. She ran from it, past the big rich houses, until she was at the top of the hill.

There was a sharp twist in the road, with a metal guard to keep cars from going off the edge. Cassie climbed over the metal guard and pushed her way through the weeds until she had a clear view of the river, where it bent, here and there, like the neck of a heron. Below, in the overcast afternoon, the railroad tracks paralleled the river to where it bent, then crossed the water and headed east alongside a macadam road. The tracks and the road narrowed to nothing and vanished into the forested hills in the distance. Gray clouds hung over everything.

— ✦ —

That evening, Lil Ma was waiting for Cassie downstairs in the kitchen, heating irons on the stove. "You took your time." Cassie came through the swinging door in the counter. "What happened to you?"

Cassie touched her hair, which felt wild, and her dirty clothes. "Nothing."

"Mrs. Hill was by. She said you hit Bethel in the mouth. I didn't believe her."

There was no denying it. "I hit her."

Lil Ma rearranged the irons. Her hair had gone frizzy in the humidity, but her dress, her shapely arms and legs were like the pictures of the ladies on the walls upstairs. Behind her, half a dozen bridesmaids' dresses, pressed to perfection, were on hangers over the back door like a dark purple curtain, as though Lil Ma was on a stage. "I told her I didn't raise my girl to be violent."

"I *did* hit her," said Cassie, "because of what she said about us."

"People say all kinds of things," said Lil Ma. "You can't live your life by what comes out of ignorant mouths." Her tone was cool in the hot room, level, like the irons on the stove. Everything Bethel had said, Cassie now understood, Lil Ma had heard before.

Upstairs the floor creaked under Grandmother's feet. Lil Ma moved two of the dresses, unblocking the door to the backyard. "You look tired," she said, "and it's awfully hot in here. Why don't you go out and sit for a while?"

"Yessum," said Cassie. She slipped past Lil Ma, past the rustling purple curtain of bridesmaids' dresses, through the door, and into the dusk.

She sat where she could hear what was being said inside and not be seen from the door. "I thought I heard Cassie," said Grandmother. "She's not home yet," said Lil Ma. "I heard another voice," said Grandmother. "You must have been dreaming," said Lil Ma.

Grandmother's footsteps creaked across the floor and back up the stairs. Cassie listened to the hissing of the irons as Lil Ma worked. She looked at the stars and the thin sliver of moon. The back door opened, and Lil Ma stepped out into the narrow frame of light that fell across the back steps. She sat next to Cassie.

"What did Bethel say?"

"She said that you . . . and Grandmother . . . and I was supposed to . . ." She couldn't bring herself to say anything more.

Lil Ma ran the hem of her apron back and forth through her fingers. She looked up at the second-floor window where Grandmother had been and lowered her voice to a whisper. "It's true."

"It isn't."

"Now listen to me. Your great-great-grandmother Cassandra saw how the lightest of the mixed children could escape. She made a plan to take whiteness, bit by bit from the white man." Lil Ma gripped her apron. "Not every daughter could keep to the plan. Your grandmother couldn't. She fell in love with a very dark man."

"Who was he?"

"I never knew him. Your grandmother left that part of Mississippi before I was born, and she told me my daddy was dead. Maybe he is. Maybe if she'd thought about what she was doing, she would have fought harder against her feelings. But here we are."

Lil Ma looked into the dark. A wind rattled the empty clotheslines against their metal poles. "What Bethel said to you, I've been hearing all my life. I would have said, 'You'll understand one day.' But I don't understand it. Things change. Just because someone keeps insisting on something doesn't mean it's the right thing." She wrapped her hands in her apron, so tightly Cassie thought the fabric might tear. "I won't let it happen to you."

There was some comfort in that.

CHAPTER ✦ TWO

Afterward, Cassie avoided Bethel, and Bethel stayed away. What were people in town thinking about Cassie and her family? After a while that question was like a dull ache. The subject of Cassie's prospects didn't come up again for quite a while. In the meantime, Beanie Simms went from carving fox heads to stick in his garden to human heads, which Lil Ma called *hoodoo* and Grandmother called *hokum*, but the new heads were just as effective as the old ones at scaring off rabbits. The circus came and went four more times, and Cassie actually got to see a magician make a woman disappear inside a cabinet while doves flew out of a hat. That was the only truly magical thing that happened until Cassie was fifteen and Judith was sixteen; that was when the albino boy came to town. His magic wasn't the good kind.

It was only late summer, but Miss Helen claimed Henry was too sickly to work and too frail to leave the house by himself. Usually, Henry was sick in the fall when the rains began, but now Judith almost always came to pick up the laundry alone.

"What's Henry do all day?" Cassie asked, on the way up the hill with the wagons.

"He lissen to the music on the reddio," said Judith. "What you-all lissen to?"

"We ain't got a reddio." It was a luxury to let her tongue be lazy, as Grandmother would have said. To speak poorly let her feel like she was someone else sometimes.

Judith opened one arm to the morning air. "Ever'body got a reddio. Even us, and we ain't got nuthin'."

"Well, we don't."

"Your granny afraid you gone hear somethin'?"

"My mother sings."

"I heard her singin' out in back. She got a pretty voice. When you need music, y'all sing?"

"Guess so."

Judith leaned against the weight of the wagon. "Even Duncan Justice and his boys got a reddio. They got one in some ol' junk car. They sit out at night list'nin' to the New York station."

Duncan Justice and his sons lived in a disintegrating house, which Cassie had never personally seen, on ten or fifteen acres just outside Heron-Neck. In his backyard, there was supposed to be a stone memorial to the Southern War Dead. Beanie Simms had told Lil Ma that Justice held a service for dead white folks every Sunday afternoon and was, besides that, a Ku Kluxer. Cassie wondered how Judith knew what the Justice boys did at night. "What's on a New York station?"

"Colored music," said Judith.

"Duncan *Justice*'s boys are listnin' to *colored* music from *New York*?"

"Maybe not them," said Judith, "but I know someone who does."

"Who?" Cassie wiped her face.

Judith stopped. "The al-biner does."

They were halfway up the hill, across from Wivells' long

driveway. Ancient maples shaded the middle of the street, but dust hung in the humid air, thick enough to choke on. "The what?" said Cassie.

"The al-biner. Over at Wivells'. He their cousin or somethin' from up North." She leaned closer and whispered. "He got *pink eyes*. Like some kinda ghost."

"The Wivells ain't got no pink-eyed ghost livin' there."

"He ain't no ghost. He's alive as you an' me. He told me 'bout the New York music. He goes out with the Justice boys to lissen to it. He got records, too. He played 'em for me so's I kin sing 'em. You want to hear?"

Cassie pushed her wagon against the curb. The fact was, Judith always sounded like she had a terrible sore throat or was just getting over one. Mrs. Duckett said Judith Forrest sounded just like a jaybird when she talked. Cassie thought what Mrs. Duckett said was true; she didn't know exactly what to say right now.

Judith let go of the wagon handle and put her hands on her skinny hips. "Don't you think I kin sing?"

"I guess you *kin* if you say so."

"Don't you make fun of the way I talk."

"I ain't sayin nuthin' about you."

"The al-biner says I could be a reddio star."

"Well, I guess you better show me."

Judith closed her eyes and clenched her hands together, swayed to music she was listening to inside her own head, and began to sing. To Cassie's surprise, the hoarseness in Judith's voice turned husky; the sound coming out of her mouth seemed to be coming from someone older than sixteen. The song was about walking out on *youuu*.

In what seemed like the middle of the song, Judith opened her eyes and stopped. "The al-biner say I sing good enough to make money at it."

"I guess he knows," said Cassie, impressed.

"I guess he does," said Judith, without a trace of modesty.

Judith knocked on the Wivells' kitchen door. Bethel answered. There was no avoiding Bethel, but Cassie hadn't spoken more than two words to her since that time five years before when she'd split Bethel's lip. Bethel hadn't spoken much to Cassie either.

"Well?" Bethel said.

"Well what?" said Judith. "We come to d'liver the laundry. Where's your momma?"

"She's here, but she ain't feelin' well." Bethel moved to one side so they could see Mrs. Hill, hunched at the kitchen table, polishing the silver. The chemical smell of polish filled the room. "I'm helping today."

"Mornin', Mrs. Hill," said Judith.

"Let the girls in," said Mrs. Hill. "You ain't gone carry that laundry by yourself."

"Where you want this, Mrs. Hill?" said Cassie.

"Be helpful if you'd drag it to the laundry room upstairs. But mind the boy."

"The al-biner boy?" said Judith.

"Crazy boy," said Bethel.

"I don't know how crazy he is," said Mrs. Hill, "but he got some music up there ain't no one else should hear."

Bethel led them to the narrow back stairs that smelled of coffee and silver polish and left them to wrestle the laundry up to the second floor. Cassie took the top end and Judith grappled with the bottom. The bag was a dead weight. They made it to the high polish of the second floor and collapsed in the doorway, panting. In the breathy silence, Cassie heard someone singing from the back part of the house where the upstairs hallway made a turn toward the bedrooms.

"That's his *phonograph*," said Judith in the exact same tone that she'd used to tell Cassie about the *pink eyes*. She picked herself up. Cassie thought Judith might walk right on down the hall, leaving the laundry and Cassie behind.

"Wait," said Cassie.

Judith turned back, lips parted and damp.

"We got things to do first," said Cassie.

The two of them dragged the laundry into the room Mrs. Hill used for ironing. The black sounds coming out of the white end of the house were harder to hear; they were a vibration through the floorboards.

Judith brushed her hands across her dress. "You wanna see what he look like?"

"That boy?"

Judith was breathless, but not from dragging the laundry up the stairs. She took a step toward the door. "Come on," she said.

Outside the door, the wood of the upstairs hallway gleamed forbiddingly. The music wasn't any louder, but Cassie could feel it, and its dancing rhythms, through her shoes. "What if Mrs. Hill sees us?"

"Mrs. Hill ain't comin' up them stairs."

"What about Bethel?"

"Bethel scared of the al-biner."

"Ain't you?"

"He ain't no ghost."

"Then why he look like one?"

"*You* scared?"

"I ain't."

"Well, then," said Judith. "Well, then."

They tiptoed down the hall until they came to the albino boy's open bedroom door and peered in. The afternoon sun filled his window, framing him from behind as he sat on the bed, tall and pale, his white hair bright as a halo. Music rose from a phonograph on his nightstand. Records lay on the bed, in and out of their jackets.

Judith stepped into full view. "Hi," she said.

"Hi," the boy said and looked right at Cassie with his pink eyes. "You're the other laundry girl."

Cassie saw what he was. There was a newspaper photo of a white tiger on the papered wall at home. *Not a true albino, as the cat's eyes are not pink, but still a pet worthy of the royal Hindu Raj.* Cassie wasn't sure what a Hindu was or a Raj, but she understood pink eyes, and this white-haired, ghost-white boy had them. He was the whitest white boy she had ever seen. She thought of Lil Ma, and she thought of Grandmother, and then she thought of herself. Her whole body went cold.

Judith walked right over to the phonograph. "What you playin'?"

"A record," said the albino boy.

"You only lissen to colored music?" said Judith.

The albino boy shifted on the bed. There was a glisten of boyish beard under his lower lip. "What about you?" he said to Cassie.

Out his window, the leaves on the trees moved in the slightest of breezes. Inside, the highly polished floor smelled overwhelmingly of wax. "We ain't got no radio," said Cassie.

"You poor?"

"No, suh, we jes' ain't got one."

"I tol' her about the reddio in that ol' car," said Judith.

"Come by some time and listen," said the albino boy. "Sometimes we have a little drink out there."

On the way home, Judith told Cassie the albino boy's name was Jack, that he was an orphan now that his parents had been killed in a car wreck, and that he had fifty, no, a hundred records, in New York City, where he was from.

Word about the albino boy was all around town. That night, while Lil Ma poured cornmeal into a bowl to make bread, Grandmother quizzed Cassie about him.

"I heard he came down from New York City," said Grandmother, as Cassie folded handkerchiefs in the light of the kerosene lantern. "Mrs. Hill says his parents died in a car crash."

"Train wreck," said Lil Ma, "wasn't it a train wreck?"

"Judith said it was their car," said Cassie.

"Did she say anything about his music?" said Lil Ma.

"She couldn't believe those white folks let him play it."

"Race music," said Lil Ma. "Somebody done made a record of what gets played in a juke joint."

"Did you remember to put salt in that mess, Adelaine?" said Grandmother.

"Yes, ma'am," said Lil Ma.

"Don't forget the milk," said Grandmother.

"I can't forget the milk. It won't pull together without milk."

Cassie finished her stack of hankies and started on another. "Why's it called race music?"

"Uncultured Negroes came up with it," said Grandmother. "It makes people act like animals."

"Makes 'em dance," said Lil Ma. She waved the mixing spoon over her head, hands spread like the women did in church, but there was more to it. More hip and shoulder. "Makes 'em sing."

She took the milk bottle out of the icebox and turned it to pour, but Grandmother said, "Warm it. You'll kill the yeast."

"We won't eat for another hour if I yeast this bread," said Lil Ma. "I'll just put it in the skillet."

"If the bread needs to rise, the bread needs to rise," said Grandmother. "We won't be common, frying it till it's black at the edges. This albino boy," she said to Cassie. "Mrs. Hill says he's paper white and white hair."

"Eyebrows too," Cassie said.

Lil Ma poured the milk into a small pan. Drops spilled over the side of the pan and burned on the hot stove. Instantly, the small kitchen smelled of scorched milk. "Doesn't sound too healthy," said Lil Ma. "Even really white white folks have color to them."

"I think Judith likes him," Cassie said, and in that moment of vague speculation, realized she was right. "She can't stop talking about him. She sings what she hears him play on the phonograph. She says he goes out to Duncan Justice's at night and listens to New York music in some old car."

Lil Ma wet a rag to wipe up the milk. "You stay *away* from Duncan Justice and his boys."

The thought of going out to the car party hadn't occurred to Cassie. She looked at Lil Ma, but Grandmother's eyes caught her attention first. They glittered in the kerosene lamplight, calculating and narrow.

Miz Tabitha Bromley died that year, Christmas Day 1954, one month after Cassie turned sixteen. Miz Tabitha had been married to the late Elmer Tawney, who'd run Tawney's Store on the south end of Market Street in Heron-Neck ever since he'd come back, one-legged, from the Great War. Miz Tabitha had never changed her last name. That and the fact that Elmer had left her the store against his family's wishes made the fate of Tawney's Store a subject of widespread speculation at the time of Miz

Tabitha's death. It was no surprise when Elmer's relatives got themselves a lawyer from up in Tennessee and announced that there would be an estate sale—not just the merchandise in the store, but every single thing left on the old Tawney plantation.

Since Miz Tabitha had sold out the front door to whites and out the back door to coloreds, on the day of her funeral, folks on both sides of the tracks were taking down the holiday decorations they'd bought from her at Tawney's Store. When the *Thompson County Weekly* announced that the estate sale would be held the next Saturday in February and would be open to all, white and colored, Grandmother marked the date on the OXYDOL DETER-GENT calendar that hung on the wall behind the laundry counter. "Miz Tabitha had a new wringer," she said.

"They'll want too much for it," said Lil Ma, ironing on the board set up beside the stove.

"They won't want it the same way they didn't want her," said Grandmother.

Cassie sat by the window where the light was best, even though rain was pouring down outside. She was scrubbing a red wine stain out of Armenia Sutter's wedding gown. Armenia's first cousin was getting married, and the wedding gown would be hers. The wedding was in three weeks, but Armenia wanted the dress back *tomorrow*. In the summer, Cassie would have used vinegar and salt, spread the dress out on the roof in the relentless Mississippi sun, and waited for the elements of nature and the kitchen to do their work. In February, weakened bleach would have to do the job.

"You'll ruin the fabric, scraping at it like that." Grandmother dipped her fingers right into the bleach water and dabbed at the fading stain. "Rub a little at a time. You can't scratch at it till it's gone."

Lil Ma came out from the kitchen with a basket of freshly ironed shirts. "Why does that woman want it so quick?"

"Her cousin's gettin' married," said Cassie. "Miz Sutter givin' it to her as a engagement present."

"If you're going to gossip," said Grandmother, "at least speak properly."

"And how would you know what kind of wedding plans white folks have?" said Lil Ma.

At that moment, Judith ran past the front window with a scarf over her head and a patched red coat. She flung open the laundry door and pulled the soaked scarf off her head with arms so lanky and long that it almost looked like a magic trick. "Rainin' like all *hail* out theah!"

"Close that door tight," said Grandmother. "You know better than to use that language."

Judith flushed as red as her coat and shut the door.

"How's Henry?" asked Lil Ma.

"He sick, ma'am," said Judith. "He ain't never been truly well since the weather turned. My momma say he coughin' too much to be runnin' round out in the cold."

"Go in back and get dry." Lil Ma opened the swinging door in the counter, and Judith passed into the heat of the kitchen. "The stove's hot. Make yourself some tea."

"Yessum," said Judith. "Thanks, ma'am."

When Judith was out of sight, Grandmother said to Lil Ma in a low voice, "That girl should not be *living* here."

"She's been wearing the same clothes for days," said Lil Ma.

"I wonder why," said Grandmother, without a hint of a question in her voice. "She's got her own people, Adelaine."

Lil Ma took a breath and said in a tone sharper than any Cassie had ever heard her use with Grandmother. "This is a test from the Lord. And it isn't just a test for *me*."

Cassie's fingers stopped above the bleach water. Grandmother whirled around and pointed at Armenia Sutter's wedding dress.

"You get that stain *out*. Don't you go back there with that white girl until it's done."

Cassie opened her mouth to say *yessum*. No sound came out. Grandmother turned around again, but Lil Ma was taking down her coat and scarf from the hook behind the counter. She tied the scarf under her chin without looking at Grandmother. Her hands were shaking.

"We're out of onions," Lil Ma said. She fastened the buttons on her coat and went out into the rain.

The door slammed behind her. Grandmother picked up a bag of laundry, dumped it on the table, and began dividing it into lights and darks.

Cassie dipped her fingers in the bleach water and rubbed the stain. She could sense Judith in the kitchen moving as quietly as possible, pouring hot water for tea. After a while, Judith seemed to be still, probably sitting at the table. Soon she would put her head down and sleep. Grandmother seemed to be listening too. It was quiet in the kitchen when she finished sorting and came over to examine the stain on the wedding dress.

"Better," she said, "but not done."

"Yessum." Cassie kept her eyes down, dabbing at the stain.

"She's pregnant, you know," said Grandmother. "That white girl."

"I didn't know," said Cassie.

"It's hard at that age," Grandmother said. "To keep it from happening. There's a feeling she got, and she couldn't fight it. All girls get that feeling. It's as strong as it is in boys, though people try to pretend it isn't."

Cassie thought of Judith's face, her parted lips, when they'd gone upstairs at the Wivells' and the albino had been playing music, which they could both feel as a vibration through the floor.

"I felt it at your age." Grandmother dipped her fingers in the bleach water. "It's strong in our family, especially in the women. Have you had that feeling?" asked Grandmother. "Have you felt it around the boys?"

The only boy she'd been around lately was the albino boy.

Grandmother took Cassie's chin, turned it toward her, and put both hands on Cassie's cheeks. "You feel it here first. In your face. A heat that comes from deep underneath your skin. Have you felt it?"

"Nome," whispered Cassie.

"You will," said Grandmother, "and soon. Then the heat comes down here." She touched Cassie's chest, over her heart. "And then lower. And that's when that little white girl quit fighting it."

Cassie's cheeks felt flushed. Her chest felt tight and strange. "I'll fight it," she whispered.

"You can certainly try." Grandmother took her hands away. "I'll be upstairs," she said. "Don't disturb me."

Grandmother walked through the small kitchen, past Judith. Cassie heard Grandmother's footsteps on the stairs. The bed creaked as Grandmother lay down. Cassie watched the street outside, waiting for Lil Ma to come back, but the rain stopped instead. When she was sure the wine stain in the wedding dress was less than a shadow, she went into the kitchen. Judith was asleep with her head down on the table, her breathing a quiet, raw snore. If she'd made herself a cup of tea, she'd finished it, washed the cup, dried it, and put it back on its shelf.

"Judith," said Cassie.

Judith sat up. "Laundry," she croaked. "I d'livered it."

"Not yet. It just stopped raining."

Judith rubbed her eyes. "I was dreamin' I had it done." She peered through the kitchen door at the empty front room.

"Grandmother's upstairs. Lil Ma went to get onions."

Judith took something metallic and golden out of her dress pocket. "Look what he give me."

It was a tube of lipstick. "Who gave you that? That albino boy?"

"Mm-hm." Judith took the top off and twisted the tube. A blunt stick of bright red came out. Cassie had seen the women in church use lipstick. Lil Ma didn't own any. Neither did Grandmother. Grandmother said the stuff was *lascivious*. But Cassie liked the way lipstick looked when it twisted up out of golden cases, always with that sharp, tapered point, always thickly colored, like summer fruit. She had seen enough new lipstick to know that Judith's had been someone else's.

"When he give you that?" Cassie sat in the chair across the table from Judith.

"Yestiddy. I ain't even used it yet. Savin' it for tonight. We got a *date*."

"Your momma kick you outta the house?"

Judith let out a tense laugh. "Why you askin' me about that?"

Cassie wanted to ask about the *feeling* and *heat*. She put her hands in her lap instead. "Grandmother says you pregnant."

"I ain't stupid. You know what we do when we're together?"

Cassie wanted to touch the lipstick case, to feel its smooth golden sheen. "What?"

"We sit in the woods in the car and lissen to the New York reddio station. He goes on and on and on about who singin' what song and when it was recorded and all that kinda junk."

"That's all?"

"Mostly that's all."

Cassie lowered her voice. "Grandmother was sayin' to me . . . I mean . . . do you ever feel . . . like a heat?"

"Heat?" said Judith. "Sure. Them boys *want* you to feel that. They say, 'Honey, you *hot*.'" Judith leaned back with an expert air. "But you cain't jus' drop your panties ever' time they say it, or ever' time you feel a little somethin'. *That's* how a girl kin git kicked out." She gave Cassie a sly grin. "Now if you're *progeny*, it's a different thing. It don't matter if you git kicked out."

"What's progeny?"

"It's what you are when someone you related to dies and you in-herit. And once you got some money, you find your own place."

"*Progeny*." It wasn't like Judith to come up with complicated new words.

"I'm progeny," said Judith.

"How you figure that?"

Judith took a folded envelope out of her pocket and put it on the table. It was addressed to *Mrs. William Forrest*. "This came in the mail," said Judith. "At home we read it the best we could, but I brought it 'cause you read better. It's all about progeny." She opened the envelope and spread out the letter. The paper was thick, the color of cream; the handwriting tight and exact. It was stamped in the top right corner with *The Veranda Hotel* in fancy script.

"Read it out loud," said Judith.

> *Dear Mrs. Forrest:*
>
> *First, let me introduce myself. I am a woman of advanced years who is a distant relative (by marriage) of your family and a friend, in some respects, of your wayward husband, William Forrest. Your Mister Forrest is alive and well here in Remington, Virginia. Though he has spoken of you infrequently, I feel I know you and your family, and as you will see from this letter, I have the greatest sympathy for your situation.*

"He's in Virginia?"

"Keep going," said Judith.

> *Lately there has been a death in the family, which has brought the division of the Forrest estate—the mansion, the furniture,*

the land—into question. It is a lengthy process and I do not trust
the lawyers, so I have situated myself here, in the Veranda Hotel,
in hopes of getting my due. Unfortunately, so has every relative for
miles, some with tenuous ties to the family, at best.

My own husband deserted me, much like yours deserted you,
when I was younger and helpless. Although I am lucky enough to
be able to sustain myself by my own small means, it is clear that
your husband is able to support himself only from the odd jobs he
took to get this far from home. I was unable to hold my former
husband accountable to my family, so I am writing this letter to
make sure you can hold your William to the responsibilities of his.
You and your children are inheritors of what ancestral wealth is
left here in the state of Virginia. I know that your husband has no
intention of returning to you or sharing with you any of the assets
that remain. It would behoove you and your progeny to make your
way northward to claim your share before March twenty-first
when the estate will be settled.

I hope that this letter finds you in time.

Yours most sincerely,
Eula Bonhomme-Forrest

Judith had been playing with the lipstick. Now she took the
letter back and smoothed the creamy paper out on the rough
tabletop.

"Do you understand it?" she said.

"Your daddy"—Cassie decided not to say *our daddy*—"he's
stayin' in a hotel in Virginia with an old lady who related to him
by marriage."

"When she says 'the estate,' she's talking about the mansion,
the furniture, and the land. Ain't she?"

Cassie read the paragraph again, to herself. The room was so warm that the paper seemed to have its own aroma, like perfume, lifting off of it. "Looks like it."

"Someone died, so they have to sell everything off. Like Tawney's."

"If it's like Tawney's, all they'll have is leftover junk the rest of the relatives didn't get a chance to steal."

"She says they got *wealth*." Judith pointed right to the word Cassie had been certain she couldn't read.

"You want to go to Virginia?"

"Why not?"

"Virginia's a thousand miles from here. How you gone get there by March twenty-first?" Cassie got out of her chair, went over to the OXYDOL calendar, and flipped the page to March. "That's just a month away. Even if you started walking right now, it'd take more'n that to get there."

"We'll find a way," said Judith. She folded the letter up again and put it in her pocket. She capped the lipstick and pushed it in as well.

"*We* will?"

"Yeah," said Judith, "You're progeny too."

The albino boy wasn't at the Wivells' that Friday afternoon and never appeared at his window, no matter how many longing glances Judith cast over her shoulder as she and Cassie rumbled the wagons down the soaked cobbles. Well into the evening, at the bottom of the hill, Judith announced that she had to get ready for her date and skipped away, rattling the two empty wagons behind her, just as it started to rain again.

That night, Cassie twisted in her narrow bed in the upstairs front room, listening to the midwinter wind rush though the bare

February treetops. Not a cold wind, never really *cold*, but carrying the distinct sound of more rain.

Grandmother and Lil Ma snored together in the bed on the other side of the room.

Cassie turned over toward the window, where the moon was edging up from the windowsill, making its way through bare branches and clouds. She thought about Judith and the letter from Virginia, Judith singing along with colored music on the radio, Judith out in the woods where the albino boy might be kissing her on lips covered with color from the secondhand lipstick. The wind and the moon and whatever Judith might be doing made her think about the open windows in summer. Through the windows on a summer night, she could hear the older boys and girls running down the dark street in pairs. At the end of Negro Street, the road dwindled into a footpath, which disappeared into the woods and then into the reeds at the edge of the Heron River. Whatever was done in secret there came out as gossip later. Cassie had heard plenty of it from James's mother, who didn't mind calling her Lil Ma *Adelaine* instead of *I'da lain down with any ol' white man.*

The ceramic jug filled with drinking water was outside on the back step. If she had a drink of cool water, she'd be able to sleep.

Downstairs, outside, Cassie huddled in her nightshirt and drank from the cold metal dipper. She had no illusions about what Grandmother, Lil Ma, or anyone else thought of Judith: Judith was sneaky, wild, dirty. Had Judith told Cassie the truth about not being pregnant? Judith could not possibly be leaving for Virginia. Judith would eventually come to no good, but no good didn't have to come tonight.

Cassie went back inside and into the front room of the laundry, where Grandmother's and Lil Ma's coats hung on hooks behind the counter. Cassie's coat and shoes were still wet from the day's delivery. She took down Lil Ma's coat and slid into it. She put on Lil Ma's new, hard-soled shoes, the leather ones that Grandmother said would last as long as a workman's brogans. They were heavy and cold on her bare feet. She went out the front door, closing it quietly behind her, and stood in the empty street. The damp air was cool and wakeful and reminded her that she had no clear idea what she wanted to do next. She glanced up at the second-floor window and saw a motion, like a shadow in a dream. It was Grandmother's short, round shape, framed by the sill, lit by the sliver moon, watching. Cassie turned and ran up Negro Street. The shape in the upstairs window made no move to stop her.

Cassie knew in a general way where the car, the radio, and Judith were supposed to be. At the other end of Negro Street, the road would take her on the laundry route if she went right, or out to the southern edge of town and Duncan Justice's land if she went left. She had never gone the south way before. She stayed close to the trees as she hurried along the edge of the road. If a car came along, she told herself she would jump into the bushes and roll into the leaves to hide. No one would see her. None of the terrible things that she'd heard happened to colored girls running around alone at night would happen to her. She was afraid, though, that they were happening to Judith.

Farther on, she saw the leafless black trees lit from behind and some distance from the road, deeper in the woods, a bonfire. She stepped off the wet macadam and into the weeds and thought immediately of snakes. She stood, listening for the rustle of legless creatures and heard, instead, music, rough and thick with static from the radio in the car.

She tried, from where she was standing, to tell who was back there in the woods. Judith's laugh was louder than the other voices. At least three other people were talking, all of them boys. Cassie moved toward the fire. When she got close enough to see her own shadow, she hunkered down behind a sticker bush.

Judith and the albino boy sat close together on a wooden crate under the trees beside the fire. Two of Duncan Justice's sons, the older boys, were poking around under the hood of an ancient, junk-looking car. The third son, who looked to be about nine, sat a little ways off under a tree with a spotted dog.

Judith and the albino poured brown moonshine into paper cups. The two Justice boys clanked tools against the engine, working by firelight. Behind the bush, Cassie shifted for a better view, and the dog pricked its ears and stood. The little boy, who had been staring up at the night sky, put his hand on the dog's back and got to his feet. There was a rope running from his wrist to the tree. Cassie thought it was a rope for the dog at first and that the dog had wound itself around the trunk, and that if she were to run away right now, it would take too long for them to unwind the dog to set it on her. She held still and held her breath, and the dog lay back down. The boy sat too, and that was when Cassie made out that it wasn't the dog that was tied to the tree, but the boy.

"Woof!" said the boy. "Woo, woo, *woof!*"

"Woof!" echoed the dog.

"Shut the hell *up!*" shouted one of the Justice boys from underneath the car hood.

The boy let out a whine and hunkered down. His dog licked his face.

"*You're listening to Radio WINS,*" said the radio. One of the Justice boys extricated himself from the engine, oily-black to his elbows, and slid into the driver's seat. The radio stuttered as he worked the ignition, and to Cassie's amazement, the engine turned over.

Judith and the albino boy cheered. The other Justice boy

slammed down the hood and jumped into the passenger seat. The
brother behind the wheel gunned the engine, and the car wrenched
loose from the dirt. It lurched around the clearing, on rims without tires. The boy who was driving swerved close to Judith and
the albino boy and opened the door on his side to knock them
off the crate. Judith screamed with laughter as her paper cup went
flying.

The car careened to a stop. "Get in, get in!" shouted the boys.
". . . *here's Muddy 'Mississippi' Waters,*" said the radio.

Judith and the albino boy got into the backseat and handed
around the bottle of moonshine while the Justice boys searched
for another radio station. There was static, then news, then static
again, then music.

The Justice boys gunned the car in a circle, kicking up twigs
and clods of dirt until the engine backfired deafeningly and
stalled. The radio went quiet. The albino boy handed them the
bottle, and the boys swigged the stuff down and got out of the car.

"Damn," said the boy who'd been driving. He kicked the dirty
metal rims. "Shoulda drove it into the fire." He kicked at the edge
of the fire. His brother, who was shorter, and who Cassie assumed
was younger, gave the car a drunken shove, but it was rooted and
didn't budge.

"Let's go," said the oldest Justice boy.

"You ain't leavin'," said Judith, still in the backseat. "You
leavin'?"

"I got some old tires," said the oldest. "I'll bring 'em down and
put 'em on. We'll fill it up with gas, and it'll burn real nice." He
went over to the boy and the dog by the tree and untied the rope.

"You ever seen a car catch fire with tires on it?" said the younger
Justice boy to the albino. "Like big torches." He made motions
with his hands, like fire reaching upward. "Then the gasoline goes,
and then the whole damn thing, *bang-o!*"

"My parents died in a car wreck," said the albino boy. "They burned up just like that. You should apologize for making me think about it."

"Did you see it?" said the younger. "Did the tires catch fire?"

The oldest Justice boy came over with the littlest boy and the dog in tow. "Ain't no body apologizin' to you," he said. " 'Cause you're a fuckin' freak." He turned unsteadily to Judith. "Why you hangin' round with this fuckin' freak?"

"Shut up," said Judith. "You got a brother thinks he's dog."

"You callin' me a freak?" said the oldest boy.

"I'm callin' you a *idjit*," said Judith. "Go home if you leavin'."

"You cain't tell us to leave," said the oldest. "This here's our land." But he grabbed his younger brother by the arm and led him, the little boy, and the dog into the darkness of the woods, more or less in the direction of Duncan Justice's house.

Judith watched them go, then pushed the albino boy out of the backseat. "Find that New York station." The albino boy fumbled under the dashboard until the radio came back on, but not the engine. First it was static, and then it was the New York station. Judith climbed out of the backseat and sat on the hood of the car with the bottle of moonshine.

"I used to listen to WINS when I lived in Manhattan," said the albino boy from the front seat. "I've got records of all their music. We can listen to them tomorrow when you come over."

"Maybe I ain't comin' tomorrow," said Judith. The fire was beginning to die, and she waved smoke away from her face.

"You and that nigger girl always come on Wednesday."

"I might take this here car and just drive myself away."

The albino boy laughed.

"I been thinkin' a lot lately." Judith took another drink. "I been thinkin', why should I stay here? If my daddy left for something better, why should I stay?"

The albino boy reached around the windshield, took the bottle from her, and took a swig himself. "I thought you said your dad ran off with a *hoor*."

"But he got some money somehow. He stayin' in a nice hotel. I don' see why I should stay d'liverin' laundry when something better's out there."

The albino boy laughed again, like she was making a joke. "Hey," he said, "is it true that nigger girl's your sister?"

Judith sat up on the car hood. In the bushes, Cassie tucked down deeper into the leaves and thorns.

"Who tol' you that?" said Judith.

"My aunt said your dad is—what's her name again? He's her dad too."

"Most ever'body in town's related one way or the other," said Judith. "Some people opens their mouth about it. Others don't."

The albino boy put his feet up on the dashboard. "My aunt said that nigger girl's grandmother made her mother sleep with a white man. That true?"

"People say all kinda things," said Judith. "They got nothing better to do with their time."

The albino boy said in a strange, soft voice, "You ever do that?"

"Run my mouth?"

"No," said the albino boy, in the same voice as before. "You ever do it with nigger boys?"

Judith took the bottle from him and drank a big mouthful. Then she slid off the hood of the car and stood up straight, as though the alcohol had evaporated right out of her. "I'm goin' home," she said. She put the bottle down by the dying fire. "It's late and all."

The albino boy sat up in the car again. The radio faded into static. "Wait," he said.

Judith walked away through the leaves and sticks and woods

and hidden snakes. She threw him a look over her shoulder. "You know your way home? It's just up that hill yonder."

"Wait!" he said, leaning out of the car.

Judith stopped by the bush where Cassie was hiding. Instead of turning back, she leaned down and said, as though she'd known Cassie was there the whole time, "I din't tell him *none* of those damn things."

The two of them walked through the trees and out onto the macadam road. The moon was up higher, a thumbnail curve in the eastern sky.

Cassie watched her own feet move in her hard-soled shoes. "Why'd you tell him you might not be there tomorrow?"

"Cause I ain't."

"You gone walk to Virginia?"

"No," said Judith. "I'm gonna take that piece of junk back there and leave 'fore they set it on fire. I'm goin' to Virginia to get my due, and then I'm goin' to New York City to become a reddio star. I ain't goin' 'lone neither."

The black macadam gleamed dully under the moon as they walked. Judith came over closer to Cassie. "What you gonna do in Heron-Neck?" she said. "The laundry? You gonna do what your granny wants for the rest of your life?"

Cassie was on the watch for headlights or any sign of motion from the dark woods behind them. She walked more quickly. Judith followed her.

"People get rich in New York City," said Judith.

"We ain't never gone get rich," said Cassie. "All I know is how to do laundry, an' all you know is how to deliver it. And Virginia ain't nowhere near New York City."

"Virginia where we gonna get our nest egg," said Judith. "We gonna find my daddy—*our* daddy—and we gonna demand our share of what he got. Whatever he's owed is owed to us too."

"You outta your mind."

Judith drew herself up, tall in her worn-out shoes. "I understan' if you feel that way. Ain't no original thinking goin' on round here near as I kin tell. You stay here and find a husband—or whatever you end up with—an' have youself a passel of young'uns. As your life goes by, you can think of me."

Cassie scuffed at the road. "How long you think you'll be gone?"

"Years likely. When I return, I'll be in a big car with a driver. An' a maid. No, two maids. And a lil ol' lap dog."

CHAPTER ✦ THREE

The next morning, the February weather had turned cool enough for heavier coats. At the estate sale, sparse clouds passed overhead, leaving the Tawney plantation in patches of winter sun, which didn't actually warm anyone. Most of the county turned out for the sale, not just the folks in Heron-Neck. Farmers and their bundled-up wives mixed with oily-shirted mechanics and share-croppers alike. The gaunt and the fat showed up to see what the Tawneys would throw out.

"Miz Tabitha's prices were reasonable," said Lil Ma, a woolen shawl around her shoulders, "but it'd be nice to pick up a few new plates now that she's gone."

"We're here for just one thing." Grandmother stepped to one side to avoid a puddle. "That wringer's going to cost enough."

"I wish you'd talk to Mrs. Tawney about the wringer," said Lil Ma. "You're better at talking to her than I am. You'll get a better price."

"You'll do what needs to be done," said Grandmother. "You need to learn to stand up for yourself. I won't be around forever."

Cassie followed Grandmother and Lil Ma, wearing the brown

wool coat she'd outgrown two years ago at fourteen. But it was warmer than the one she usually wore, which was still a little damp from yesterday's laundry delivery. She pushed her hands into the too-small pockets, not wanting to get in the middle of this argument. Lil Ma was afraid of old Mrs. Tawney, who would surely be in charge of the selling of the wringer. Every time Lil Ma took Cassie to Tawney's Store, she kept her eyes down and acted ashamed when old Mrs. Tawney was there instead of Miz Tabitha. When Grandmother went along, she looked old Mrs. Tawney straight in the face and had no problem with the dealing that had to be done to get a new pot or a set of towels or even clothespins. Lil Ma hung back. Cassie knew Grandmother didn't like the way Lil Ma behaved, but it was the first time she'd heard her Grandmother say, *I won't be around forever*. It was like a threat, but in some ways a relief to the imagination.

Cassie let herself trail farther and farther behind, looking for Judith in the crowd. The Tawneys' old barn was down the hill from the crippled-looking house. The house was surrounded by bare oak trees and a variety of run-down sheds. Miz Tabitha had the store on the first floor, leaving the second and third floors to the aged relations who lived with her. Cassie knew from being brought around to the back of the place once a week for most of her life that no one young had lived there in a long time. The winter weeds, old rusted cars, and a tilting, three-wheeled tractor in the front yard told the story of years of neglect.

The auctioneers had set out every last thing from the store behind the house on the kind of long tables used for church picnics. Lil Ma had taken Cassie to flea markets before, but none of them were as big as this. This was an *estate* sale, and to see the amount of stuff on the tables was to wonder how Miz Tabitha had fit it all inside the house.

There were Pyrex dishes, cookbooks, bolts of fabric, hats,

clothes, tinned tobacco, cups and saucers, cereal, bags of flour and coffee beans. Washtubs, irons, ironing boards, various hardware like hammers and saws, everything anyone might need except for maybe milk and anything else that could spoil. To Cassie it looked like the riches of the world.

She lagged farther behind Grandmother and Lil Ma until she couldn't really see them anymore in the crowd. She knew where they were going. The wringer was at the old house. She would be yelled at for wandering away, but she needed to find Judith. Judith was here somewhere.

At a table covered with costume jewelry, Judith was circling for the best view of the fake pearl earrings and shiny necklaces. Three women with red-and-white striped ribbons pinned to their bosoms strode around the table, guarding it. Miz Armenia Sutter was one of them.

"Gal," Miz Sutter said to Cassie, "when your momma gone to have my weddin' dress clean?"

"We working on it, ma'am," said Cassie

"You tell your momma I be by this afternoon to git it, y'heah?"

"Yessum, I tell her."

Miz Sutter fixed her eyes on Judith. "You too near to them necklaces, Judith Forrest! You ain't got the money to buy ennythin' heah. You keep your hands in your pockets and *scoot*."

Judith put her hands in the pockets of her patched red coat and sauntered off. Cassie trailed after her down the grassy incline, where the rest of the tables were arranged in uneven rows.

"I just finished packin' up the car," said Judith. "Got a bit of smoke ham, a bag of cornmeal, an' some aigs."

Cassie tried to picture Judith driving off in the junk car, heading for her future. It was surprisingly easy, considering she had never seen Judith do much but pull a wagon. At seventeen, though, maybe it was time for Judith to stop pulling wagons, time to move on. This made her think about the question Judith had asked her the night before—*you gonna do what your granny wants for the rest of your life?* The answers made her feel bad in her stomach.

"Them boys put on the tires?" said Cassie.

"Not yet, but they filled it up with gas. Fact is, I need to get out of town 'fore them idjits remember to come down tonight and set fire to it." Judith pulled her red coat tighter around her skinny frame. "Now look. Here's the reddios."

Some of the radios were brand-new, still in boxes. Others were clearly secondhand, with their prices written on bits of tape wrapped around the plugs. Judith examined these while women with ribbons pinned to their bosoms watched her without bothering to hide their suspicions. None of the new radios were less than three dollars, and Cassie moved away, down the table until she and Judith came to a clump of older-model radios with chewed-looking cords. The cheapest was two dollars.

"What you gone do with a radio?" said Cassie.

"Lissen to it when I git to my ho-tel room in Virginia," said Judith. "Sometimes I get tarred of my own singin'." Judith put a hand in her pocket and pulled out a dirty, folded bill so that the women guarding the table could see it. It was a single dollar. She must have saved her laundry nickels for a month. "Now if you had a dollar, we could go in on one o' these reddios."

"I ain't got a dollar," said Cassie, which was true.

"Well," said Judith, "these look a bit junky. If I was gonna buy one, I'd get me a brand-new model." She looked back at the ladies and put her chin up, as though the whole county was watching. "Come on an' let's look at the guns."

Cassie followed her through the thick of the crowd, which was white folks closer to the barn, where the auction would be later that afternoon, and colored farther away. Cassie knew Grandmother and Lil Ma were over by the house negotiating for the wringer and would be looking for her. She tried to see through to where the wringer might be on the porch of the crumbling old house, but there were too many people in the way. She stuck with Judith as Judith pushed past old women and little children, until she got to the table with the guns. Most of the people there were men. Judith shoved right in, turned, practically under some farmer's armpit, and waved Cassie toward her.

"Looky here." A sledgehammer-sized revolver lay in a row of rusted pistols. "You know what that is?"

The barrel was big enough to stick a finger in. Its trigger was thin and rusted. Cassie shook her head.

"That there's a horse pistol from the war a-tween the states. We got one at home, exceptin' ours in better shape. Still got some shootin' left in it." Judith picked up the gun with both hands and held it out straight, aiming in the general direction of the barn. "He a heavy old thing. I wonder if he got a name."

What always impressed Cassie about Judith's lies was that she never seemed to spend even a second coming up with them. It was like she had a store of spontaneous stories at the tip of her tongue. "Why would it have a name?" said Cassie.

"Ours do. He's called Big Red."

"It's a red gun?" said Cassie.

"Nope," said Judith. "He's named for the horse he had to shoot. My great-great-great-granddaddy came home on his horse from the war a-tween the states with that pistol, and there weren't nothin' to eat. And my great-great-great-granny said to him, 'Suh, we gonna have to shoot Big Red an' butcher him, or we gonna plumb starve.' And my great-great-great-granddaddy said, 'Over my dead body, woman,' so she shot him, and then she shot the horse."

"She *killed* your granddaddy?"

"She shot him in the leg so he couldn't get in her way. Then she held onto his gun so if he got vengeful about the horse, she could defend herself. She taught my great-great granny how to shoot it, and she taught my great-granny, and granny taught my momma, and my momma taught me." She hefted the pistol with both hands. "I'll teach my daughter one day."

Cassie left Judith to decide where to spend her dollar. She found Grandmother at the back of Tawney's old store. The wringer sat at an angle on the ancient, sagging veranda. Lil Ma stood near the veranda, on the ground in the weeds, her hands pulled back into the sleeves of her coat. Grandmother stood under an oak tree a little ways off. One of Miz Tabitha's aged female relations was on the disintegrating porch, holding herself up with a cane, counting bills. Cassie recognized old Mrs. Tawney, Mister Elmer's great-aunt. It was rumored that she was over a hundred years old and had shot at the Union troops from the top story of the Tawney house. Cassie had always believed this because her age made all the other elderly women around her seem young in comparison.

Old Mrs. Tawney pushed the bills into her apron pocket. The bargaining was over, and Lil Ma had done her reluctant part. "It ain't enough," old Mrs. Tawney said to Lil Ma, "but I reckon nobody else wants the damn thing." Old Mrs. Tawney looked down from the porch like she owned the whole place and every-one on it. "You-all better have it out of here by tomorrow, or I'll have it sent to the junkyard. I don't want no niggers round here after dark, y'hear?"

"Yessum," said Lil Ma. "We have a man come by."

Old Mrs. Tawney went back into the house with the money. Lil Ma looked up and saw Cassie, and for a second Cassie saw the unhappiness in Lil Ma's eyes. Not just today's unhappiness, or the way she felt about the insult of the moment, but the years of it, a lifetime's worth.

Grandmother came out from under the tree. "Good," Grandmother said to Lil Ma, "good," like she was talking to a dog. Lil Ma
let her shoulders slump. Grandmother motioned to Cassie. "You
run on back to the laundry. Get a dollar out of the moneybox and
give it to Beanie Simms. Tell him to bring his truck. Right *now*."

Through the back door of the laundry, past the neatly folded ironing and the dresses waiting to be pressed, Cassie went to the front
of the store, took the cash box out from where it was hidden under
the counter, and opened it. Inside were five quarters and seven
one-dollar bills. She took a dollar for Beanie Simms and put it in
the pocket of her old woolen coat. She looked at the rest of the
money. She took out three more bills, one at a time, and held
them like a fan in her hand, thinking about the New York voices
that could only be heard at night. She thought about Judith living
in Heron-Neck forever, just like Judith's mother, and her mother's
mother, and all those horse-pistol-wielding women in Judith's
past, never getting away, never going to Virginia to fulfill her des-
tiny as *progeny*. She thought about the look on Lil Ma's face just
now at the Tawneys', and about the albino boy sitting in his sunlit
bedroom listening to the blackest music he could find. She wanted
a radio. She would listen to it in the middle of the night, and she
would hear what other songs black voices sang when it was blackest outside. She put the money back in the cash box, just to see if
she could still make an honest motion with her hands, took it out
again, and pushed it deep into her coat pocket.

Beanie Simms's truck coughed and shuddered. It seemed ready to
rattle right apart. Beanie Simms let Cassie sit in the passenger
seat while he drove.

SOM'S DAUGHTERS 51

"I wisht I still had my ol' mule some days," said Beanie Simms, loud over the noise of the engine. "There was a reli'ble critter." Beanie Simms held onto the steering wheel as though he thought it might come off in his hands. "I ever tell you 'bout my ol' mule?"

Cassie knew most of Beanie Simms's stories by heart. She looked out the window as the town crawled by.

"Why you so quiet, gal?" said Beanie Simms. "You sick?"

"I ain't sick."

"Better *ain't* let your granny hear you talk like that."

"I'm not sick."

"Then what's the matter with you?"

Cassie rubbed her knees. "You got a radio, Mister Simms?"

"Sure, I gots a reddio. Over at de shoe-shine."

"What you lissen to?"

Beanie Simms ground the truck's gears. The road started to rise as they neared the Tawney place. "I lissens to de gospel music."

"All week long?"

"Well now, a man kin git tarred of the same thin' all week long."

"You ever lissen to colored music?"

Beanie Simms laughed. "What you know about colored music?"

"I heard about it."

"Your mama and your granny ain't gone want you list'nin' to that."

Cassie put her hand over the money in her pocket. Outside, bare trees crept past the car. Exhaust puffed up from between the floorboards. "You ever think about leavin' here, Mister Simms?"

"Shore," said Beanie Simms. "Alla time."

"You do?"

"Shore. Ain't nothin' here t'keep me."

"What about the shoe-shine?"

"Well, if'n I still had my ol' mule, I'd jus' put the shoe-shine inna back o' the cart and take 'em on to th' next town."

"But you have a truck."

"This truck ain't got no dur'bility. A mule ain't gone do nothin' stupid. This truck don' care if I drive it inna ditch." He turned down the road that would take them to Tawney's. "Mule *object* to bein' driv' inna ditch. What about you, lil gal? You ever think o' leavin'?"

Cassie shifted in the seat, thinking of Judith, the car in the woods. "I couldn't leave my mama and my grandmother."

"I guess I'd be thinking 'bout leavin' if I was you," said Beanie Simms. "'Specially with that new white boy in town."

Beanie Simms was a tall man with close-cropped hair. In the cramped noisiness of the truck, he loomed over her. Cassie felt herself cringe in the threadbare seat. Did the entire town of Heron-Neck know about Grandmother's scheme? Was the entire town waiting to see what would happen next?

"Some folks do ennythin' to get themselves whiter," said Beanie Simms. "There an easier way than what your granny got in mind."

"I heard you talk about it when I was a little girl," Cassie said.

"It ain't jus' talk," said Beanie Simms. "It a town called Porterville, where white folks and black folks live in perfeck harmony. All them white folks useter be black as tar."

Did Beanie Simms know about the car in the woods and Judith's plans to escape to become a reddio star? There was no telling what Beanie Simms knew.

"Why don't you go there yourself?" Cassie said.

Beanie Simms drew himself up in the truck, taller than ever. "I's the messenger. One day I'll go, but in the meantime, I's got to stick around to help folks out."

He let her off by the Tawneys' barn and pulled the truck back to where the house was. Judith was nowhere in sight, not by the table with the miscellaneous and ancient guns, or the jewelry. Cassie made her way through the crowd and through the smells of sweat and tobacco to the table with the radios, where a white lady she didn't recognize was standing guard.

The two-dollar radios were gone. The only one left was a brand-new three-dollar model, still in its box. The box was white with a picture of a white man on it, obviously enjoying the music coming out of the radio inside.

"'Scuse me, ma'am," Cassie said to the white lady. "I'd like to buy that, please."

"You got three dollars?" said the white lady.

Cassie took the money out of her pocket and felt a prickle of naked curiosity from the white woman as she wondered where a little colored girl had gotten that much cash.

"What a girl like you need with a radio?" said the white lady.

"We ain't got no radio inna laundry," said Cassie. "We ain't got no ways to lissen to de gospel music less'n we sings it ourselves."

The white lady held her hand out for the money. "You're Adelaine's girl?"

"Yessum."

"So *this* is why she charges so much for pressing." The white lady snatched away the three dollars and pushed the boxed radio into Cassie's hands.

When she got home, Cassie could hear Beanie Simms and another man shouting advice to each other out back about where to set the new wringer. She crept in the front door, careful first to see that no one was inside. The back door was open and gave up a narrow view of the backyard through the kitchen. The men steered the new wringer into the sheltered space where the old wringer was with Lil Ma and Grandmother darting back and forth, giving directions. Cassie slid past the stove and ran up the stairs before anyone could see her. She reached the second floor just as the screen door slammed downstairs. Someone clinked glasses together. Beanie Simms shouted something from outside, and from the bottom of the stairs, Lil Ma let out a musical laugh. Cassie knelt on the floor and opened the thin cardboard box and lifted the radio out of its silky paper wrapping.

The radio was tiny compared to its box. It was the size of a pocketbook or of a neatly folded shirt. It was white plastic, with a smooth gray knob that made a little red needle swerve across numbers in a neat row in a window.

5.8 6 7 8 10 12 16

Cassie twirled the knob back and forth, watching the needle move. What kind of music would come out of this little thing? She hadn't thought about it, but maybe there was a special kind of radio you needed for the colored music that made your feet want to move and your hips want to swing. What if this radio only played gospel or music that white folks wanted to hear?

She unwound the cord, and the cord answered her question, but in a different way. She looked up from the radio to the walls papered in yellowing newsprint, magazine pages, and letters in blue ink from strangers. There was no electricity in these walls. Heat and light came from coal, kerosene, and candles.

Out the window, Beanie Simms gulped down a glass of cold water. Water came out of a pump. Water cooled outside in a ceramic pitcher. Instead of indoor plumbing, there was an out-house. Everyone on Negro Street lived like this.

Cassie hid the radio under her own thin mattress, not know-ing what else to do with it. She folded the cardboard box and the silky paper into the smallest wad she could manage, and when she was sure she wouldn't be seen, she took the wad downstairs and dropped it into the furnace heat of the stove.

Judith didn't show up that afternoon. By three, Grandmother told Cassie, "You'd better get those wagons loaded. That laundry isn't going to deliver itself."

While Lil Ma and Grandmother disparaged Judith's lateness, her family's hopeless problems, her character in general, Cassie loaded the wagons, then pulled the wagons down the street, across the tracks, and up the hill. She tried to sing to herself as she dragged the heavy, squeaking things, but in her heart she could feel that Judith was gone, gone in the car, supplied with her family's old horse pistol and a trunk full of ham and cornmeal. Maybe the albino boy had gone with her, heading home to New York City, encouraging her to be a reddio star. Cassie pushed one of the wagons off the side of the road and into the bushes, where she could find it later for the second half of the deliveries. The first stop was the Wivells'. Cassie tried to make herself tall and straight. If the albino boy was there, it meant that Judith was still in Heron-Neck and for whatever reason hadn't shown up for work. Cassie leaned into the weight of the wagon and hauled it up toward the Wivells'. A car came out their driveway, paused, and turned toward her. Cassie stepped aside. It was the Wivells' car, and she peered in to see if the albino boy was inside. He was in the passenger seat and smirked at her through the glass.

"Where's Judith?" Cassie shouted at him.

The albino boy ignored her, and Mister Wivell, who was driving, frowned as though he'd heard something go wrong with the engine.

Back home in the early evening with the empty wagons, Cassie found Lil Ma in the yard, hanging sheets. "Judith's gone," Cassie said.

Lil Ma looked at her in surprise. "Gone where?"

"She's up and left to find her fortune in Virginia," said Cassie. "She's going to be a big singing star." Even as the words left her mouth, she could hardly believe it. "I thought she left with that albino boy, but he's still here."

Lil Ma pulled the last of the sheets from the basket but didn't pin it up. "Judith would never go anywhere without you."

Cassie held out a handful of clothespins. "She has a car; she's got food and a gun. She has a plan."

"That girl never had a plan in her life," said Lil Ma. "She can't leave without you." Lil Ma let the wet sheet drop back into the basket and looked up at the second-floor window. She lowered her voice. "When your grandmother heard about that albino boy. The look in her eyes. You just can't imagine."

Lil Ma took her back under the roof of the porch, where they couldn't be seen from upstairs. "That boy's the dream she's been having all these years. She thinks your baby's going to be like a white shell. Before it's born, we'll leave and go further north, where your grandmother thinks there are plenty of children like that, and we would fit right in."

"But it isn't true?"

"Child, how do I know if it's true?" She grabbed Cassie's hand. "Come inside. I have to give you something."

Cassie followed Lil Ma inside, through the kitchen, past the irons on the stove, through the door, and into the space behind the counter. Lil Ma reached under the counter and pulled up one of the floorboards. Underneath was a cigar box tied shut with butcher string. Lil Ma opened it, revealing the neat piles of bills, counted out ten, and gave them to Cassie. "Sit," she whispered.

Cassie sat. Lil Ma took off her own hard-soled shoes and knelt on the floor in front of Cassie. She pressed the bills into the shoes and put the shoes onto Cassie's feet and tied the laces. Upstairs the floorboards creaked.

"Be sure no one's looking when you take them off," whispered Lil Ma. "Use them for a pillow when you sleep." She was crying. "I don't want you to leave," Lil Ma said. "But find your sister. Go with your sister." She pulled Cassie to her feet, kissed her, pressed her out the front door of the laundry, and closed it.

Cassie stood for a moment in the February chill. Then she ran. The brogans clunked, and the money slid back and forth under her feet. She ran into the sunset dark of Negro Street.

Was Judith in the woods? Cassie knew what the Justice boys would do to the old junk car if they found Judith with it. Everyone would be able to tell something was wrong in the woods by the column of black smoke that would rise from the burning tires. What they felt like doing to Judith would leave no column of smoke.

To her relief, she heard a car coming as she came to the end of Negro Street. She couldn't see it yet, but it coughed and choked like the car in the woods. Its engine sounded clogged and unreliable. Cassie's heart both leaped and sank. Judith was coming to get her, in a car that wouldn't make it to the other side of town.

It wasn't Judith, though; it was Beanie Simms, coming back from the shoeshine.

He leaned out the window. "Where the heck you runnin' like that, gal?"

"Mister Simms," she said, already breathless, "where's Porterville?"

His face compressed into instant understanding. "I don't know 'zactly where," he said. "But it's east o' here. You ask the folks in Hilltop. Follow the railroad tracks. You be careful, gal."

It was dark by the time Cassie got to where the road crossed

Duncan Justice's land. She saw the familiar flicker of firelight in the trees and crouched down to peer through the weave of naked branches. The car was a boxy shadow in the dim light. Empty liquor bottles glittered in the leaves on the ground. No one seemed to be around, but the fire was lively. Someone had stirred it recently.

Judith was singing in a drunken, mournful voice. Cassie stepped into the cool murk of the winter woods. Twigs snapped under Lil Ma's hard-soled shoes. Maybe Judith wasn't alone with the bottles and the fire. Cassie crept to the edge of the clearing. She huddled behind a spreading briar until she could see into the shadows of the car.

"Judith?"

Judith looked up like a surprised pigeon. She swung her legs over and slid out of the driver's seat, wobbly. *Inebriated*, Grandmother would have said in her most disdainful tone.

There were smears of lipstick across Judith's chin and the side of her mouth.

Cassie stepped out of the bushes into the light of the fire. "Where them boys? Where's the albino boy?"

Judith gestured into the night with a bottle. Her dress was torn at the sleeves. "They been here an' gone." She fell back into the seat behind the steering wheel.

Cassie looked at the wheels and saw the tires—not new, but not flat either. "They comin' back?"

"They wenta git more booze."

Cassie went around to the back of the car and opened the trunk. It was too dark to see much, but sure enough, there was a fist-sized hank of smoked ham, a sack of cornmeal, eggs, and an iron skillet. She didn't see the horse pistol. She shut the trunk and came around to the driver's side. She leaned in the window. "Can you make it start?"

Judith pulled halfheartedly at a handle in the dashboard. Smoke poured out from under the hood. The engine sputtered, and the car shook like Beanie Simms's old truck, but it kept running.

Judith's lower lip pushed out, and tears ran down her face. "You comin' with me to Virginia?"

"I'm comin' with you," said Cassie. "An' I guess we're gonna find your daddy."

CHAPTER ✦ FOUR

In the morning, with Heron-Neck hours behind them, Mississippi looked no different. Flat muddy roads, straight lines through stands of piney woods. They followed the railroad tracks. Now and then they rattled past a mean little shack, where ragged colored children and their equally ragged relations stopped what they were doing to watch the old junk car go by, white gal behind the wheel, colored gal in the passenger seat.

Judith always waved, singing out *Hey y'all,* like she was already a famous reddio star. Cassie would pretend to read the map spread over her knees. She'd found the map in the glove compartment. It had been folded and refolded so many times that most of the roads and names of counties had worn down to nothing. Vague areas of color and intermittent lines covered the map like stains. There was no sign of a place called Hilltop or of a town called Porterville.

That morning Cassie managed to convince Judith that she'd driven Beanie Simms's old truck plenty of times, and Judith finally let her get behind the wheel. Cassie shoved the gearshift until it seemed to hook onto something. She moved her feet on the clutch and gas pedals until the car jerked forward. The ride wasn't smooth, and Cassie didn't look like she knew what she was doing, but Judith settled into the passenger seat with her bare feet up on the door. Cassie tried to make herself comfortable between the lumps and springs of the driver's seat. They would have to find a cushion somewhere. Maybe two or three.

Cassie gave the car a little gas, and it rattled down a shallow hill. A breeze blew between Judith's dirty toes, and Judith smiled at the morning. Cassie drove and Judith dozed. The car clattered and smoked. Winter fields became sparse pine forest, which gave way to scattered shacks. Shacks faded back into the trees, and the forest diminished. Now felled lumber, now rotten stumps, now a field. The landscape repeated itself. Were they going in a circle? Once in a while a stray cow or chicken stared at them from the middle of the road, too dumbfounded to run.

The scenery interrupted itself once with a church in pieces on the side of a hill. The steeple sat on cinderblocks. All four walls leaned against one sturdy tree, looking like they had been sawed from some other building. Someone had dug a foundation. The sturdy tree and the four walls were right beside the road, and going uphill, the car went so slowly, they had plenty of time to examine the church as they passed.

Judith combed out her hair with her fingers. "What church you go to back home?"

"We din't go much, but when we did, First Baptist. Where'd you go?"

"Missionary Baptist."

"That little white one off Main Street?"

"Wasn't little."

"Weren't big neither."

"You sing in your church?"

"Ever'body sing in church."

"Not deaf folks."

Deaf folks. How did Judith know anything about deaf folks and what they did in church? Were there any deaf folks in Heron-Neck? Not that she knew of, neither white nor colored. This was Judith bored. Judith making up anything just to pretend she knew what she was talking about. This was how she entertained herself. Was Cassie herself bored enough to care what Judith would say next? She concentrated on the road, though there was no traffic in sight. Was Judith busy trying to decide, like she was, if this trip was actually a good idea? They had no real plan and no idea how to get to Virginia, much less Hilltop—and Porterville. What if there was no Porterville? What if those were places Beanie Simms had made up? People paid him for the information, she was pretty sure of that, but what if following the railroad tracks was a wild goose chase? And even if they made it, then what? Would she turn white and leave Judith? And if Judith made it to Virginia, would Bill Forrest hand over whatever inheritance was left? He'd been gone for years, and the letter from Eula Bonhomme hadn't said how much money there was. What if it was pennies? In the rearview mirror, dust rose behind the car, hiding the road to Heron-Neck. What would happen back home? With the albino boy lying in wait for colored girls or even women, was it safe for Lil Ma? Cassie should have brought Lil Ma; this was the mistake she'd made, the mistake lurking at the edges of Judith's certainty. The three of them could have made it to Virginia, where, no matter what, there would be laundry to do. Should she turn around and head straight back? She wouldn't escape a second time. She made a silent pledge that whatever she did, wherever she and Judith ended up, she would get Lil Ma to safety.

They reached the top of the hill. Cassie pushed the clutch in to let the old heap roll down the other side at its own speed.

"Give it gas," said Judith. "Floor it. Like this."

She shoved her foot over the top of Cassie's and pushed it all the way down. The car lurched, then surged. Wind gusted in, blowing their hair and coats, pushing out the smell of exhaust and rotting upholstery. As they picked up speed, Cassie opened her mouth to let the air fill it. The vibration of the road through the seat went all through her. Trees flashed by. Her stomach lifted. Judith let out a yell, and Cassie yelled too, into the wind, without words.

By sundown of their first full day, they'd reached a low line of hills and bare winter fields. On their right, the railroad tracks disappeared into the mouth of a tunnel; on the left, their road vanished into the evening.

Cassie stopped the car. There was a railroad crossing. Patches of dirt showed that others had crossed the tracks in front of the tunnel, heading up into the hills.

"Where are we?" said Judith.

On the map, the print closer to the edges was easier to see, but no matter how Cassie studied it, she was more and more certain that they had driven off the eastern edge of the map some time ago. She showed Judith. "We'll need a new map."

"Where we gonna find a new map?" said Judith.

"I guess at a gas station."

"You reckon we should stop fer the night?"

"I reckon we should."

They got the car off the road and under some pine trees. Judith opened the trunk, found a box of matches, and struck one. The light showed what else was in the trunk: the sack of cornmeal and the hunk of ham lying unwrapped in the cast-iron skillet.

"I got aigs in here." Judith shook out the match, lit another, and poked around in the musty space. She pulled out a chipped bowl with an apron stuffed into it. The eggs, wrapped in the apron, were miraculously intact. Judith shook out the second match and pushed the eggs at Cassie. "Go on an' mix us up some corn bread. I'll start the fire."

Cassie sat on the running board and mixed cornmeal batter with her fingers, since there was no fork or spoon in the trunk. The bread would be flat and tough. Lil Ma would have added warm milk and yeast; the bread would have risen into something respectable instead of burning black in the pan. On her knees, Judith blew on a tiny flicker between dry pine twigs.

The fire caught and flames rose up. They showed Judith's uneven teeth in a grin. "There y'are." She brushed her hands on her knees. Cassie scooped the batter into the skillet and squatted by the fire with the pan.

Judith put in a few more sticks. The flames jumped and crackled. "We should slice up that ham and put it in too."

"Did you bring a knife?"

"Din't you?"

"Didn't really think I'd be leavin'."

"I thought 'bout leavin' alla time after that albino boy, Jack, started talkin'. Started thinkin' 'bout, you know, marriage an' travelin' an' New York." Judith put in some bigger sticks. Behind her, the dark shoulders of the hills showed as an ebony edge against a sky slowly filling with stars. The fire gained some heat, and the warmth made Cassie feel achy from hours of sitting in the car.

"Which way you want to go tomorrow?" Judith pointed left with a stick, following the road. "I don't think this ol' thing'll ever get up that hill."

"Then I guess we should take the road." Cassie hadn't eaten since last night and felt lightheaded enough to ask the question that had been on her mind since she'd seen Judith drinking and horsing around with the albino boy and the Justice boys.

"You gonna have a baby?"

Judith pushed a burning stick around. "I don't know." She took the skillet and set it into the fire. In a minute, the batter began to hiss, already burning at the edges.

"What're you gonna do if you have a baby?" said Cassie.

"I dunno. Plenty of them singin' stars got babies."

"I guess."

After they ate and scrubbed out the pan with sand, Judith tucked herself into the frayed ruins of the backseat. She dug the enormous pistol out from under the driver's seat and laid it by her head. "I'm gonna use it fer a piller," she said.

Cassie used her shoes, the way Lil Ma had told her to. The shoes were hard. She rolled onto her back, pushing them to one side. From where she was lying in the front seat, she could see the stars through the windshield and the same sliver of moon she had run away from home under last night. What might Lil Ma be saying to Grandmother right at this moment? How long would they stay in Heron-Neck now that she was gone?

In the morning, the car refused to start. Judith rattled the key in the ignition. Something inside the engine flapped like a bird trying to get out. They put up the hood and stared at the oily-black workings inside. A train rumbled into view and went into the tunnel, moving so slowly that they could have kept up with it at a fast walk.

"We should find a freight car and get on," said Judith. She seemed ready to do just that when a freight car with an open door passed, and the railroad hoboes riding it hooted and hollered at them.

"My daddy—*our* daddy—useta ride them freight trains," Judith said. "He got robbed when he was asleep, and that was the end of that. Said he thought he was ridin' for free, but turned out he was payin' tramps for a ticket."

"Shoulda kept his money in his shoes" said Cassie.

"He did. They took his shoes too."

"They took his shoes?"

The train, with its hooting hoboes, vanished into the tunnel.

"Sure as I'm standin' here."

The bills in Cassie's shoes slid under her heels. Her sense of safety—which she hadn't actually been aware of until this moment—evaporated. If she were robbed, nothing she had was safe. Not her shoes. Not her body.

"Which way you think we more likely to run into somebody?" Judith said.

The road looked more exposed, but the wagon track into the woods made her think of the Justice boys. "Let's take the road."

They ate what was left of the burned corn bread. Judith put the pistol in a sack over her shoulder. It was a cold, overcast morning. The unfamiliar road, the fields, the wire fences looked unfriendly. After they'd walked for a while, the sun came out from behind a few thin clouds. It shone down on the rows of cut corn and made the earth smell like spring might not be too far off, but it didn't make Cassie feel any more comfortable. Who could say they hadn't wandered into a world filled with Duncan Justices or oil men looking for dark-skinned women?

"What if you can't find your daddy?" said Cassie.

Judith just walked along holding the sack with one hand, swinging her other arm. "You homesick already?"

"I'm not homesick." Cassie tried to mimic Judith's walk, but her arms didn't seem to have the same confidence. "I'm just wondering what you're gonna do if you can't find Virginia."

"Ain't it too big to miss?"

"It ain't too big to miss. It ain't even on the map."

Judith snorted and pushed hair away from her face. "I never thought I'd be out travelin' in the great big world with some scairt lil homesick nigger girl."

Lots of terrible things, all accurate and deserved, got ready to rush out of Cassie's mouth. She picked the most cutting thing she could think of. "My mama say you sound like a jaybird when you talk."

Judith stopped in the middle of the empty road.

Cassie stopped too. "Every nigger in town says so."

Judith took a funny little breath, like she'd never considered the opinions of the Heron-Neck niggers. "Every nigger in town ain't heard me sing."

"I'm the only nigger in town who heard you sing," said Cassie. "An' I say, don't you never use that jaybird voice to call me that again."

"I jus' kiddin' you."

"I'm not scared, an' I'm not homesick," Cassie said, though truthfully, she was, and she was bothered—a lot—that Judith's dreams and illusions shielded Judith from any of Cassie's fears, fears which seemed to get bigger the farther they got from the car.

"Well then, I'm sorry," Judith said.

They started walking again. Winter birds sang in the trees. Cold wind blew under the clothes they'd slept in. Cassie said, "Do you worry about getting robbed?"

"I thought we shoulda brought a dog," said Judith, the same way she always said anything—like she'd given it deep thought at some earlier date and had prepared the perfect answer. "Shoulda brought that little Justice boy. The one with the spotted hound."

"That boy who thought he was a dog?"

"He din't jus' think it. He really a dog born into a boy's body. They say when he was a baby he never cried. He whimpered, like he was a puppy."

"Even you don't really believe that," said Cassie.

Judith put her nose up as though offended. "I do try to keep my mind open."

The sun had cleared the horizon when they saw a colored man driving a mule hitched to a wagon. The man didn't seem to see them until he was very close; then the mule let out a snort, and the man looked up from under his hat. Cassie thought he'd been sleeping while the mule made his way to wherever they were going.

The man pulled the wagon to a stop and tipped his battered porkpie hat. "Mornin', ladies." He looked like he thought he might be having a dream, and part of his dream was Judith and Cassie walking together. "What brings you-all out on such a fine day?"

Judith elbowed Cassie as though it was her job to speak for the two of them.

"Mornin', suh," she said. "We got us a car done broke down back a ways."

His eyebrows went up when she said *car* as though he was sure he was dreaming now. "You gals got a car?"

"Ain't much of a car," said Cassie. "You know anythin' about gettin' 'em to run?"

"My nephew up 'crost the hills there, he know sumpin' 'bout cars." The hills were behind them now, on the other side of the railroad tracks.

"You reckon we could get a ride partways?"

"I reckon you could," said the man. "But you might think twicet 'fore you gets in." He angled his head at the bed of the wagon.

Both girls peered over the side at a pinewood coffin.

"Oh hail!" said Judith. "Somebody in there?"

"Oh yessum," said the man. "That there my wife's cousin, Lisette. Dearly departed just this mornin'. I takin' her up to the church to her eternal rest."

"We sorry for your loss," said Judith, looking as repentant as she could after *oh hail!*

The man moved over on the wagon bench, and the two of them got up next to him. He introduced himself as Ovid Beale, spoke to the mule, and the wagon lurched forward.

Cassie, in the middle, told him their names and said, "We sorry to run into you on such a sad day, but we 'preciate the ride."

"It sadder than it look," said Ovid Beale. "Lisette was a young woman. She died from her heart done bein' broke. Her man foolin' round on her, and she found out about it. She run off. We look and look. Ain't no one kin find her. She come back on her own, but she wasted away. She so sick that no matter what folk do—even the white doctor and the root woman—cain't do nuthin' to save her."

"That's terrible," said Cassie.

"We sorry for you loss," Judith repeated.

"Her husband know it?" said Cassie. It felt good to be riding instead of walking, even if she was squashed into the middle of the wagon seat. And she was warm now, between Judith and Ovid Beale, which made her realize how cold the walk had been.

"He know," said Ovid Beale. "He gonna make a good showin' at the funeral, then he think he goin' back to his hoochie mama." The mule shook its head and laid its ears back. Ovid Beale let out a laugh, but not like anything was truly funny. "Git up, y'damn mule," he said and took a quick look at Judith. "'Scuse my language, ma'am."

"Ain't no problem," said Judith.

"He's a nice-looking mule," said Cassie, and he was a nice-looking mule, brushed clean and shining like polished mahogany in the early sun.

"Nice lookin'," said Ovid Beale, "but a lazy sonuvagun. We calls him Miles, 'cause ever day 'fore he go out to work, he think to himself, *Man, I got miles to go 'fore I kin git back to bed.*"

"How you know what he thinkin'?" said Judith.

"I knows this lazy mule like I knows a lazy man. He hate bein' a mule. Hate havin' to work. He the meanest critter in the yard. Chickens skeered to death of Miles. You know some mules useter be human folks?"

"As a matter o' fact," said Judith. "We know a lil boy who's really a dog inside."

"Oh, it's true," said Ovid Beale. "A hunnert percent. Miles useter be a man until recently."

"Then why you need reins?" said Cassie. "If he was a man, whyn't you jus' tell him where to go?"

"You cain't tell this mule nuthin'," said Ovid Beale. "He din't understan' nuthin' when he was a man. He real stubborn as a man. He'd fight an' mess around jus' as soon as talk to you. Ain't no different now he a mule. Now all he got to do is contemplate on his situation. Hey!" he shouted at Miles and slapped him with the reins. "Git up thar, mule!"

"He act like enny other mule I ever seen," said Cassie.

"You never know 'bout de mules you see," said Ovid Beale. "Half them useter be colored folk. Turnin' into a mule simpler for colored folk than turnin' into some other critter, 'cause a mule already half one thing and half another. Mule the most nigger of all the critters."

Judith started to laugh. "Ain't no such thing as a nigger critter."

"If you think that, then you ain't truly studied on the mule," said Ovid Beale. "The mule got his outside self what gots to work all day without complaint or be whupped. But inside hisself he got his own thoughts, and he got plans."

"What kind of plans?" said Cassie.

"Well, a mule only got two plans," said Ovid Beale. He tipped his hat back in the cool morning air. "He want sumthin' to eat and to lay down an' sleep. But his other plan—he got it in his mind at all times—is when the right time come, he gone to be out the barn, out the field, gone away to someplace better. No matter how hard he work, he got the other plan in the front of his mind."

"How's that enny different from enny other critter?" said Judith. "Ain't a horse the same way? What about a dog? Or a cat? Or people even?"

"Horse a more noble an'mal," said Ovid Beale, "An', I admit, it less common for a man to turn into a dog, but like you say, you already knowed one. An' as fer a cat, cat ain't worked a day in its life, 'cept fer mousin', an' mousin' recreational fer a cat."

"What about a mule turning into a person?" said Cassie.

"Sho, they kin turn back into the person they was. That happen. Miles waitin' fo' it to happen to him. Ain't that so, Mister Miles?"

The mule shifted one ear.

"I mean a real mule," said Cassie. "One that never was a person before."

"A real mule turnin into a man?" said Ovid Beale. "Sho, that happen too. I known plenty of mules become men. But most mules turnt into wimmin."

About that time, they came upon the stand of pines and the railroad tunnel, and Judith said, "Now here's the car."

Ovid Beale stopped the wagon and eased himself off. He peered under the junk car's hood and had Judith try the ignition a time or two. There was no noise from the engine.

"How far y'all come in this ol' trap?" said Ovid Beale. "Mebbe you plumb wore it out."

"You heard of Heron-Neck?" said Judith, with some snootiness. "It some miles off. We done drove all day yestiddy to git this far."

Ovid Beale looked around at the scuffed pine needles, the burned remains of the fire, and the skillet, still sitting out behind the car. "You slep' out here las' night?"

"Yessuh," said Cassie.

Ovid Beale pushed the hood down. "That ain't safe. 'Specially here by the railroad track. Don't know what-all kinda riff-raff come through here ridin' them freight cars. I kin haul this here car up over the hill, see what Slick kin do with it, but it might be you need some kinda spare part." He gave Cassie a penetrating squint. "You gals in any kinda hurry?"

The look made Cassie feel guilty, even frightened, but Judith took it as a cue to start talking about bein' a New York reddio star. Cassie put a hand on Judith's arm to stop her before she got to the part about how they shared a father, how the two of them were progeny and would soon be rich. "No, suh," Cassie said, "we ain't in any kinda hurry 'tall."

They started off again with the car tied up behind the wagon. The cart, the coffin, and the car all bumped over the railroad crossing. Ovid Beale turned the mule onto a half overgrown track that led up the side of the hill.

The track wove between trees and stony outcroppings, narrow here, wider where a low spot had become too muddy to drive a wagon. Hoof prints showed as carvings in the cold mud. Wagon wheels left a double imprint along the sides of the trail.

The mule leaned into his harness. In the back of the wagon, the coffin slid heavily back and forth as the track shifted. Behind the wagon, at the end of a short dirty rope, the car looked ancient and disreputable. Cassie and Judith had probably looked like vagrants when they were driving in that junk car; that's what Grandmother would have said. Up the hill, ahead of them, the track twisted through the woods. Would they be able to see Heron-Neck when they reached the top?

By noon, they'd reached the crown of the hill. Trees had been cut and the stony ground cleared for planting. The wind rushed between stone fences and rows of corn stubble.

"What's the name of this place?" said Cassie.

"Welcome to Hilltop," said Ovid Beale.

Cassie straightened in surprise. Was this Beanie Simms's Hilltop? She'd imagined something grander. This Hilltop was a dozen unpainted wooden houses clustered under the remaining trees. There was a brick church that had no steeple—not yet, Ovid Beale told them. There were planks over the holes where the stained-glass windows would someday be. The sun was out, and despite the wind, the day warmed. As the wagon rattled into town, two elderly women with shawls around their shoulders came into the street from the church.

They came over to the wagon, and the one who looked the more wizened said, "Well now," to Ovid Beale. "Look what-all you picked up on the road."

"These gals travelin' from Heron-Neck," said Ovid. "They car broke down. I tol' 'em Slick could fix it."

The second woman, a slightly younger version of the first, and almost as wrinkled, said, "Heron-Neck?"

"Well," said Ovid Beale, "I ain't never heerd of it neither, but lotta folks ain't never heerd of Hilltop."

"One thing I ain't never heerd of is a colored gal and white gal drivin' round in a car together," said the older woman. "You gals done stole that car." She didn't say it as a question.

"Nome," said Cassie.

"Then what you doin' way out here?"

"We goin' to Virginia," said Judith. "My daddy's there, an' we his progeny."

"You his what?" said the younger woman.

"Progeny," said Judith. "We gettin' our share of my daddy's inheritance."

The older woman studied their faces. "You got the same daddy," she said. "You half sisters."

"Yessum," said Cassie.

"An' he ain't no colored man."

"Nome," said Judith. "He skirt-chasin', adulteratin' white trash."

The older woman raised an eyebrow. "An' you think he gonna give you anything?" She waved a hand, dismissing their crazy idea and Ovid Beale too for bringing them to town.

"You got Lisette?" The younger woman looked in the wagon. "Drive on down by the church, and we'll take her inside." She and the older woman turned to cross the dirt road to the church. As they passed the mule, it reached its head toward them, to nuzzle or to bite. The older woman slapped him away. "And *that* ain't gonna help you neither!"

The mule tossed his head. Ovid Beale smacked him with the reins and drove forward. The church door opened, and out came five young men in black suit jackets and pressed white shirts. Four went to the back of the wagon to ease the coffin out. The fifth came over to Ovid Beale.

"Mornin', Uncle," he said.

"Slick," said Ovid Beale. "Slick, boy, let me make some inter-ductions."

Behind the church was the cemetery, where two men with shovels sat next to a freshly dug grave, smoking cigarettes. Some little distance away, a bright red convertible was parked under a tree. Slick and Ovid Beale untied the old junker from the back of the wagon, unhitched the mule, and tied the mule to a tree. Slick rolled up his freshly pressed white sleeves, opened the hood, and examined its innards.

"Don't be gettin' dirty," said Ovid Beale.

"I ain't. Prob'ly jus' needs some gas."

Ovid Beale went over to the red car, opened the trunk, and took out a red can. Slick circled the junker until he figured out where the gas went and put in most of the can.

"Try it now," he said to Judith.

Judith turned the ignition. The engine flapped and sputtered. Slick poked a finger into something under the hood. "Try it now."

Judith cranked the ignition, and the oily engine groaned. Foul blue smoke billowed out from underneath the hood and rose around the tires. The junk car shuddered in its rusty frame, but it was running.

Slick gave the engine a doubtful look. "How far you goin'?" he said.

The engine was so loud, Cassie knew Judith couldn't hear her reply: "Judith's goin' to Virginia, and I'm trying to find Porter-ville."

"Porterville?" said Slick. "You have to ask my uncle about that."

"Haven't you heard of it?" said Cassie.

"I heard of it. He knows where it is." Slick shut the hood and carefully rolled down his sleeves. "I know where Virginia is," he said, "an' I can tell you, this heap might git you to Alabama, but Virginia a *long* way."

"Hey," shouted Judith from the driver's seat. "That all we gotta do? Put gas innit?"

Slick gave Cassie the gas can. "You put that in the back and fill it when you get to Newcome." He pointed down the road, away from the church. "They gotta gas station there, but only for white folks."

"You think they gotta map in Newcome? Our map so old, the roads done worn off."

Slick went over to the convertible, where Ovid Beale had pulled a crisp new map out of the glove compartment. Slick helped him spread it out on the convertible's silky red trunk. Cassie pressed herself close to Ovid Beale before Judith could climb out of the shuddering junk car and gallop over.

"Slick says you know where Porterville is."

"Shore I know," said Ovid Beale. "Who tol' you 'bout it?"

"You ever hear of Beanie Simms?"

Judith was there, pushing the hair out of her eyes, hands on the map.

Slick tapped an unmarked point near the leftmost edge of the map. "We here," he said. "This the railroad you bin followin'." The railroad showed as a hatched line across the green background of the state of Mississippi. The road from Heron-Neck beside it was marked in black and as thin as mending thread. The state roads and highways cut wide paths in reds and blues.

"Newcome down here." Ovid Beale pointed out a dot no bigger than a speck of pepper. "Two hours away." He traced the length of the road from Newcome to the next intersection. Two thready black lines ran together; the one paralleling the tracks, the other crossing them. The road crossing the tracks was marked STATE HIGHWAY 18. "This here crossroads is Porterville."

"Porterville?" said Cassie in amazement. So close?

"A good twenty miles from Newcome, and you got to be there by sundown." Ovid Beale straightened and held Cassie by the wrist, looking right into her face. "I don't want you gals to think we inhospitable, but you need to be well past Newcome by afternoon so you can git to Porterville by night."

"What's in Porterville?" said Judith.

"Colored folk," said Ovid Beale. "It ain't safe campin' by the tracks after dark. Y'hear me, lil white gal? An' telling folks this lil colored gal is you sister is jus' plain stupid. Get you both wuss'n kilt. Y'unnerstand that?"

Judith looked like the idea had never crossed her mind. "Yessuh."

"When you git to Porterville," said Ovid Beale, "you ask for Mistah Johnson Mallard. He one of my uncles. You tell him Ovid Beale sent you, and he give you a place to stay."

Behind Ovid Beale, more and more people were arriving at the church. Most were wearing black and red. The women had red head-wraps, and the men wore red sashes across black suits. One of the women made her way over to the cars with a basket on one arm.

"You gettin' that shirt dirty?" she said to Slick. "That the only white shirt you got."

"I ain't," he said and showed her the sleeves, which were pristine.

"Service 'bout to start," said the woman. Cassie thought she was probably Slick's wife. The woman turned to Cassie and gave her the basket. It was heavy and smelled of ham and fresh bread. "Don't want you to consider us inhospitable, but you cain't stay. This a private service."

"Yessum," said Cassie. "Thank you, ma'am."

"Thank you, ma'am," Judith said.

Ovid Beale folded up the map and handed it to Judith. "Don't dawdle now," he said and went to untie the mule from the tree.

They got into the car, Judith in the driver's seat. She put the car in gear, ready to roar out of town as soon as the mule was out of her path. The junk car belched a cloud of blue smoke right into the mule's face. Cassie expected the mule to startle or balk; instead, it turned its head toward them and curled its lips across its teeth. Judith twisted in her seat to watch Ovid Beale lead it toward the church.

"What's the matter?" said Cassie. "We got to go."

Judith swung around in the seat. "Din't you hear that?" Judith gunned the engine, and the car jerked into motion.

"Did he say somethin'?" said Cassie.

"You did too hear it."

"Mister Beale?"

"The mule!"

Cassie glanced back at Ovid Beale and the mule. The rest of the street was empty, and the tall, leafless trees framed the houses in shades of brown and gray, like an old-time photo.

"You din't hear it," said Judith.

"What din't I hear?"

"The mule." Judith kept her hands on the wheel and her eyes on the road, her mouth fixed. "Said, *'Hep me, lil white gal. Hep me!'*"

Cassie laughed. "You outta your mind." She looked back once more at the trees and rough houses just in time to see Ovid Beale lead the resisting mule up the steps of the church and in through the front door.

CHAPTER ✦ FIVE

By midafternoon they found the city limits sign for Newcome. The sign was pocked with bullet holes.

TOWN OF NEWCOME

POP. 212

"Even Heron-Neck had more folks than that," said Judith.

Newcome was big enough to have a general store with a pair of gas pumps. On the near side of the tracks were the same run-down houses, loose chickens, and tied-up dogs as in Heron-Neck. On the far side of the tracks, where the general store was, grand brick houses sheltered under tall oaks and maples.

The general store was called *Ellie's*. Judith pulled into the rutted dirt lot in front of it, alongside two other cars and a wagon with a mule. The wagon driver was a colored man, who looked at the two of them out of the corner of his eye. One of the cars was an aging pickup truck with bales of straw stuffed into the back. The other was older even than the junk car and had weeds growing under it.

Judith surveyed the cars and then the store. "You think I should go in?"

"I ain't," said Cassie. "So it's got to be you."

"Think I should take Big Red in with me?"

"What?"

"The gun."

"Lord Jesus, Judith, you want them to think you're robbin' 'em?"

"I ain't got money, so I guess I'm gonna be doing jus' that."

"You ain't got no money?"

"Where would I git enny money?" said Judith.

The colored man on the wagon was staring right at them. Cassie leaned over her knees so he couldn't see what she was doing and pushed off one shoe. The damp dollar bills had traveled in a wad toward her toe. She peeled off two. "Here," she whispered and pushed the money at Judith from under the dashboard, out of sight.

"You got money in yo' shoes?"

"Jus' get the gas."

"Lucky we ain't jumped on no freight cars."

"And get another map."

"But we gotta map."

"You tell 'em you want a map that go north an' east. Alabama's east of here and Tennessee's north."

"I ain't gonna member. Write 'em for me."

Cassie took a stub of pencil from the glove compartment and wrote on a scrap of paper bag:

Alabama
Tennessee

Judith took the scrap of paper and the empty gas can and went into the store. As soon as she was out of sight, the man got down off the mule wagon, sauntered over to the car, and leaned on the door.

"Aftuhnoon, miss," he said.

Cassie nodded curtly without looking at him, like Grandmother would've done.

"Where y'all from?" he said.

"Yonder a ways."

"I been all round Mississippi. Likely I know your town. Where y'all from?"

He made her uncomfortable. "You know Hilltop?" Cassie said.

"Hill folk don't come down here too often."

"That's right."

"Cain't say I ever seen 'em with white folk, neither."

"Prob'ly not."

He studied her and leaned in closer. "If you hill people, I'm king o' de niggahs."

Cassie glanced at the front of the store. There was no sign of Judith or anyone else. She thought of the horse pistol under the driver's seat but couldn't see how she could lean over, grab it, get the hammer cocked, and point it at him in one smooth move.

So she pointed at his mule. "Where you git your mule from?"

"Ain't my mule."

"Always been a mule?" said Cassie.

"What the hell you talkin' 'bout, girl?"

She could remember the gist of what Ovid Beale said on the way to Hilltop, but not the details, which had been ridiculous at the time, but now felt too important to be left out. "You never know 'bout mules," said Cassie. "Half of 'em use to be colored folk."

The man didn't say anything, but he moved back a bit.

"An' your mule got a certain—a certain *'pearance*."

"What kinda *'pearance* you talkin' 'bout?"

"He got plans," said Cassie, trying to sound careless but informed, like Judith when she lied. "Eatin', sleepin', and gettin' out. That mule useter be a man, jus' like yourself." She paused for effect, because this would be where Judith would pause. She gave the man a look right in his eye, because that was what Ovid Beale would have done. "He musta said the wrong thing to somebody sometime, 'cause now jus' look at 'im."

"Girl," said the man. "You crazy as shit." He walked away, slow, like he really wanted to run, and climbed back onto the wagon. He sat with the reins in both hands, watching the front of the store until a white man came out and motioned him to drive around the back.

Judith came out not long afterward with a full gas can, maps under her arm, and a fist full of beef jerky. She climbed into the driver's seat, handed the jerky and the maps to Cassie. One was ALABAMA AND SOUTHERN GEORGIA. The other was TENNESSEE AND EASTERN MISSISSIPPI. To Cassie's surprise, there was a calendar, too. An OXYDOL one, just like at home. Judith had already folded it open to February.

Judith started the car. "What that ol' man want with you?"

"We jus' talkin' 'bout his mule," Cassie said.

Late in the afternoon, they took a break from driving and sat on the cold ground to eat two of the half-dozen ham sandwiches in the basket. Cassie spread out all three maps—two from the gas station and one from Slick. She could see all of Alabama and most of northern Georgia, as well as the southern edge of Tennessee riding in the upper margins. Virginia was nowhere in sight.

"How far we come already?" said Judith. She was crossing out days on the calendar as though she knew the date. She had made x's all through the month of January and halfway through

February. Cassie wasn't sure of the date exactly, but if Judith was right, they had about four weeks to get through all these states and more that they couldn't see yet.

"Here's Newcome." Cassie showed her.

"Where them Hilltop folk?"

"They ain't marked. But these the hills. Heron-Neck over here someplace." She tapped her finger on the ground, off the map, to the west.

"Well," said Judith, "then I guess we come a fair piece."

Cassie placed her hands side by side by side and counted four hands between where they were and the Mississippi and Alabama border.

Judith put the calendar aside, chewing jerky. "You think there somethin' special where Mississippi ends and Al'bama starts? Like a golden gate? Or a soldier in a little red house?"

"I think that'd be nice," said Cassie.

"I hope there is," said Judith. She got up and wiped her hands. "Let's get goin', or we'll never git to Porterville by dark."

The farther they got from the hills, the smoother the road became. With the winter sun low behind them, the junk car made good speed. Soon they were going fast enough for the wind to flutter their clothes and lift Judith's limp hair. The car was still noisy, but there was no more blue smoke. It seemed like the junk car had cleared its throat and could breathe again.

Judith drove as they passed through the slight hills of the countryside. As it got later, the air became chilly but not unbearable.

"How close're we to Porterville?" Judith asked about an hour before dark.

"Pretty close." Cassie was fairly sure she knew where they were. The railroad was on their right like a dependable river. Ahead State Highway 18 would cross the tracks and the road, and there would

be Porterville. Cassie wasn't sure what she would say to Judith
when they got there or what exactly she would do, but Judith had
a car that ran and maps to find her way. And if there was an inheritance, it would be all hers.

"You know what I'd surely like," said Judith.

"What?"

"A little reddio music." She pointed at a dirty, dented plastic
box on the floor under the dashboard. "Get it up here. Turn it
on. See if we kin git a station."

The radio was a boxy thing under layers of greasy black finger-
prints and of dirt from the footwell. Cassie had thought it was
some part of the car that had fallen out under the dash. It slid
back and forth on a long cord. As long as it lay there and the car
still ran, Cassie had figured leave well enough alone. She squeezed
down over her own knees and reached for the boxy thing gingerly,
a banged-up version of a two-dollar model she'd seen at Tabitha
Bromley's estate sale. She pulled herself and the radio out from
under the dash, holding it with her fingertips. It was just as filthy
as it could be. Even the little bit of glass covering the dial was
filthy.

"Turn it on!" said Judith. "I knows it works."

There were two knobs. Cassie turned one all the way to the
right. Static roared out of the radio. She yelped in surprise, and
Judith laughed so hard the car swerved on the road. Cassie turned
the other knob. There were voices talking, then singing, then
static, then something like gospel, then more static.

Judith said, "See if you kin find New York City!"

Cassie turned the knob the other way, slower.

. . . and the woman fled into the wilderness, where she hath a
place prepared of God, that they should feed her there a thousand two hundred . . .

"If it ain't Sunday, we ain't gotta lissen to the preacher," said Judith. "Keep goin'."

In the beginning was the Word . . .

"*Is* it Sunday?" said Judith. "Mebbe we should check the calendar."

"I don't think it is."

"Then keep lookin'."

Today, President Eisenhower told the press that . . .

Cassie turned the knob once more. There was music, thin and sweet.

"That Doris Day," said Judith. She sang along full-throated but stopped in the middle. "Oh, I hate this song. You like this song?"

"I never heard it before," said Cassie. "Sounds like she singin' inna tin can."

"Her voice all right," said Judith, "but that *song*. La la laaaah, lala." She let her tongue loll out on each *la*.

Doris Day faded into an announcer's voice and more music. Judith listened intently to the first few notes, then crooned along. It was a song about someone's papa, how good and gentle and lovable he was.

Cassie snorted. "He don't sound nuthin' like *your* papa."

"No, he don't," said Judith. "Now here's how the song go about *your* papa."

> *Oh, your pa-pa, he run out on your mama*
> *Oh, your pa-pa, he ran out on mine tooooo*
> *No one could be so turr-i-ble*

Lyin' an' incur-gi-ble
He a skirt-chasin', adulteratin' white trash mannnn!

They laughed so hard, Judith had to steer with one hand while she wiped her eyes. "You think we could git that on the reddio?"

"It don't even rhyme," said Cassie, and they started laughing again.

Another song came through the static, and Judith reached over to turn it way up. "I know this one! Jack played it!"

She started to sing along but stopped again. "This ain't right. These ain't the same guys."

The voices were smooth, like an ironed sheet. "They white," Cassie said, so suddenly she surprised herself.

"They *white*?" Judith fixed her eyes on the radio as though she could tell more by looking at it. "Singin' a black song?" She belted out the chorus the way they'd heard it upstairs at the Wivells'.

"They on the reddio," said Cassie. "They must be doin' somethin' right."

"I wonder if Jack know ennythin' about this." Judith reached over and switched off the noise.

It was dark by the time the railroad tracks turned slightly north and their road met a paved two-lane road marked MISSISSIPPI STATE HIGHWAY 18.

Without even a sliver of a moon, the two of them looked around for Porterville.

They looked for lights or houses or even someone's back fence. There were tracks on the right and open pastures on the left. The one thing that made the intersection remarkable was a billboard, and it was too dark to see what it was for.

"Town's s'posed to be right here," said Judith.

It was too dark to check the map, but Cassie had been check-ing all afternoon. "Right here," she said.

"Mistah Ovid Beale couldn't bin lyin' to us 'cause he showed this place on the map. What's it called again?"

"Porterville. You think we missed it?"

"We din't miss nuthin'," said Judith. She peered into the night. "Kin you hide a whole town?"

"Colored folks maybe want to keep out of sight of the road."

"If that the case, whyn't ennybody say ennythin'?"

Maybe the town would become obvious in the daylight, but Cassie had a terrible feeling in her stomach. She pointed at the billboard. "See if we can get the car back behind there. Just stay here for the night."

Behind the billboard Judith ran the car back and forth in the dry winter brush until the brush lay down in a thick mat. They cleared a space and built a fire out of the broken sticks. Cassie put the rest of the eggs in the skillet, took the ham out of the sand-wiches from Hilltop, and cooked them together. When the eggs were cooked and the ham was hot, Judith shoveled hers back between the two slices of bread. Cassie toasted hers and ate the ham and eggs with her fingers out of the cooling skillet.

"Good ham in Hilltop," said Judith. She opened her mouth for another bite and hesitated and lowered the sandwich. "Hey now. You don't s'pose they turnin' men into hawgs, too—like that mule. I bin thinkin' about it, an' I think he was the husband of that woman in the coffin. They was makin' him haul his own dead wife." She leaned forward and lowered her voice. "You think they was witches?"

"I don't think anyone can turn a man into a mule."

"So why was they takin' him into the church?"

"Maybe the whole church was already fulla mules an' chick-ens an' hawgs."

"You ridiculous. I cain't even have a sensible conversation with you."

"You the one think you eatin' a man-sandwich."

"Well, do you want it?"

Cassie held out her hand, and Judith slapped the warm remains of the sandwich into her palm.

"I feel bad for leavin' that ol' mule back there on his own," said Judith.

"Maybe he deserved to be a mule. Mister Beale was talkin' 'bout him just like he was a skirt-chasin' adulterator."

Judith poked a stick into the fire and let out a laugh. "You s'pose they could do *that* to my daddy?"

In the morning there was no more trace of Porterville than there had been in the night. They crossed the tracks and drove on State Highway 18 for miles in each direction only to find more piney woods. Judith drove, and Cassie turned on the radio for company. It was Sunday, February 20, according to Judith's OXYDOL calendar, but instead of gospel music all they got was static, and Cassie turned it off. They backtracked alongside the railroad tracks, searching the fields and forests until they were halfway back to Newcome. There was no sign of a town or any human habitation.

Judith yawned to show how tired she was of driving in circles. "Mebbe we din't go far enough las' night."

"He said it was at the intersection," said Cassie. She felt far away from everything. "Maybe I saw it wrong when he showed me."

"Mebbe he wuz wrong. He said we wouldn't be safe by the tracks at night, but here we are, so why we still wastin' time lookin'? We got to git goin'. We only got eight days left in February, an' who knows how long it'll take this ol' heap to git to Virginia."

"What if his uncle was expecting us?"

"How Mistah Ovid Beale gonna send word 'bout us to his uncle? Smoke signals?"

Judith put the car in reverse, looked over her shoulder, and steered with one hand as she backed up in a wide curve until they were facing east again. "Course," said Judith, "if they was witches, mebbe they usin' crystal balls." She shoved the car into a forward gear. "You ready?"

Cassie turned the folded map to show the eastward road. She felt desperate, but she didn't know what else to do. "I guess so."

After Johnstown, which was just a collection of shacks, came Larvadale. After Larvadale, where there was no more than two houses and a barn, they began to see signs for Wilburville. Judith decided she was done with driving for now, and they switched. Judith turned the radio back on and soon found gospel choirs up and down the radio dial.

"Mus' be a big place, Wilburville," said Judith.

"Find a station where they singin' 'Ol' Rugged Cross,'" said Cassie.

Judith spun the dial. "That your favorite?"

"Lil Ma likes when I sing it."

Judith hunched over the radio and searched, skipping through various renditions of "Rock of Ages." "I ain't finding it." Judith shut the radio off and sat up straight in her seat. "Reckon I'll have to sing it for you." She tapped Cassie's shoulder, like a schoolteacher. "I'll do the main part. You sing the harmonies."

> On a hill far away stood an old rugged cross,
> the emblem of suffering and shame;

Judith's voice was like a thick piece of chocolate cake. Cassie's own voice was plain beside it, but they sounded good together, and it was easy to make the harmonies heartfelt.

Cassie thought of Lil Ma ironing white women's sheets and pillowcases, sweating late at night over stained table napkins. For the first time the song filled her with a sense of terrible shame. Was Lil Ma's Rugged Cross the light-skinned child she was supposed to bear? Was Cassie's own darkness the suffering and shame? With Cassie gone, how was Lil Ma supposed to redeem herself? What would Grandmother come up with? Cassie shivered. Was Lil Ma strong enough now to refuse her own mother's wishes? Had Cassie thrown away family to set herself—and only herself— free?

"Judith . . ." But Judith let out a yelp.

"Slow down! Slow down! Stop an' pull over! Lawd Lawd! Them Justice boys come to git us for stealin' they car!"

Cassie looked up at the rearview mirror and saw a police car behind them. He flashed his lights and turned the siren on, and Cassie's hands froze on the wheel. Here was God's consequence. But the Justice boys had been ready to torch this car, so how could it be stolen? Hadn't she and Judith saved the car, like a disintegrating rotten old soul?

Cassie managed to pull the car over. The Justice boys—and their father—were not in the police car. There was only the one policeman. If this was God's consequence, He was sending the police a long way for a banged-up car that hardly ran. She turned to Judith, huddled against the passenger door, muttering "Jesus! Jesus!" in her jaybird voice, and it struck Cassie that Judith should have been driving—or was it better that she was the passenger? Where Judith was sitting right now made a difference in how to explain why they were *together*, and where they were going *together*.

"Hush now!" said Cassie. "You actin' like a criminal. All we tryin' to do is find your daddy, right?"

"Jesus!" whispered Judith.

"Right?"

"Right! Right!"

"Now hush and try telling the truth for once."

Judith swallowed and sat up straight in the car seat as though she were in a church pew. The policeman got out of his car, put on his hat, and walked up the driver's side. He leaned down to rest an elbow on Cassie's window and saw Judith. His breath smelled of Wrigley's Spearmint Gum. His sleeve smelled of cigarettes.

"Where you ladies goin' so fast?" said the policeman.

Cassie stared at the steering wheel. It was better not to say anything, better not even to take a breath. Judith answered him all in a rush.

"Suh, we tryin' to git to *church.*"

"What church?"

"Missionary Baptist, suh. I's s'posed to sing for the evening service. Mah girl drivin' cause I's too nervous to drive on days when I sings."

Cassie bit the inside of her cheek. She felt his eyes come to rest on her, then travel back to Judith.

"Which Missionary Baptist?" said the policeman. "The one in Jefferson?"

"Is that the nex' town?" said Judith. "I ain't got no map, an' mah girl don't know what direction she goin' half the time."

"Next town is Madison. Jefferson's ten miles on from there."

"That's where we headed. I jus' hopes we gits theah on time."

The policeman studied her. "Young lady, I don't mean to be disrespectful, but you don't sound like you got no singin' voice. And your girl here was weavin' like she'd had a drink or two."

"She ain't drinkin'. She jus' a turrible driver." Judith stuck out her chin. "In fact, in Heron-Neck where I's from, mah singin' voice is well-known and respected. In fact, I's headed to New York City for an aw-diction with the *Main* Missionary Baptist Church."

Cassie made herself be still. It was too late to say anything now.

"That so?" said the policeman. "Then why don't you step out that car and let me hear your well-respected voice."

"Come on out, Cassie," said Judith. "You kin sing harmony."

Something bad was going to happen. Cassie could feel it as she sat in the lumpy seat. She had no idea what she could do to stop it except physically grab Judith, throw her into the car, and try to outrun the police.

"Yessum," said Cassie.

The two of them stood in the road by the car, which was still half in the lane, half under a barely leafed tree along the side of the road. There was no other traffic, only the sounds of birds, and dogs barking in the distance.

The policeman stood in the middle of the empty road on the white line that divided the lanes. "I'm waitin'."

Judith said to Cassie, "Precious Lord, Take My Hand."

Cassie nodded. She'd half-expected Judith to say, *Get in th' car! Les run fer it!* but Judith clasped her hands before her chest as though in prayer, took a breath, and sang.

> *Precious Lord, take my hand,*
> *Lead me on, let me stand.*

Maybe it was the chill air that made Judith sound so grown, so full of feeling, or maybe it was the way the road resonated. She sang without drama or her usual wild hand motions. She sang the song as though she'd known the man who'd written it, a man whose wife had died in childbirth along with the child itself, and come to understand his pain. Cassie looked out of the corner of her eye to see if the policeman had any appreciation for what he was hearing. He had taken off his hat. He had taken a shuffling step across the white line into the other lane as though pushed. He looked amazed.

Judith shut her eyes and let her voice rise through the refrain into the parts where a soloist would leave the choir behind. Cassie looked at her shoes and thought about Lil Ma. She would never go back and make a baby with a white man for Grandmother. If that was selfish, then that's what it was. If there was a punishment down the road for being selfish—and she knew there would be—it wouldn't be a light-skinned child and a sudden move to another town farther north. It would be something unexpected and perhaps awful. She looked at the policeman again and wondered if God would punish her and Judith both by compelling him to escort them to a church at which they had no appointment.

> *Take my hand, precious Lord,*
> *Lead me home.*

Another car approached from the east, slowed, and stopped as Judith came to the end of the second verse. Two elderly white women poked their heads out and began a fluttering applause. Judith smiled, gracious and sweaty, and looked like she could use a drink of water.

"The spirit moves in you, sister!" shouted one of the women.

"The Lawd done touched her," cried the other.

"She singin' at Missionary in Jefferson tonight," said the policeman.

"Oh, ain't that exciting!" said one of the women. "My grandson goes there with his wife's family."

Another car pulled up behind them, a battered old heap in worse shape than the one they were driving. A gaunt white man and his gaunt children stared out the windows.

Judith, sensing an audience, pushed her hair back with her usual drama. "An' now I'll be singin' 'Wade in the Water.' Y'all join with me!"

The gaunt man got out of the car. His children, so thin and dirty it was impossible to tell which were boys and which were girls, got out too and stood in a barefoot row. Judith began to sing and they clapped along without rhythm.

> *Who's that yonder dressed in red*
> *Wade in the water*
> *Must be the children that Moses led*
> *And God's gonna trouble the water*

Another car, this one from the west, slowed and stopped. A white man in a pressed suit got out and gave a nod to the policeman. Judith, singing, slid her eyes over to him and swung her arms wide like she was fending off hornets.

More cars stopped, and people got out of them, as though all the churches in these parts had let out at once, and all the folks who'd been in church had to travel home along this road.

> *You don't believe I've been redeemed*
> *Wade in the water*
> *Just see the holy ghost looking for me*
> *God's gonna trouble the water*

Judith finished and everyone applauded. The policeman put his hat back on in an approving way, so that it seemed that instead of stopping a car for weaving, he had actually discovered Judith's talent, and having her stop traffic in the middle of a Sunday was a blessing to everyone.

Judith coughed delicately into her palm and nudged Cassie with her elbow.

"We gone be late, Miz Judith," said Cassie loudly. "Lawd bless these folk for stoppin' and list'nin' to you sing."

"The Lawd bless you *all*," said Judith. She took a step back and slid as gracefully as she could into the car and across to the passenger side. Cassie could hear people saying, "Missionary Baptist in Jefferson tonight!" She got into the car and turned on the ignition, praying to Jesus and every angel that the car would start without trouble. It did. She put it in gear and inched it forward. People in the road smiled and waved as Judith blew kisses. Cassie pulled away, and the collection of cars and locals diminished in the mirror.

"Mah goodness!" said Judith. "Go faster, Cassie. I'm overheated, and I need a breeze!"

Cassie glanced in the mirror. There was no sign of a police car, but she didn't speed up. "Aw-diction in New York City? The *Main* Missionary Baptist Church?"

"It jus' come into my head. I cain't help it. I reckon I get it from my daddy."

"Lucky no one from Jefferson was there," said Cassie. "We'd be in jail."

Judith wiped her forehead on her sleeve. "Seen any signs for Jefferson?"

"Not yet."

"If you do," said Judith, unnecessarily, "we better go in a diff'rent direction."

CHAPTER ✦ SIX

Someone had lied about Porterville. Beanie Simms or Ovid Beale, and for the life of her, Cassie couldn't understand why. She felt a strange twinge when she thought about herself as a white girl instead of a black one, like she wouldn't know who she was anymore. Using some kind of magic was different from using the albino boy to create a light-skinned baby. Surely turning white wasn't something that could happen overnight. It must be something that took time and some study. Judith wouldn't want to wait around. She would go on to Virginia and leave Cassie behind.

With only four weeks to get to Virginia, it seemed sensible to get off the secondary roads and try the more direct highways. An east-west line on the map was marked HIGHWAY 80; they ran into Highway 80 later that afternoon. There was a man parked at the intersection in his pickup truck selling from a crate of apples and a stack of cheeses. The apples were mealy, what you'd expect this time of year, but the cheese was good. In another few miles, just past Compton's Bluff, they found a gas station.

Cassie sat in the driver's seat needing to pee, but the bathroom was for WHITES ONLY. She didn't want to go around back behind the bushes. There were houses nearby, and besides, there was this pimply white boy. He was wearing a white gas station uniform. His job was to pump gas and wash all the car windows. He sopped the side mirrors and the headlights, which didn't even work. Why was he being so thorough with the windows when the rest of the car was such a mess? He looked at her through the windows as he washed, which made her uncomfortable. For the most part, though, he stood by the side of the car and rattled the gas pump until the sounds of flowing sputtered to a stop and the tank was full.

Judith had gone inside craving Red Hots. Cassie had given her a nickel, saying, "You sure you ain't pregnant?" Judith had laughed.

Farther down the road, Judith showed Cassie what you could get for a nickel—Red Hots *and* about fifty jellybeans in *all* different colors, even the licorice ones which Cassie hated. Judith reached into the bottom of the bag. "I got this for you."

It was a postcard of a town square with a statue in the shape of a woman holding a vase over her head. Water sprayed out of the vase and cascaded down. People in their Sunday best stood around, admiring her.

"You like that?" said Judith. "The man behind the counter give it to me for free."

Cassie slowed and took the postcard.

"Keep your eyes on the road now."

"Where's this?"

"That in Enterprise, Al'bama, straight ahead, 'bout eighty, hunnert miles. We goin' right through."

"They have a statue?"

"It's a *monument*."

"To what?"

"He din't say." Judith took the postcard, squinting at the printing on the back. "Hail, I cain't read this. Here, les switch, an' you kin read it to me."

"My turn to drive."

"Well." Judith dug in the bag again and took out a freshly sharpened, bright yellow pencil. "I got this for you too."

"What for?"

"Well," said Judith. "I thought you might want to send a post-card to your mama." She pulled out an identical second postcard from the bag. "An' while you're at it, mebbe you kin help me write to my momma too."

In the evening, well behind a billboard for KELLOGG'S CORN SOYA TWIN TREATS, they built a fire, ate the rest of the jellybeans, and Cassie wrote out postcards as Judith scratched another day off the calendar.

"What you want to say?" she said to Judith.

Judith put the calendar down. "Dear Mama an' Henry,"

Cassie had already written that part. Her letters looked blocky, unpracticed. Not like the flowing script in blue ink from the newspapered-over walls back home. *My dearest sister; I am sorry to tell you that our father is dead.*

"I am almos' in Al'bama."

Cassie wrote it down. In spite of the candy taste in her mouth, the sense of accomplishment in driving so far, and her own denial, she felt homesick.

"It is cold," said Judith, and Cassie wrote that down too, but Judith made her erase it. "Then she'll try'n' send me new socks or somethin'. Here, write this. 'I am on my way to New York City to be-come a singin' star.'" She watched Cassie print the words. "Now write, 'You keep list'nin' to the reddio, and you'll be hearin' from me.'"

Cassie wasn't sure how to spell *radio*, so she wrote it the way Judith always said it. *Reddio.* "You want to mention your daddy?"

"It'd make her spittin' mad if she knew I was gonna see him. Now lemme sign it."

Cassie gave Judith the pencil. Judith took the card and made smeary black marks in the remaining space at the bottom that spelled *Judith Forrest,* as though her mother might be confused about which Judith had sent her a postcard.

Later, when Judith was asleep, Cassie wrote her own postcard.

Dear Lil Ma.
  I am doing good. We have a car and people help us when it don't run.

Grandmother would see it too, maybe first. The postman might just hand it to her. She erased everything and started again, with proper grammar this time.

Dear Lil Ma and Grandmother,
  I am doing well. We have a car and people help us when it doesn't run.

Wind blew under the KELLOGGS billboard, making the fire thin. A wall of thorny bushes separated the billboard from the road, and birds chirped sleepily from inside. She wondered what to write next. *I miss you.* Even though it was true, that would make Lil Ma cry. Cassie couldn't bear to have Lil Ma's crying in her mind.

I have met a mule that once was a man.

They would think she'd taken up drinking.

Soon we will be in Enterprise in Alabama . . .

That seemed good. She wrote it down.

where there is a monument to . . .

She turned the postcard so she could see the caption on the back. In the firelight, at first she thought she'd read it wrong. She read it again. She turned the card over and finished her sentence.

. . . where there is a monument to the Boll Weevil. I will write more soon.

                                           Love, Cassie

She addressed it to Lil Ma at:

The Laundry on Negro Street,
Heron-Neck, Mississippi

Cassie put the card on the dashboard and lay down on the seat. She was tired, but the last two days had been so full of strange things. She found herself thinking about the two elderly women up on Hilltop who had spoken to her in such hard tones—as stern as Grandmother—but then another woman had given her the basket full of ham sandwiches, which she'd probably been taking to the funeral. Which made her think about Judith's fears about the man the ham might've once been, which made her laugh. Judith sat up suddenly in the back and sucked in a quick breath through her teeth, like she'd scared herself out of a dream.

"You 'wake?" Judith said.

"Yes."

"You hear that?"

Cassie listened but could only hear the low sound of the wind coming around the billboard. "Hear what?"

"Voices."

"You dreamin', Judith. You was sound asleep, and I bin 'wake this whole time."

"I wasn't asleep." Cassie could hear her unwrapping the pistol.

Cassie sat up. "*Please* don't go out there an' start shootin'."

"I'll shoot enny damn thing that needs to be shot." Judith climbed out of the car.

Cassie scrambled after her. "There ain't nothin' out there."

"*Shush!*"

The pistol was immense, even in the dark. It was as long as Judith's lanky forearms and heavy enough that she had to hold it with both hands. It was so big, it made her look too small to do anything with it.

Cassie followed her around the front of the car to where they had a clear view of the road. The area directly underneath the billboard was filled with thorn bushes and briars grown so thick and high that they presented the illusion that there was nothing behind the sign but briar patch, but there was actually a hedge of barbs and thistles. Judith and Cassie hunkered down on their heels, close enough to the thorns for their sleeves to catch.

"I heerd somethin'," said Judith. "It weren't no dream. Look."

Across the road, two figures—as flat as a cardboard in the dark—were walking toward the billboard.

One of them said distinctly, "Dave said he saw 'em pull in back year."

"He sure it's them?"

"He said it was a junky ol' Model A with a coupla nigger gals drivin' it."

"Thought one was white."

"One was 'tendin' she was white. The other one too dark to fool ennyone."

Was one of them the pimply faced boy from the gas station? It didn't really matter who they were. The boys sauntered closer to the sign coming around the opposite side where Cassie and Judith were. Cassie pushed Judith forward, keeping the island of thorns between them and the boys.

Judith let herself be pushed, but not far. She craned her neck to see. Cassie could tell by the crunch of brush that the boys were coming around to a point where they couldn't help but see the car. She gave Judith a shove, but Judith didn't budge.

"They gonna de-stroy the car," Judith hissed. "They ain't no different than them damn Justice boys. They prob'ly brought a canna gasoline." She took a step toward the car. Cassie grabbed Judith's arm to hold her back and pulled. She pulled with such force that Judith lost her grip on the heavy gun. It fell out of her hand and into the mass of briars.

"Jesus *Christ*!" Judith plunged her hands in to find it.

"Hey," said the voice of the pimply faced boy, which Cassie could now hear clearly. "Hey, here's that piece o' crap now."

She could just see the tops of their heads and heard them kicking the cast-iron skillet around and slamming the car doors.

"Where you reckon they went?"

"They heard us comin', idjit. I tol' you to shut yer mouth. They miles away by now."

Judith pulled herself loose from the bushes, wiping blood from where the thorns had raked her arms. She didn't have the gun. "God dammit," she panted. "Come on!" She lunged forward, but Cassie grabbed her again.

"It don't *matter* what they do to the car! What you think they gonna do to *us*?"

"Well, if I had my damn *gun*, they wouldn't do *nuthin'*." Judith yanked away and ran before Cassie could get another hand on her.

"Hey!" Judith shouted. "Hey, you git the hail away from mah car!"

Cassie hunched in the shadows, wondering what the *hail* she should do now. There was only one thing. She snaked her hands into the briars.

"Well, now," said one of the boys. "Looky year. Where's yer friend?"

"She saw how ugly you was, and she run off," said Judith. "You git the hail outta here. You got no bizness botherin' folk in the middle of the goddam night."

"My, my," said the other boy, "we din't realize this was yer personal billboard. An' look how nice you got it set up. Where you sleep? Inna backseat?"

"I said git out," said Judith, and Cassie heard the iron skillet ring as she picked it up off the ground. "An' I mean, *git out.*"

"Lil lady, you needn't get all excited."

Cassie's fingers touched cold metal. She got a two-fingered grip on the barrel of the gun. Thorns stuck into the backs of her hands.

"I'm gonna crack your haid wide open!" yelled Judith, and a second later, Cassie heard one of the car windows smash. Male voices laughed. Cassie got a better grip on the gun, her hands scored. She wrenched it out, and the skin of her wrists tore like the cuffs on an old shirt. The gun glinted in the dull night. It weighed more than she'd thought, as heavy and graceful as two bricks. She almost dropped it again. She stuck the pistol straight in front of her, bolted around the billboard, and burst out in front of the car, where Judith was swinging the frying pan with furious desperation. The boys were close enough to grab it.

"You stop right there!" shrieked Cassie, and both the boys stopped. She'd never shot a gun in her life. She pointed the heavy thing at the pimply faced boy's heart. Judith looked scared. Cassie could see that and the scratches and blood trickling down her own arms all at the same time.

"Whoa, now," said the pimply faced boy. "There ain't no need fer violence."

"You get out right now! Or I'll blow your head off!"

"Looky year," said the other boy.

"*Get out!*" Cassie screamed. Her arms were giving way under the weight of the gun. "*Get out!*" She'd never heard herself scream before.

The pimply faced boy took a nervous step away from Judith. Judith raised the skillet without hesitation and swung it into his elbow. The bang and howl made Cassie think that the gun, inspired by the situation, had shot of its own accord, but the sound was the impact of the cast iron on bone. The pimply faced boy howled again. The other boy grabbed the back of his friend's jacket and practically carried him past Cassie. She swung around to follow them with the barrel of the gun and this time remembered to put her finger on the trigger. She wanted to kill them. It had something to do with the driving and the wind and being away from home. She wanted to kill them, and then Judith was behind her, pulling the gun out of her hands. Cassie dropped into the dirt on her knees. Judith fell down beside her. Out by the road, the boys were still running, into the trees on the other side.

"We have to go," said Cassie.

"We goin' right now." Judith picked herself up and helped Cassie to her feet. She held the gun against her chest like a pet cat, and when they got to the car, she only let go of Cassie long enough to pick up the skillet and toss it in the backseat.

"I thought you was gone to hit him in the head with that thing," said Cassie.

"I wanted to. But I din't wanna kill 'im. You want to drive?"

Cassie shook her head and got in the passenger side. Judith slid in, shut the door, and started the engine.

"I wanted to kill 'em," said Cassie. "I cain't believe how much I wanted to."

"You was truly terrifiyin'," said Judith. "They saw you standin' there, a lil nigger gal with a big ol' gun, pointed right at 'em. I bet that keeps 'em up at night fer a while."

She pulled onto the road and sped up. They watched the trees and the shadows. After a mile or two, the trees opened up into newly plowed fields. Cassie watched the road behind them until she was sure they weren't being followed.

"They's something you should know 'bout that gun," said Judith.

"Don't it shoot?"

"It shoot," said Judith, "except there ain't no bullets in it. They right here in my pocket." Judith produced three bullets, huge even in the dark, each the size of a man's thumb.

"Why ain't they in the *gun*?"

"These here is the very last three bullets that goes with this gun, and I cain't see wastin' 'em on no trashy white boys."

"What do you mean 'the last three bullets'?"

"Miss Cassie, as you well know, Big Red is right at one hunnert years old, and so far as I know, they ain't makin' bullets for it no more."

"What if they don't work?"

"All a bullet's gotta do is fly out the gun and stick itself into something. Ain't no one gonna bother us with a bullet stickin' in 'im."

"Have you *ever* shot that gun?"

"Lotsa times," said Judith.

It felt pointless to ask any more questions. Cassie looked out her side of the car, at nothing in particular, not even the dark.

CHAPTER ✦ SEVEN

After the episode with the pimply faced boy and his friend, both Judith and Cassie stayed in the car when they went to gas stations, and both watched suspiciously as the service man pumped gas and sopped the windshield with soap. The broken window from when Judith had smashed it with the frying pan was in the back, and they found a piece of cardboard big enough to fill the hole and sturdy enough not to be blown away as they drove.

Judith still wanted candy and jerky, but instead of getting these at gas stations, they agreed that a stop at a five-and-dime in some tiny town wouldn't put much of a dent in their schedule. Judith would use the WHITES ONLY bathrooms to keep herself cleaned up. Cassie would find an isolated patch of trees to relieve herself and various cold creeks to wash in.

February was almost over, March was fast approaching, and Virginia was a long way off. Cassie worried, but with the calendar in hand, Judith seemed confident that they would get there with all the time in the world to spare. In the meantime, the car ran, if not smoothly, then at least steadily. At night they camped behind billboards for KENT CIGARETTES, FUNK'S BUTTER, and

OLDSMOBILE. Usually there was enough brush to keep the car hidden from anyone driving by. If there was enough moonlight, Cassie would study the maps before she went to sleep. Judith would puzzle out city names, and they would follow the courses of rivers and railroads with their fingers.

By the end of their first week, they'd reached the Alabama border. There was no golden gate or candy-striped guardhouse. There was only a sign:

WELCOME TO ALABAMA
THE HEART OF DIXIE

"Dammit," said Judith.

Cassie was driving.

"God dammit."

Cassie looked over to see a bloody stain spreading on Judith's skirt.

"Ain't we got a god-damn rag somewhere in this heap?"

Cassie pulled off by the first creek in Alabama. The car bumped off the road and into the grass. Judith kicked her door open and ran down a narrow pebbly beach and into the water, up to her knees. There were houses nearby, so instead of taking the dress off to wash it, Judith twisted around in it so that it was on backward, dark buttons running up her chest instead of her back. She squatted in the water, took off her drawers, and scrubbed them.

Cassie waded out into the cold creek and stood next to her. Judith was crying. Her tears dripped off her chin and into the chill water. "I can get the blood out for you," said Cassie.

Judith stood up, soaked. The stains on her dress were on the back and the front. It wouldn't matter which way she put it on. She wiped her eyes with the backs of her hands.

"Why're you cryin'?" said Cassie.

"It ain't my time of the month," said Judith. "It was a baby. I was gonna have a baby."

Cassie built a fire on the riverbank and hung the dress on a stick to dry. It was still stained. Only vinegar and salt, or bleach would truly clean it.

Judith sat among the pebbles in her undershirt and discolored drawers. "I wonder if it woulda looked like him. All pale like he was."

Cassie pushed twigs into the fire. "Din't you think he was good-lookin'?"

"I guess. Those pink eyes bothered me. Did you think he was? You know. Handsome?"

"I kinda thought so. He wasn't too nice to you, though. Good lookin' don't mean nothin' if he ain't good to you."

Judith hugged herself. Her skin showed gooseflesh. Cassie got her patchy red coat from out of the car and draped it around Judith's shoulders.

"That what your mama said?" said Judith

"My mama never talked 'bout no men."

"Your gramma?"

"What your mama tell you 'bout men?" Cassie stirred the fire.

"'Fore daddy left, she'd say, 'Find yo'sef a man just like yo' daddy.' She used to make me an' Henry get down on our knees an' pray with her every night 'fore bed and thank God for our lil fam'ly. We did that until the day Daddy run off, an' after he left, she'd say, 'Don't never marry no man like that! He gonna bamboozle you, an' no one gonna forgive you for bein' so stupid! Not even God.'" Judith studied her own bare feet. "You know how in fairy stories the pretty girl gits rescued by a knight on a white horse? She'd tell Henry stories like that when he was sick. She loved them stories more'n she loved the ones in the Bible." Judith looked up at Cassie. "But unless you a beautiful princess locked in a tower or in some magical sleep, ain't no man ever gonna come rescue you. They ain't interested in your misery." She hunched over her belly.

The fire smoked and gave off no heat to speak of. Cassie tried to think of something to say to make Judith feel better. "Beanie Simms used to tell me stories, but they never made no sense. They was animals instead of people. Like this monkey who found gold in the river behind his house. So he gets his friends—the elephant and the lion—to help him dam the river and dig up the gold. He says he gone share it. When they're done, he breaks the dam and they all drown, and he keeps the gold."

Judith pushed her arms into her coat and gave that some thought. "How you drown a elephant?"

Cassie poked the fire. "Guess it was a big river."

"Din't that monkey's friends know he never gonna share nothin' with 'em? What kinda story's that—one monkey gits rich, but ever'body else dies in the end?"

"It's just a story," said Cassie. "What kinda lady stays locked up in a tower till the right man come along?"

Judith put her head in her hands. She looked weary, like an old woman. "I'm gonna go lay down."

"You feelin' all right?"

"Just tarred."

"Well. G'night then."

"G'night."

Later the moon rose over the bare trees, so full it woke Cassie out of her sleep. She knew it was the moon, not a noise, and she sat up in the front seat, not afraid but alert.

She got out of the car as quietly as she could. Judith was curled up in the back, sleeping too deeply even to snore. Between the river and the car, Judith's dress hung drying on its rack of sticks. The dress was a light color, possibly white at one time, or maybe

a pale pink. In the moonlight, the stains spread down like maps
of unknown places. Maybe they could pick up some bleach, or
vinegar and salt at a store, soon, depending on which was
cheaper.

Cassie went back to the car and took Lil Ma's shoes out from
under the passenger seat and went barefoot to the creek to count
the money they had left. One dollar bill, four quarters, and some
change, which added up to another forty-six cents. She put all of
it back into one shoe, put both shoes on, and stood.

It was a warm night. Satiny moonlight reflected from the surface of the creek, shimmering on tree trunks on the opposite bank.
Spring peepers chirped in the shadows. The intruding moon made
her restless. She walked along the river until it reached the road.
The bridge there was concrete with 1947 molded into it at the near
end. There was no trace of traffic. Cassie looked across the bridge
and thought she saw lights on in a house, but it was the moon
shining through the trees. The trees stood in a perfectly straight
line, thick-trunked but branchless. Were they telephone poles? She
squinted against the moon. They weren't trees or telephone poles,
but columns that had at one time held up some part of a mansion. The other trees around them were saplings growing inside
where the veranda had been. In the dark from where she was
standing on the bridge, the shape of the vanished house was surprisingly distinct.

Cassie crossed the bridge and stood at the edge of the road,
where short-stemmed brush had broken through the remains of
a flagstone terrace. Some of the flagstones had fallen away, leaving
open holes, which were filled with water, maybe from when the
creek ran high. A pool glittered in the moonlight in an opening
behind the columns where the front hall or the foyer might have
been. The moon shone on the water through the five remaining
pillars. Water lapped against what was left of the house.

Someone was kneeling in the ruins of the house. The lapping was the slap of wet fabric on stone.

A short woman, a colored woman, was scrubbing clothes in the flood of the house's foundation. Two wicker laundry baskets flanked her. Cassie heard herself make a surprised sound, and the woman stopped her washing.

"Who's that?"

Cassie said her name and stepped down into the ruin, where the woman could see her from the opposite side of the pool.

"Come on over heah," said the woman. "Stan' wheah I kin see ya."

Cassie came around the edge of the pool, carefully across cracked flagstone. "We just passin' through. Sleepin' in a car by the crick."

"We?"

"Me an' 'nother girl."

"Where you from?"

Cassie told her.

The woman looked her over. "Ain't you et properly?"

"We et what we brung."

"You friend thin like you?"

"No thinner'n she ever was."

The woman wrung out the shirt she was washing and put it in one of the wicker baskets. "You hep me tote this'er laundry, an' I'll fix you up some ets." She put one of the baskets on her head and pointed to the other. "Follow me."

Cassie picked up the basket and set it on her hip. It was heavy with wet wash. Down the road was an old house set back about ten feet from where cars went by during the day. There was a light on in the front room downstairs, and when the woman with the laundry basket opened the door, another woman, very elderly, looked up from a rocking chair.

"Now who's this?" she said.

"This a vagrant chile who sleepin' by the river."

The house reminded Cassie of her home on Negro Street. Stairs went up along one wall of the house. Upstairs there would be two underheated rooms. Were there bits of newspaper covering the walls? She felt terribly homesick.

The younger woman took the baskets into the kitchen. Cassie heard an outside door open and knew the younger woman was on her way to hang the laundry on lines out back.

"Why you a vagrant?" said the old woman.

"I'm no vagrant. I left home is all."

The back door slammed again, and the younger woman, the daughter probably, came back into the front room. A puff of cooking smells followed her from the kitchen.

"You done let the stew burn," said the daughter.

"Ain't burnt," said her mother.

The daughter turned to Cassie. "You like rabbit stew?"

"Yessum."

"Your friend like rabbit stew?"

"I think so."

"You know how to make corn bread?" the daughter said and eyed her mother. "This old woman was s'posed t' make some, but she so damn old she plumb fergot."

"Lawd," said her mother. "I plumb fergot. I was bein' so keerful 'bout the damn rabbit stew."

The daughter turned back to her. "It a wonder you still alive. One o' these days you gone plumb fergit to take yo' nex' breath."

"I kin make the bread," said Cassie.

"I ain't so old you got to bring vagrant gals inna middle of the night to make the corn bread," said the mother.

"Oh you *ain't*, is you?" said the daughter. "Then how come

we *ain't* got no supper?" She caught Cassie by her wrist and pulled her into the kitchen.

"You yeast your bread?" said Cassie, as the daughter dragged her under the drape separating the kitchen from the front room. The daughter looked back like Cassie was crazy.

"We ain't got time to let it rise, gal. I got to git up in two hours and clean the damn houses."

The kitchen was wide and warm and brightly lit, and the rabbit stew simmered on a white enamel gas stove. Cornmeal, baking powder, salt, a big bowl, three brown eggs, and a pitcher of milk sat on the kitchen table along with a metal baking dish. The daughter handed Cassie a wooden spoon.

"Mix it up," she said, "an' git it inna oven. I got to finish hangin' these damn clothes." She went out the kitchen door into the dark. Her mother came in under the drape, limped over to the table, and sat in one of two rough wooden chairs.

Cassie poured cornmeal in the large bowl, guessed at the amount of baking powder, broke in the eggs, and poured the milk. She stirred until the old woman said, "You fergot the salt."

Cassie added the salt, mixed, and was about to pour it into the pan when the old woman said, "Butter it!"

Cassie got butter from the refrigerator—not an icebox like the one at home but an actual electric refrigerator—found butter and greased the pan. She poured the batter and faced the stove. She'd never used a gas stove before.

"Here, now," said the old woman, "see them knobs?" She told Cassie how to turn them for the right temperature, which struck Cassie as being something like tuning the radio in the car. She put the cornbread in and brushed off her hands.

"You think you done?" said the old woman. "Grab out them collards from the sink." She took a long paring knife out of the folds of her skirt and handed it to Cassie. Cassie trimmed the collards and cut them into neat strips, stems in a pile for the garden, like Grandmother had taught her. "Ma'am," Cassie said. "If you don't mind my askin'. Do you gen'rally do cookin' and cleanin' in the middle of the night?"

The old woman let out a snort. "We do what we got to do when we got to do it." She pointed to a door by the refrigerator. "Look in the pantry and slice off a little of the ham hangin' there."

Cassie took the knife and opened the door. The pantry was tiny, no bigger than a small closet. It was dark inside and almost as cold as stepping outside on a winter day. Cassie's breath let out as steam.

"Ham's in the back," said the old woman. "Over them baskets of dried apples."

A dozen little jars of clear water sat in a row just inside the door. Cassie stepped over them and ducked under braided hanks of onions hanging from low unpainted beams. Baskets full of potatoes, turnips, and roots she didn't recognize were stacked close together on the cold stone floor and gave the air a brittle fragrance. The pantry was so dark, she could barely see the smoked ham. She took a step, stumbled on a potato basket, and flung out a hand for the back wall, but there was no back wall. Her hand touched a surface like a stair instead, filthy with age and icy to the touch. And there was something else, densely cold, almost solid. Whatever it was, when her hand brushed through the icy space, something sighed a melancholy sigh. Cassie stiffened, the smooth wooden handle of the knife in her hand.

"What you doin' in there, gal? Don't be steppin' in my baskets!"

The ham swung in an unfelt breeze. Cassie stepped back, eyes locked on the invisible thing in the dark.

"What you doin' in there, gal?" demanded the old woman. "Ain't you see that ham? Git me two good slices an' come on out!"

Cassie jammed the knife into the ham and hacked off two pieces. The presence on the stairs moaned as if it had known the hog personally. Cassie reeled backward between baskets, spun around, ducked the onions, and with two thick strips of ham in her fist, jumped the line of glass jars. She emerged into the kitchen to see the old woman rocked back in the kitchen chair.

"You look chilled, gal."

"Cold in there," whispered Cassie.

"Sure as hell," said the old woman. "Bit crowded, too. Now get that ham in the pan."

Cassie dropped the ham into the skillet and stood half-frozen while the meat sizzled. She remembered to put the collards in, but her feet itched with the desire to run right out the door. Grandmother had always sneered at people who told stories about ghosts. She dared to look over her shoulder at the kitchen door and the front door beyond. The old woman had blocked any clear escape. Cassie turned to the collards.

"Gal, you like yams?"

Cassie wished the younger woman would get back from hanging the laundry. "Yessum."

"You knows where yams comes from?"

Cassie concentrated on the collards, stirring them as they wilted down. "From the garden?"

"Yam come from Africa, gal. Some people call it *sweet potato*, and sometime I expect the yam think of himself as a sweet potato, but the sweet potato and the yam two different things confused for each other." She scowled at Cassie. "You knows where you come from, gal?"

"Mississippi, ma'am."

"Right there, you like the yam. You think of yo'self as one thing, but then there's another thing. You don' know it. Nobody round you know it, but there ain't no way you cain't be it. No more'n a yam kin be a sweet potato."

"Is it like the mule, ma'am?" said Cassie.

"What you know 'bout mules, gal?"

"They the mos' nigger of all critters."

The old woman leaned forward in the chair so that it gave a deep, aching creak, and gave her the same disbelieving look as the man who'd been sitting in the mule wagon back by Ellie's store.

The kitchen door opened, and the younger woman came in. She sniffed at the smells coming from the stove, eyed the ham frying in the pan, half-hidden by the limp darkening collards, and gave her mother a look, as if she knew exactly what Cassie had felt in the pantry.

"Dammit," she said to her mother. "I kin see the gooseflesh on her where you gone and scairt her witless." She pushed in front of Cassie and took over the stove and everything on it. "Gal," she said, "this ol' woman send you into the pantry?"

Cassie nodded wordlessly.

"We got some cold spots in this house." She gave the collards a good hard stir. "Some people likes to think of them as spooks. This the overseer's house back in slavery time."

The old woman leaned back in her chair. "Cold norm'ly drift down, but not in this house, cause this house ain't normal."

"There ain't no damn spooks," said the daughter. "An' even if there was, I ain't letting 'em have the run of this place. This place belongs to me, an' I got things to do."

The younger woman scooped half the collards into a big, chipped bowl. She took the hot corn bread out of the oven, sliced up two big hunks, and put them in the bowl with a generous scoop of the rabbit stew. She put in two big spoons and covered it all with aluminum foil.

"This vagrant gal stayin' with us for supper," said her mother.

"No, she ain't," said the daughter. "I ain't gonna let you play with her jus' cause you got nuthin' better to do." She opened the pantry door without hesitation and took out an empty basket. A cold draft curled through the kitchen, but there was no moaning or sighing. The cold smelled of old wooden beams and onions.

She packed the food into the basket and handed it to Cassie. "Share that with your friend out there by the crick. Careful you don't spill. You need help findin' your way?"

"Nome." Cassie held the heavy, fragrant basket in both hands. She wanted to bolt out the door, but there was one more thing she needed. "I was wonderin', though, if I could bother you for some vinegar and salt."

"Someone bleedin' on they clothes?" demanded the older woman.

"Yessum." Even though it was a harmless lie, the words sounded suspicious and hung in the room like the cold air from the pantry. "The blood done set," she added, because at least that was true.

The younger woman reached into a cabinet and took down a bottle of vinegar and a box of salt. She poured out about a quarter cup of salt into an empty jam jar and screwed the lid on tight. She put it and the vinegar in the basket with the food. "You leave this and the basket by that pond inside the mansion." She led Cassie to the door. "Where're you goin'?"

"Virginia," said Cassie.

"Long way," said the older woman.

"You an' your friend be careful," said the younger woman.

The old woman got up from her chair and grabbed Cassie's arm. "Take yo' friend's bloody draws to the pool. Not that li'l crick—the *pool*. Scrub it with that salt and vin'gar an' save the squeezin' water off it in that jam jar." She angled her head at the pantry door and the row of glass jars, unseen behind it. "Blood and salt water. That's how we keep evil things away." The old woman sat down in the straight-backed wooden chair again; righteous.

The daughter led Cassie to the front door and opened it to the night.

Cassie crossed the bridge and followed the creek back to the car. Judith was huddled in the front seat, shivering in her coat.

"Where the hail have you bin? Mah Gawd! I thought you run off."

Cassie got into the junk car and handed Judith the basket. "Folks gave me supper. And stuff to wash out your dress."

"You knockin' on doors and doin' laundry inna middle of the night?"

"I couldn't sleep." Cassie pulled the foil away to show Judith the food. She took one spoon and gave Judith the other, and they ate every bit of the rabbit stew and corn bread and collards. Cassie let Judith eat all the ham.

In the morning Cassie washed the dress in the pool where the old mansion had been. Judith sat cross-legged in her draws and undershirt. The basket, empty except for the bowl and two spoons, sat in the shade by one of the disintegrating columns.

"I'll wash it," Judith said for the second time. "It's my dress."

"That's all right."

"Don't scrub so hard."

The dress was old and thin, but a stain was a stain. "Don't worry about the dress," said Cassie.

"I'll worry if I want to," said Judith. She waved away gnats.

The salt roughed itself into the damp fabric, gritty, then slippery as it dissolved. Vinegar added something to the mix that made the stains slide out and vanish in the rinse. In the cool light of sunrise, the dress was dark with water but clean. Cassie squeezed the dress where the stains had been and let the water trickle into the empty jam jar. The water had a brackish look to it, an unpowerful look.

Judith propped herself up. "What in the world are you doin'?"

"What's it look like I'm doin'?"

"It *look* like you saving the damn bloody washin' water."

"I guess I am." How could she say what the water in the jar was really supposed to do?

Judith picked up the jar and threw it into the pool. She took up the dress and wrung it until it was as dry as it would get without being hung. She put it on. "It'll dry when we get drivin'," she said.

"You'll catch cold," said Cassie.

Judith straightened her damp dress. "Cain't you tell it gonna be a hot day?"

Cassie drove, east through Alabama. The land looked a little different. The pines taller and thicker in the woods and a smoky quality to the air, especially higher up in the hills. Overall, though, the flatland was still flat, and where the land was farmed, there was always a man and a mule. Two times there was a man and a tractor. Always, there was a tumble of shacks, and in the distance, a big house on a hill, falling to pieces under huge old trees.

Cassie thought about the jar and the water, mixing with all the other washing water in that pool. She thought about what Lil Ma might be doing, which was easy. She was doing the wash while Grandmother kept an eye on her, and from beyond the grave, the mothers of grandmothers and grandmothers before them kept an eye on her. Clear back to slavery mothers. Maybe beyond. Was the ghost in the pantry kin to the older woman and her daughter?

"You b'lieve in ghosts?" Cassie said.

Judith had been frowning at the road, not really seeing it.

Any other time this would have been enough to launch Judith into some convoluted story she'd made up on the spot; this day Judith just hunched into her shoulders. "Don't you?"

CHAPTER ✦ EIGHT

For the three days it took to get to Enterprise, Judith didn't say much. The junk car puttered along the two-lane highway. People in other cars yelled at them to *git outta the way*. Even other junkers passed them.

Cassie turned on the radio and found a station with a man playing a melancholy guitar and singing cowboy songs. Judith didn't sing along. She cried at night. Cassie tried to say things she hoped were comforting, but when nothing seemed to help, she said, "Is you sick? Mebbe you need a doctor to look at you." Back in Heron-Neck, Mrs. Duckett had known about every female trouble. She knew who was confined to bed rest, who'd miscarried, who'd had twins (each by a different daddy). She knew who was trying hard to get with-child and who didn't need "enny more chillun ennyhow." Mrs. Duckett talked about male troubles too, but those were discussed mostly with raised eyebrows and hand gestures, and only when Grandmother wasn't around. Cassie felt far less informed about male problems.

At the end of the third day, the land turned hilly, and the car, unaccustomed to climbing, began to overheat. Even though it was early in March, the day had been hot. Cassie had stopped often to make sure there was water in the radiator. Judith slept in the backseat, oblivious.

In the late afternoon while Cassie was peering into the heat and darkness of the radiator, Judith woke up. "Where are we?"

"Alabammy hill country." Cassie shut the car hood and picked up a galvanized bucket she'd found on the side of the road. The bucket had been shot at, but the holes were only in the upper half, so the bottom still held water. She'd been keeping it in the foot well of the passenger seat. There seemed to be a creek in every little valley.

"I mean where on the map?"

"I guess about a day away from Enterprise."

Judith sat up in the backseat. She looked better, not so bloodless. "Where we gonna stop?"

"I ain't seen a safe place. I seen a lot of lil shacks with white folks an' big dogs. None o' the coloreds been wavin' back."

"Ever'body think you stole this car, an' now you drivin' round showin' it off." She got out of the backseat and made her way gingerly to the front. She sat down with her feet on either side of the bucket without acting like she'd even seen it. "You lucky you ain't been shot at."

"Nobody wants this car but us. You want somethin' to eat?"

Judith leaned her head back on the ragged upholstery. "I'd like a steak 'n' taters, please. An' a ice-cold Coca-Cola to wash it all down." Cassie laughed, and Judith smiled a pale smile. "Let's find us a big ol' billboard for the night."

A billboard for TIDE detergent was at the top of the hill and had been for such a long time that the bright orange-and-yellow bull's-eye box had faded to gray. Cassie and Judith hid the car in thorny weeds and ate stale corn bread, all they had left. Judith marked off the past three days on the calendar and turned the page uneasily to March. Two weeks left and still in Alabama.

"We gonna hafta drive day and night," said Judith.

"We don't have the money for gas to drive day and night."

"Well now," said Judith, sounding a little desperate. "We cain't git stuck out here after comin' all this way."

"We'll find a way," said Cassie, "isn't that what you said?"

"I know it's what I said."

"We got to eat," said Cassie. "We'll think better with something in our stomachs."

They picked dandelion greens and tried boiling them the way they thought they remembered their grandmothers had, but the greens were bitter and tough. Not far behind the billboard, Cassie found a stand of mulberry trees with enough fruit for the two of them to feel less like they were starving. In the long grass under twisted trees they found a rotting arrangement of crates, which had once been set up as a table and chairs. Judith pushed a crate over with her foot, and that was when they found the bottles of moonshine whiskey. One was corked, nearly full, and only dirty on one side, where it'd been lying in the leaves for who knew how long. Judith scuffed around it until all the spiders ran off, and took it back with them to the car.

It had been a clear hot afternoon, and the evening was no different. From the top of the hill, their view of the sky was uninterrupted. Stars came out. Crickets, frogs, and night birds sang all around them. There wasn't so much as a porch light showing in the valley. Had they fallen between the crisscross of roads and landed somewhere on the old map they'd started with—on which the markings had worn away?

Judith uncorked the bottle, took a deep whiff, and handed it over to Cassie. It smelled like paint thinner.

"I hope you don' think I'm gonna drink this," said Cassie.

"Din't nobody in your fam'ly drink?" said Judith. "Not even when your granny wasn't lookin'?"

"You know my momma din't."

"She shoulda." Judith reached for the bottle. Cassie handed it back and watched Judith put the mouth of the bottle between her lips and lean back so the whiskey just rolled in. Judith swallowed twice, silently, with a terrible expression on her face, leaned forward, and coughed like she was drowning. Cassie tried to pound her on the back, but Judith held her off.

"'At's how it s'posed to be." Judith gasped and pushed the bottle at her and made encouraging motions with both hands.

"I felt so sorry for your ma," Judith said. "She din't wanna sleep with my daddy. She coulda done better by you. I'd see people lookin' at your mama, jus' *lookin'* at her. I felt so sorry for her," she said again. "Din't you?"

Cassie looked out at the dark and the moon, aware of a pain in the middle of her chest.

"You wanna go home," said Judith.

"I don't."

"You do," said Judith, "but you cain't." She giggled, got up, and stumbled to the car. The radio came on. Static hissed. A white man's voice read an agricultural report. The idea that white people were right here, talking about how the corn crop was coming along, not just among themselves around a kitchen table, but on the radio where everyone could hear, made Cassie's chest hurt more. Judith had left the bottle on the ground, and Cassie picked it up. It was about half gone. *Cain't. Ain't.* She shut her eyes and tears came out. She took a gulp, fast, so as to bypass her tongue; it was like a mouthful of gasoline. The fumes came up behind her eyes and made them water. She choked for breath.

"Don't you be drinkin' the whole bottle!" Judith said.

The stuff ran down into Cassie's stomach and lay there. Her mouth and throat felt like she'd swallowed lit matches. There was nothing to do but drink again. She did and had to lie down on her back in the grass. She blinked at the moon. Her chest seemed not to hurt as much.

Judith was fiddling with the radio.

"We out in the middle of nowhere," Cassie kind of sang. "What you gone get 'sides hillbilly music?"

"You lissen an' see." Voices flickered through static, faint, then stronger, sharp-edged, distant accents from a different world.

I'm young, I'm loose, I'm full of juice.

Drums and horns and a man's voice spilled out of the radio. Judith pranced back through the darkness and stood over Cassie. She pattered her hands across her hips, shook her hands around, and rolled her eyes. From Cassie's ground-view, Judith looked like a boneless waggle of limbs, which was funny. Judith reached down and pulled Cassie to her feet. "Come on an' I'll show you how to dance. Do what I do." Judith threw her hands over her head and wiggled all over. Cassie tried it, and the silliness of it made her burst out in a laugh. Judith swung her arms and kicked her feet and sang along with her chin jutted out until static overwhelmed the song. She whirled over to the car to find another station. Cassie rubbed at where the pain had been in her chest. The ache was gone, and she felt fine now. Even the worry about getting to Virginia on time was fading. Where was the bottle? In Judith's hand.

"They only play this kinda music at night?" Cassie said.

"Ain't legal durin' daylight hours. Jack tol' me."

Judith squinched up her face in the moonlight, listening for something in particular amid the shreds of music and yelps of voices. There was a *Woohoooo! Woooohoo!* Not a human sound. Barely an instrument. Judith bounced out of the car, kicked off her shoes, and stood tiptoe in the long grass. "I wanna show you how Jack showed me to dance," she said. She took a long suck on the bottle, steadied herself against the car, and wiped sweat off her forehead.

It was the moon, Cassie thought, the moon was making everything so hot. The liquor, which had numbed her stomach and her chest, seemed cooler in the bottle than the night air, so it only made sense to take another drink, and even though it still felt like fire, her throat was seared now, so it didn't really matter what went in there. She was surprised to see how the moon shone through the dirty glass of the bottle, and how the light from the moon looked on her own skin, like a wash of thin white paint, which made her think of Grandmother, and how she must look at the world—coated in shades of white. How complicated all Grandmother's plans seemed, when just standing under the light of a nearly full moon with Judith and her reddio music and a bottle produced the same results. As long as it was night, she was white. Cassie laughed until she thought she might vomit.

Judith laughed too. She snatched the bottle back. "Was you watchin'? Didja see?" She rocked her shoulders one way and rolled her hips in the other direction. "This how Jack taught me to dance." She grabbed Cassie's hand. "You be me," she said. "I'll be him. Here now, spin round!"

Judith spun her. The moon circled around unexpectedly, and the ground felt wobbly. Cassie caught Judith's other hand, the bottle still in it. Together they gripped it, Judith swayed, singing along, to the sounds coming out of the radio. Even though she didn't know the song, Cassie felt like she did, and the words just came out of her mouth, words about love and regret and leaving and return. Judith took another gulp from the bottle, and Cassie did too. The song changed to something slow. The grass was flattened where the two of them were dancing. The moon shone straight down on everything.

"Now," said Judith, "you be him, and I'll be me."

Cassie felt Judith become heavier, and the heaviness pulled Judith into a long, woozy spin. Cassie reached out to keep her from falling down in the flat white grass and saw her own arm, white, white, white.

The albino's whiteness. It had descended on her. The music was slow and sad. Their sweaty hands touched. Judith looked up with weepy eyes. She clutched Cassie's hands and said, "Want to see how Jack showed me how to dance? This 'ere, this's how we did it," and she collapsed against Cassie's chest, buried her wet face into Cassie's neck. The two of them held each other, sweating whiskey through their clothes, whiskey tears soaking into each other's hair, in the middle of the night, at the top of the hill in the trampled grass, where only deer and foxes had been before.

CHAPTER ✦ NINE

The next morning, they got up later than usual. By Cassie's judgment the height of the sun made it almost noon. The weather was cool, which was good, but a light morning mist had settled into their clothes, chilling them both. Their mouths were dry and their heads hurt. The noise from the old junk car made their heads hurt worse. Judith said "Time's a-wastin'," and they got started driving. The highway opened up in front of them. Soon they saw a sign that read ENTERPRISE 10 MILES.

Judith, who was driving, said to Cassie, "What you got left in your shoe?"

Cassie took off her shoe and counted the change. "Ninety-six cents."

"We ain't gonna get to Virginia on ninety-six cents."

"We can get work in Enterprise."

"No one gonna hire us for nuthin'," Judith said. "We jus' vagrants far as ennyone concerned. Besides, earnin' money gonna take too long. I got an idea."

Cassie put her shoe back on. "What's your idea?"

"I ain't telling you," said Judith. "'Cause I ain't sure it gonna work, an' I don't want you thinkin' I'm'n idjit."

"I'll tell you right now if it's a stupid idea, and then you don't have to worry 'bout me thinking you'n idjit."

"You don't have to do nuthin'. An' if it don't work, then I guess we'll clean ourselves up an' find a place needs help with the laundry."

Up ahead signs announced ENTERPRISE'S RARITAN and LIONS CLUBS and a host of others, including the FRATERNAL ORDER OF POLICE.

"You ain't gonna try to do hoorin', are you?" Cassie said.

"Even *I* ain't idjit enough for that."

By the time they got to Enterprise, the cool March morning had turned into a warmer March afternoon. Highway 80 led directly to the center of town, which was where the statue in the picture postcard was. Cars and pickup trucks were parked at an angle along both sides of the street in front of a hardware store, a grocery, and a diner. The monument to the boll weevil rose from a concrete island in the middle of the street. A gleaming white woman stood on a pedestal, dressed in something flimsy that was decorated with gleaming golden curlicues. She looked like she had fallen from the sky, from somewhere completely different than the dusty ordinariness of downtown Enterprise, Alabama. She towered over everything. Her bare arms were raised over her head, hands joined as though in a victorious gesture. In the postcard picture, water had come rushing out of a vase. Now the fountain was dry, and the top was blocked by something dark and oddly shaped.

Judith parked the car by the fountain. "What she holdin' up there?" said Judith.

Cassie squinted into the brightness of the day. What object was that woman holding over her head in both hands, like a trophy?

"Damned if that ain't some kinda insect," said Judith. "Is it a tick?"

"It's a weevil," said Cassie. "See its legs stickin' out on the side?"

Judith stepped into the street and walked over to the edge of the fountain's dry pool. Cassie waited for a pickup truck to chug by, then followed Judith. She could feel people staring at them from the windows of the diner. Cassie shaded her eyes to get a look at the top of the statue. Judith squinted in the sun.

"This ain't how it looked in the picture," said Judith. "It looked better without the bug."

"Maybe no one could tell what it was a monument for."

"Why'd you make a monument to a pest?" said Judith. "It ain't like it died inna war."

They studied it for a while longer. Cassie said, "People looking at us."

"I know." Judith put her hands on her hips. "We got a hat?"

"I don't think so."

"We got somethin' like a hat?"

"Nothin' even like a hat," said Cassie.

Judith eyed the car. "Bring me that ol' skillet."

"Why you want the skillet?"

"We ain't got no hat for folks to toss pennies into."

Cassie looked up at the weevil. "What you plannin' on?"

"I aim to start my fame and fortune right here and now," said Judith. "This the biggest town we come to. Time to stop wishin' an' start doin'. Will you bring me that skillet?"

Cassie went and got the skillet out of the trunk. At the foot of the monument, standing in its afternoon shadow, facing the half-seen people behind dusty windows, Judith cleared her throat and did some humming to warm up her voice. Cassie put the skillet on the ground to Judith's left. Sparse traffic veered around them and the monument. Cassie didn't know where Judith thought her admirers were going to stand and listen. She could have told Judith that she had a better chance at pennies if she stood on the sidewalk in front of the diner, but Judith had a vision in her mind, and there would be no changing it.

"What you gone start with?" said Cassie.

" 'Amazin' Grace,' " said Judith. She cleared her throat and began to sing to the afternoon street.

Cassie sat on the edge of the dry fountain and kept her eye on the diner. On the other side of the plate-glass window, paunchy white men in overalls drank coffee and cut into slices of pie. *What was that girl doin' out there, singin' in the afternoon sun?*

Judith was building steam. Her outsized grown-up voice lent itself to gospel, and she let the sound of it ring off the dusty fronts of the brick buildings. She sounded good today. Cassie smiled at her to let her know she thought so. Judith raised her eyes to the afternoon sky and sang her song as though it was a prayer to God Almighty for success to hit her like a lightning bolt.

She got all the way through "Amazing Grace." People were looking at them from inside shops on both sides of the street. No one came out except for a couple who got in their car and drove off.

"Maybe these ain't religious folks," said Judith, dabbing sweat from her chin. "Maybe I should sing somethin' more country."

"Country don't sound good without accomp'niment," said Cassie, though the truth was, she was starting to get nervous about the lack of interest here in Enterprise. It felt like hostility was coming together behind those shop windows. Gospel might protect them from the worst things. "It's getting late. Mebbe we should get goin'."

Judith started into "Surely God Is Able." More folks got in their cars and drove off. The ones that drove past the monument glared disapprovingly until a woman shouted, *"Git outta here, you raggedy tramps!"* and someone else in a truck yelled, *"Nigger beggars!"*

"I think it is time for us to go," said Cassie.

"I ain't goin' nowhere until I finish." Judith raised her voice for anyone listening. *"The Lawd don't like bein' innerupted!"*

"You better hurry up."

Another car pulled out, two-toned brown and white, like a fancy shoe. It came slowly down the street and stopped in front of the fountain. The windows were open. A pudgy white woman in a hat too nice for a diner sat on the passenger side. A man in a black suit was driving. Judith, still singing, didn't miss a beat. Cassie held her breath, half expecting a shotgun barrel to poke out, but the woman waited for Judith to finish, tugging on a pair of white gloves, adjusting her hat, and examining Cassie all the while.

Judith spread her arms wide for her finale. She ran out of air, clasped her hands, and smiled at the woman in the car.

"Where y'all from?" said the woman.

"Heron-Neck, Mississippi, ma'am," said Judith.

"What y'all doin' here?"

"Singin' to get a little money, ma'am. I's on my way to New York City to make mah fortune."

"Singin'?" said the woman.

"Singin'," said Judith.

The woman reached behind her seat and opened the back door. "Now come on an' git in," she said. "We real impressed with you singin', and we gone to introduce you to the members of our church."

Cassie jumped up from the edge of the fountain. "Miz Judith! Miz Judith! Cain't you follow long in yo own car? You know I cain't drive, and you cain't leave me heah by mahsef!" She rolled her eyes at the impending evening and the marble monument and the boll weevil topping it all.

"I cain't leave her here, ma'am," said Judith. "This gal already half died from fright a dozen times. She ain't got too many frights left in her."

The woman examined their car. "We'll go slow. It's just a mile or two."

Cassie slid into the passenger seat, and Judith got behind the wheel. The car wheezed to life.

"What you think?" said Judith breathlessly.

"Mebbe they witches."

Judith giggled. "They ain't *witches*. You think they got enny connections, you know, with the singin' bizniss?"

"I think they gone to make you sing for they prayer meetin' and send you off with a big basket of fried chicken."

"And mebbe some tater salad?"

Cassie poked her. "Be sure you tell 'em you need money for gas. You kin tell 'em ennything you want about New York City, but *please* don't say anythin' 'bout our daddy."

They followed the car into one of the nicest neighborhoods either of them had ever seen. The houses weren't big houses like the ones up the hill in Heron-Neck, but all were white with fresh paint, neat front lawns, and flowers. The lady's car pulled into the crowded parking lot of a dainty church. Lights inside the church shone through stained glass windows.

"You think they Baptists?" said Judith.

"Don't even ask," said Cassie. "Just do what they want you to do an' come back out."

"Ain't you comin' in?"

"What-all would I do? They'll make me sit in the back and give me dirty looks. I ain't going in there."

"What if somethin' crazy happen?" said Judith.

"Like what, a man turning into a mule? These normal folk."

"What if I need you? You gots to come in." Judith lowered her voice. "You my *sister*."

The woman and the man were getting out of their car. The man, Cassie saw at last, was a minister in a minister's black suit. The woman was pudgy, dressed in blue. "All right," Cassie said. "They gone to make me sit on the hardest chair in the room."

Judith bounced out of the car. "Y'all got the prettiest church I ever seen!"

"Thank you," said the minister. He introduced himself as Father Ash and the woman as his wife, Beatrice. "Won't you come in?" he said, just to Judith. "You'll want to see the windows before you meet our members."

"An' mah gal here?" said Judith.

Beatrice pointed Cassie to the rear of the church and led her around the back, while Father Ash took Judith up the front steps to see the stained-glass glory inside.

"We don't usually have a lot of singin' on a Wednesday night," said Beatrice. "It's our prayer meetin'. But that gal got quite the singin' voice."

"Oh, yessum. Miz Judith got the callin', an' I guess th' callin' took us here." Cassie smiled with all her teeth. "We prayed on it together that someone who know good singin' would hear her."

At the back of the church, stairs led down to a basement door. Beatrice waddled down and rattled the knob. "Anna May? Anna May! Open this door!"

Anna May was just as round as Beatrice and wore her blondish hair in a varnished swirl at the top of her head. When she saw Cassie, she frowned, but Beatrice made impatient gestures with her hands, and Anna May stepped aside.

The basement was brightly lit. Two dozen white ladies sat

around long tables in fancy prayer-meeting hats. They turned as one when Cassie came in, and Cassie wished she'd insisted on waiting in the car. It wasn't like Judith would crumple from stage fright if she was here by herself. Judith could sing hymns for a pack of wild dogs. Beatrice sat Cassie in a folding chair by the back door, right up against the cinderblock wall. All the while, not one of the prayer-meeting ladies took their eyes off her. Then Father Ash escorted Judith down the stairs on the other side of the room and heads turned like a flock of geese.

Father Ash introduced Judith and helped her up onto the kind of low stage the churches back in Heron-Neck used for Christmas plays. Judith smoothed her cleaned-up dress, shuffled her worn-out shoes, and cleared her throat. Beatrice sat at an old upright piano looking self-important.

Father Ash nodded at Judith. "What'll you start with, Miss Forrest?"

" 'Precious Lord,' " said Judith, with terrible gravity, "Take My Hand.' "

Beatrice played the opening chords. The basement was like a shoebox, and the piano was out of tune. The smells of rosewater and hand lotion thickened the air, but none of that could stop Judith. She opened her mouth and the song spilled out.

It crammed itself against the walls and low ceiling. It practically drowned out the piano. Judith clenched her fists and squeezed shut her eyes. She crouched over the lyrics and sweated real sweat across her upper lip. Her drama carried across the long tables, revealing a girl who believed and who had been saved by every word that came out of her mouth. On the low rise of that church stage, Judith threw off her drunken nights with the Justice boys and her days of hauling laundry for nickels. The Judith Forrest who lied like she knew everything but wasn't experienced enough to recognize a tube of used lipstick had disappeared; this Judith

Forrest was a decent young gal of little means, traveling 'cross the southland to bring the message of Christ Our Lord to everybody, high and low, and so on and so on. Cassie leaned against the cool cinderblock and watched Judith work the room. The church ladies fanned themselves and clapped politely at first, fanned themselves a bit harder as Judith picked more energetic songs. They wiped their eyes over time-worn favorites and rose up and sang in their lily-white church lady voices when Judith called everyone to their feet.

When she was done and had patted her brow, and the ladies had finished their applause, Father Ash stepped forward to pass the collection basket. Cassie watched from the back of the room as the dollar bills and silver dropped into the basket. Just about everyone put in something. Cassie counted twenty-four prayer-meeting hats. If each one put in only a quarter, it would be enough to buy gas for a couple of weeks. The basket made its way to the front of the room again, and Father Ash and Beatrice presented it to Judith with huge smiles and invited her to dinner. Cassie watched Judith nod graciously and walk away, up the stairs, and into the church proper, without a backward glance.

Judith came back to the car hours later. The church bell had chimed nine o'clock. Cassie was lying on the grass. The night was warm and clear, and the stars were thick as bees.

Judith plopped down cross-legged beside Cassie on the grass. She had a worn fake-leather purse over one arm and a little basket covered with a picnic napkin over the other. "You hungry? I got fried chicken, mashed taters, an' chock'lit cake."

Cassie found a drumstick and bit in. Barely warm, and the crunch had gone out of it. "They give you that purse?"

"Yep." Judith dangled it. "Prob'ly sumpin' they woulda thowed out, but I don't care. They put the money in it. And I think the gun'll fit in there too."

"How much money?"

"Thirty-one dollars and seventy-two cent."

Cassie blinked in amazement. Why even stop in Virginia when they could make more money than Bill Forrest would ever inherit? But this wasn't the time to bring that up. Cassie finished the drumstick, found a fork in the basket, and started on the cake. "This good cake."

"Ain't it? Kinda wisht we coulda started with it. The taters got too much water in 'em, and the chicken's just all right."

"You din't say that to 'em?"

"Hail no. I knows how to be a guest." She wrapped her arms around her knees. "How'd it sound to you?"

"What? The singin'? It sounded good."

"Good like real good? Or good like real, real, *real* good."

"Now I ain't gone say nothing to swell your head."

Judith picked a piece of grass and rolled it between her fingers. "It was good?"

"Pretty good."

Judith got up and twirled around. "I kin do ennythin'!" She skipped in a circle around the car. "Ennythin'! Ennythin'!"

CHAPTER ✦ TEN

After that, the trip seemed to get easier at the same time it got harder. They tried driving all day and all night, but the car overheated, and they had to stop to let it rest. Judith sang for folks in a big Baptist church in the middle of a town called Sunderland. The Sunderland people gifted her with seventeen dollars and a basket of fried chicken. The following Wednesday she performed for the Ladies Auxiliary of the Halsey Church of the Nazarene. They gave her three dollars in dimes, two dresses, and a pair of shoes. In Elliston she got ten dollars and pork ribs. In Daysville she got a basket of apples, a loaf of bread, and a chunk of farmer's cheese. Cassie and Judith kept their calendar up-to-date by looking at the local newspapers in the towns they passed through. They saw headlines in the papers about Elvis Presley and President Eisenhower, but all they really needed were the dates, not the news.

Before long, it was March tenth, and they were barely through Georgia. Cassie sent Judith in for more maps at a gas station and saw how far away Virginia really was.

"We ain't never gonna git there at this rate," said Judith. Cassie could tell how worried Judith was by how quiet she was as they drove.

Cassie put in her left shoe the money Judith earned, and in her right, the money remaining from what Lil Ma had given her. At night when she took off her shoes, she took the right one off first, so as to think about her mother, and then the left, so as to think about what might be ahead the next day. In the morning, she put the shoes on in the opposite order with the same thoughts for each shoe, so she was prepared for the day but with a thought for Lil Ma foremost in her mind.

At the South Carolina border, which they crossed on Tuesday, March fifteenth, Cassie asked Judith what was the point in going to Virginia. With less than a week until Eula Bonhomme-Forrest's March twenty-first deadline, they weren't going to make it on time. Cassie was carrying close to fifty dollars, not counting the change, which was so uncomfortable to walk on that she hid it in the trunk.

"We could just pass through Virginia," she said as they drove along on a county highway. Every day the weather was warmer, and it felt like spring. "You can sing and earn money and go on through without no trouble. We can get you some nice new clothes for New York City."

"Well now, you're right," said Judith, "an' I bin thinkin' 'long the same lines for a while, but you know what I come up with each time I considers it?"

"What?"

"I knows I'll spend the rest of my life wishin' I'd stopped in Virginia. I want him to see what he lef' behind. I don' care if he got enny money. I don't care if he drunk as a skunk and hoorin' around town."

"Yes, you do."

"All right, I do. But I want him to know he cain't jus' run off an' never see his fam'ly again, like we was somethin' that never mattered."

"You gone follow him like a curse."

Judith looked out the window at the flowering trees and then back at the road. "What you gonna do in New York City when we gits there?"

"Ain't I staying with you?"

"I 'magine you could do mos' ennything you wanted. It's s'posed to be different for colored folks up there. Ennyway, half the singin' money's yours."

"Now what'm I gone do in New York City if I ain't helpin' you get to be a reddio star?"

"Mebbe start a laundry bizniss? Mebbe git your momma outta Mississippi?"

These ideas had been at the edge of Cassie's mind. Hearing them come out of Judith's mouth made her stomach flutter the way it did when the car went down a steep hill. She opened her mouth to say *I'll think about that*, when the car, which had been running just fine for weeks, belched blue smoke from under the hood. The greasy innards gave a clattering convulsion that shook the hood wide-open. The engine gasped, shuddered, and quit.

Judith guided the car off the road into a damp patch of weeds and poison ivy. They got out and looked at the smoking engine without touching it. The last town was an hour behind them. It was late in the afternoon. It looked like it was going to rain.

Judith took a sniff of the smoke and coughed. "Smells like a *daid* thing."

They sat back from the road eating the last of the apples. Judith drank a warm bottle of Coke from the trunk. Coke made Judith jumpy, and Cassie considered the stuff a waste of money, but hot or cold, Judith swigged it down with gusto.

Before long they heard a car coming down the road. Judith

stood up from behind the tall grass and thorny shrubs and shaded her eyes.

"That a new car," she reported. "Two-tone paint. Red an' white."

"It'll be a car fulla drunk white boys."

"They stoppin'. I kin hear their reddio playin'." She took a quick little breath as though the best thing in the world had just happened. "Oh, Cassie, they *colored*. They colored men in suits!"

She jumped out on the road shouting, "Hey y'all! Hey! Y'all know ennythin' 'bout fixin' cars?"

Cassie followed, hoping they wouldn't be scared off by the crazy white girl leaping out of the roadside weeds.

Two cinnamon-colored men in dark suits—church or funeral suits, Cassie thought—were just getting out of their car, so new, the sidewalls of the tires were still sparkling white. They were about the same height and age, and when they looked up, Cassie thought they were at least brothers if not twins. She saw their eyes flicker between herself and Judith and watched their faces fill with the usual questions. One took off his hat and made a wide, gallant motion. "Ladies? Do y'all need some assistance?"

"We shorely do," said Judith. "Is you gentlemen know anythin' 'bout cars?"

"We're mechanics," said the second man. "We got a garage over in Porterville."

"Porterville?" said Cassie in amazement. Judith had already bounced off to ogle their car and its radio. "We been looking for Porterville," she said. "You know a man by the name of Mistah Johnson Mallard?"

One of the brothers was wearing a red kerchief in his breast pocket. "He's our daddy. How you heard about him?"

"Someone in a place called Hilltop told us to ask for him. We thought he was talking 'bout a town in Mississippi. We thought we missed it."

Judith skipped over, full of sugary energy. "Kin you git it to start? Ev'ry time I tries to start it, I wonder if it's gonna turn over."

The brother with the red kerchief got into the car and tried the ignition. The engine clicked lifelessly. "Alternator?" he said.

"Alternator," said the other.

"We'll give you a tow into Porterville," the first one told Cassie. "We'll have you fixed up before suppertime."

"We kin pay," said Cassie, "but how much you think it'll be?"

"Rebuilt model?" said the one with the red kerchief.

"Rebuilt model," agreed his brother.

"New one costs twenty dollars," said the one. "We can get you going for ten."

"Good as new?" said Cassie.

"Good as new," replied the other.

Charlie Mallard was the one with the red handkerchief. Junior was his twin. Their garage was in Porterville Township and took up the front yard of their family's house. The house was set well back from the road behind newly leafed locust trees and looked the same as the dozens they'd passed—rough boards with a tin roof and a sagging front porch. The garage was a different story. It was new, painted white, built of cinderblock, with a big glass window that looked in on a neat little office. MALLARD BROTHERS AUTO REPAIR was painted over the double garage doors in professional-looking script. The two dozen cars in the gravel lot beside it were parked in rows, washed and waxed. Even in the overcast afternoon, the cars gleamed like they were new.

Charlie got out to open the garage door. Junior smiled at them in the rearview mirror. "Have a bite to eat at the house while you're waiting. Dad'll take care of you."

He led them past the garage, where Charlie had already shouldered into his stained blue mechanic's coverall and was untying their car from its tow rope.

Up close, the house wasn't as raggedy as Cassie had first thought. The boards needed paint, but they'd been scraped recently. One side of the porch did sag, but the other was covered with pine boards so new, they smelled of the sawmill. Junior opened the front door into a parlor crowded with furniture, an upright piano, and bric-a-brac. It took a minute for Cassie to see Mister Mallard the elder sitting in an armchair by the room's only window. He looked up from reading a newspaper, and Judith nearly stepped on Cassie's heels as Cassie stopped short.

His skin stretched tight over his wide cheekbones and the deep sockets of his eyes. He was so thin in the face, it made Cassie wonder if he could even stand, but it wasn't just his starved appearance that stopped Cassie in her tracks. It was his eyes, which were pink, and his skin, which was the color of chalk.

"You're like Jack!" Judith blurted.

Cassie caught Judith's shoulder to keep her from saying any more. "It's just—we know someone else who's—the same."

"'Nother albino," said Mister Mallard, in a tone too flat to tell if he was offended. "A true albino?"

"Yessuh," said Judith, ignoring Cassie's grip. "He was as true an al-biner as I ever did see. Till now, course."

"He a Negro albino?" said Mister Mallard.

"No, suh," said Judith. "He just a white white boy."

"We rare," said Mister Mallard. "Negro albinos real, real rare. Prob'ly more albino white folks than you think. Hard to tell with some of 'em. Now, I knew two colored albino boys when I was comin' up; they both got lynched for 'tendin' to be white men. Wasn't neither one of 'em more'n sixteen years old."

Junior cleared his throat. "These girls waitin' for us to fix their car. I said you'd give them somethin' to eat."

"Sho, sho, I ain't inhospitable." Mister Mallard folded his paper and laid it by the chair, revealing the rest of his body, which was just as thin and bony as his face. He lifted himself onto his feet and beckoned them into the kitchen but stopped Judith at the door. "You a white gal, ain't you?"

"Yessuh. I shore am."

"Why you travelin' with this colored gal, here?"

"We sisters," said Judith before Cassie could say anything. "We got the same daddy."

Mister Mallard fixed his pink eyes on Cassie. "That true?"

"Yessuh," Cassie said reluctantly and waited for Judith to bring up their being progeny and so on, but to Cassie's surprise, Judith showed more sense.

"Seen that," said Mister Mallard, like this was just what he'd expected her to say. "All that mixin'. I seen plenty of that."

He poured coffee for them from a battered metal pot, scrambled them some eggs, fried a ham slice, and put a big biscuit on each of their already loaded plates. Cassie thought his arms would snap, but he ignored her when she offered to help.

"Hope you ain't mind eatin' breakfast so late in the day," he said when they were settled at the kitchen table. "That's all I cook since my wife done passed. If not for my boys, I'd be eatin' ham'n' eggs three times a day. Taste all right?"

The two of them nodded, mouths full.

"That's good." Mister Mallard set his frame down at the third chair at the table and pulled the kitchen curtain aside. "You gals see the back of that garage?"

"Yessuh," said Cassie, around her biscuit.

"What you see in the back of that garage?"

"They got themselves a window lookin' out the back," said Judith. It was so big and clean, Cassie could see the road on the other side.

"Window lookin' out the front make perfect sense. You got to see who pullin' into your lot. Who pays good money for a window in the back, where all you kin see is you own house? I'll tell you who—a man who's too sure that there's gone be money comin' in tomorrow, the next day, the next month. That's two men too sure that the white folks gone to keep bringin' in they cars to a coupla colored mechanics."

"They only do work for white folks?" said Cassie.

Mister Mallard made a dismissive motion. "Sho, they got colored folks comin' in, but half them cain't pay and half they cars ain't fixable."

"But if the colored folks cain't pay and they cars ain't fixable, who else they gonna get for work 'sides white folks?" said Judith. "Less'n you got some other kind of folk round here."

Mister Mallard scowled. "We got other kinda folk round here. They start out humble, that's for sho. They family's been here since slavery times. Then they pick theyselves up and get a little money, and then they gone. Once they gone, they ain't never come back, not them, not they chillun, not they chillun's chillun."

"You mean colored folks?" said Judith. "They make some money and move someplace better? There ain't nothin' wrong with that." She nudged Cassie. "That what we're doin'."

"Oh," said Mister Mallard, sitting up in his chair, "there ain't nothin wrong with that, if *that* was what we talkin' 'bout, but *that* ain't what we talking 'bout." He leaned over the table with fierce urgency. "We talkin' 'bout the future of colored folks. And 'scuse me, lil white miss, if I starts talkin' in a way you don't understand." He turned to Cassie. "Now your white daddy ain't somethin' you planned on, but now you got to be thinkin', *If I so light now, if I git me a light-skinned man, maybe my chillun be light 'nuff to pass for white.* You ever think 'bout that, girl?"

"My grandmother thought 'bout it," said Cassie. "That all she ever thought 'bout."

"Well now, here the part she ain't thought 'bout," said Mister Mallard. "She ain't thought 'bout things like knowin' the difference tween a damn yam an' a damn sweet potato. Like standin' up in church shakin' yo hands up to the sky. She ain't thinkin' 'bout things colored folks do that white folks don't cuz we coloreds and we come from some place there ain't no whitefolks." He pointed toward the garage. "Them boys jus' come back from a funeral. They tell you that?"

"No, suh," said Cassie.

Mister Mallard leaned over his elbows on the table, his frightening emaciation filling the space. "This mornin' they buried a man a hunnert and twenty-five years old. He born into slavery by a woman straight from Africa. He growed up in slavery but kep' his Africa in him. Not just cuz he black as tar—he was frightful black—but cuz he 'membered what his mama taught him 'bout Africa." He gave Cassie a hard look. "Your mama teach you ennythin' 'bout Africa?"

"No, suh."

"You think she know ennythin' 'bout Africa?" Cassie shook her head, and he said, "How 'bout her mama? Her mama 'fore that?" Mister Mallard eyed Judith. "You know where your folks come from, lil white gal?"

"Mississippi, suh."

"I mean 'fore that."

"Been there as long as I know, suh."

"You there 'fore the injuns?"

"Far as I know, suh," said Judith, and Mister Mallard made a *phfft* through his teeth.

"See now?" he said to Cassie. "Ain't no white folk in Mississippi 'fore the injuns, but white folks done put that fact outta they minds. It don't fit in with how they see theyselfs. Colored folks doin' the same thin' now. They gits whiter, and they fergits everthin' 'bout they past. One day they ain't gone to be no past, jus' folks behavin' like today the only day that ever was."

"Maybe that's not such a bad thing," said Cassie.

"Girl," said Mister Mallard, "you shut your mouth." He reached for her plate. "You done?" She wasn't, but he took it anyway and then snatched Judith's. "Now set yourself down in t'other room whilst I wash up."

"You mighta insulted him," Judith said in a whisper as they stood in the parlor.

"I was sayin' what I thought. He was sayin' what he thought."

"Ol' folks ain't innerested in what you have to say. Like your granny. You ever have enny real kinda conversation with her?"

Back in the kitchen, Mister Mallard banged pots and ran water and didn't seem like he was going to come out. Judith glanced around the jammed little parlor and squeezed between a pair of ladderback chairs to look at the framed black-and-white photos lined up on top of the upright piano. "Here them two boys when they was little."

Cassie made her way over to see. One photo was of Junior and Charlie with Mister and Mrs. Mallard when the boys were three or four. Mister Mallard was younger looking but as thin as ever. The black and white of the photo picked up the highlights of his face and deepened the shadows until he looked positively skulllike. Mrs. Mallard was a dark, pretty woman with high, round cheeks and fetching eyes. The boys looked just like her—*thankfully*,

Cassie thought. The other photos were from baseball teams Junior and Charlie had played on.

"Lookit how cute." Judith pointed to a row of serious-looking little colored boys in striped shirts and pants. "I cain't see which ones is them in this'n. But see here in this high school picture?" Junior and Charlie were off to the left, distinctly identical and noticeably lighter than any of the other young men. "How kin they be dark as the dickens when they was little and turn out so light in high school?" Judith raised an eyebrow at Cassie. "I never noticed y'all get lighter."

"It's just a bad picture," said Cassie, but there was really no arguing it. The most recent photo showed Junior and Charlie grinning in front of the gleaming white garage, arms over each other's shoulders, lighter-skinned than they were in any of the other photos. A banner stretched over the office door behind them which read, GRAND OPENING!!

"When you think that was took?" Judith said and answered her own question. "Not too long ago. See? The trees're all leafed out like summer."

The brightness of the white paint should have made their darkness even darker, but it didn't. It obviously didn't.

"It's just a bad picture," said Cassie again. "It's jus' how they look in front of that white garage."

The front door opened, and Charlie came in. "Turns out you threw a rod," he said. "Means we got to order some parts, an' that means we ain't gone be able to fix it till tomorrow."

"Tomorrow?" said Judith. "We got to be in Virginia in less than a week!"

"Don't see how you'd get there even if that trap runnin' smooth," said Charlie. Judith started to object, but Charlie said, "You need somewhere to spend the night, and it ain't proper for y'all in a house fulla men. We gone take you to the minister, the

Reverend Glade. His wife'll fix you up." Charlie sniffed the air, which was still heavy with the smells of their late, short break-fast. "Daddy feed you?"

"Yessuh," said Cassie.

"He let you finish eatin'?" Cassie looked down at the plain brown carpet, and Judith twisted her fingers together. "I 'polo-gize," Charlie said. "Daddy got some real set ideas. You think you havin' a discussion. He think you dead wrong. I cain't tell you how many dinner plates I had yanked out from under my nose. Mama wouldn't put up with it." He opened the door. "Come on. We'll drive y'all down to the church."

The church was at the other end of town, which, in Heron-Neck, would have put it on the wrong side of the tracks. But the railroad didn't seem to pass through Porterville or anywhere near it, even though Ovid Beale had shown them the speck of the town in relation to the tracks. Cassie tried to shake Ovid Beale and his wrongheaded directions out of her thoughts and study the town passing by. The houses were modest, well-kept, and most had a car in the driveway. Back home on Negro Street, Lil Ma would point out the places where people paid rent to landlords and how those places were always more run-down than the places people owned for themselves. In Porterville, Cassie saw no renters. She also saw no white people.

"At the church," said Junior, who was driving, "there's a wake goin' on for Mister Legabee. That's the fella we done buried this mornin'."

"The man who's a hunnert and twenny-five years old?" said Judith. "The fella borned into slave-ry?"

"That's right," said Charlie.

"If you don' mind, I'll stay here in this nice ol' car." Judith ran her hands over the smooth leather upholstery. "I ain't impolite enough to make a big disruption."

"You'll be welcome," said Junior. "Both of you'll be welcome. There'll be plenty white folks."

"Mister Legabee was a respected man. His family been here a long time," said Charlie.

"He gave advice," said Junior.

"Good advice," said Charlie. "He'd help you find the right direction for your life."

"Like a preacher?" said Cassie. "Or minister?"

"Like an elder," said Junior.

It would have been hard for Mister Legabee to be anything but an elder at a hundred and twenty-five, Cassie thought.

Junior had to park way down the street because the dirt lot behind the church was full. They ended up walking half a mile only to be the last of the latecomers.

Junior pulled the basement door of the church open for them. Inside, the room was filled with mourners and with the aromas of home cooking. People sat in groups in folding chairs. Others chatted at tables piled with casseroles and hot dishes. Among all shades of darker folk, the crowd was salted with white faces.

"Let me introduce you to the Reverend Glade," Junior said. "Then you can help yourselves."

The Reverend Glade was a light-skinned colored man in the middle of the crowd, shaking hands heartily with a well-dressed white man. He shook Junior's and Charlie's hands too.

"Your father didn't come," said Reverend Glade.

"I hope you weren't expecting him," said Charlie.

"I'm glad to see him once in a month of Sundays." The Reverend Glade smiled at Cassie and Judith.

Charlie introduced them to the Reverend Glade and told him they'd been directed to Porterville by a man in Hilltop.

"Back in Mississippi?" said Reverend Glade. "Did you meet Mister Beale?"

"Mister Ovid Beale told us you were just down the road," said Cassie. "But we didn't find you until South Carolina."

"Maybe you were using an old map." The Reverend Glade clasped his hands in front of him. "Where're y'all headed?"

Judith took a breath to answer, but Cassie laid a hand on her arm. "Judith's on her way to becomin' a big singin' star in New York City, but our car broke down."

"We fixin' it," said Junior, adding that Judith and Cassie needed a place to stay for the night.

"Let me find my wife and tell her." The Reverend Glade clapped Junior on the shoulder. "You young ladies help yourselves to the food. The Mallard boys can introduce you to the widow Legabee so you can pay your respects." This last the Reverend Glade directed to Cassie, excluding Judith, but Judith didn't seem to notice, or if she did, she didn't care. Judith lost no time finding a plate and filling it with fried chicken, potato salad, collards with bacon, and a delicious-looking piece of apple pie. Cassie tried to take less than Judith but found herself just as hungry after their interrupted breakfast. She and Judith sat together at the end of one long table and dug in, starting with the pie.

"We ain't never gonna get to Virginia," Judith said. "They're gonna fix that ol' trap, an' it's gonna break down again, just outside Remington."

Cassie thought Judith was probably right but kept forking in the collard greens with bacon. "Maybe they'll sell us a car that's more reliable."

Judith took another bite of the pie. "You think they got somethin' faster?"

"Anything would be faster."

"You think they got somethin' that'll get us to Virginia in less'n six days?"

"All we can do is ask."

Judith straightened up to look for Charlie. A colored woman came around, offering squares of corn bread on a platter. Judith declined the offer, and the colored woman moved on. "I'm so sick of corn bread," said Judith. "When I'm famous I ain't never eatin' corn bread agin'. I be drinkin' champagne and eatin' ka-vee-yar."

An elderly colored lady scooping black-eyed peas from a floral bowl moved closer to them. "Honey, you know what caviar is?"

Judith wiped her mouth. "Somethin' famous folks eat, so I hear, ma'am."

"It's fish eggs," said the woman. "They scrape 'em out of a kind of carp."

"I might've got the name wrong," said Judith.

"Tiny little black eggs," said the woman. "Like pinheads, floatin' round in salty oil."

"You had 'em before?" said Judith.

"Oh yes," said the woman, "and champagne too." She took a neat square of corn bread from the next platter and put it beside the peas on her plate. "Caviar is an acquired taste, honey, let me tell you." She disappeared into the crowd.

"You think she famous somewhere?" Judith said.

"I think she playin' with you."

Just as they were thinking about a second helping of every-thing, Charlie Mallard came over. "Come on, now," he said before Judith could start asking him about a new car. "Let me introduce you to the widow Legabee."

He led them to the far end of the crowded basement hall, where there was a stage with a red velvet curtain. People of all shades and ages stood on one side of the stage, chatting in low tones, dressed in solemn black, waiting to go behind it. The women wore fantastic hats. The men wore shoes so shiny they reflected the red drape of the curtain.

"That where the widow is?" said Judith to Charlie, and he nodded. "Why she back there?"

"Just the way her family does things. Her daughter's there too, and her grandson."

"This like Miz Tabitha's estate sale back in Heron-Neck," said Judith. "When she passed, the whole county showed up. She a white woman. But she run a store and she sell to ever'body, so all kinds of folks came down. Course," she added, "they didn't mingle so."

The Reverend Glade waved at them from the other side of the stage and came over with a trim, light-skinned colored woman in a demure black dress. "Here they are," he said. He took Judith by the elbow. "This is my wife, Mrs. Glade, our choir director. She's very interested in your singing career."

Judith, happy to go into detail, allowed herself to be guided away by Mrs. Glade. Charlie caught Cassie's shoulder.

"You should meet the widow," he said.

A mass of people were waiting in line to speak to the widow. "Ain't all these people first?"

"You're a visitor," said Charlie. "She'll see you ahead of them."

"I never even met her husband," said Cassie.

"Still," said Charlie. "You should pay your respects."

Cassie didn't understand this. She hadn't paid her respects to Tabitha Bromley, and she'd seen Miz Tabitha once a week for her entire life. She followed Charlie around to the side of the stage and behind the red curtain. A heavyset colored man sat in a folding chair, straight-backed, like a soldier. He wore a patterned brown-and-white cape and a hat made of the same fabric. It wasn't a normal hat—it had no brim and came up straight from the sides of his head, like something military, except for the colors. He nodded to Charlie and gestured to the darker, back part of the stage.

Cassie had expected the stage to be crowded behind the

curtain, but she and Charlie were the only ones. A table was covered with candles and plates of food, as though people had left their dinners as offerings, but neither the widow nor her family were eating. They were sitting together on a big armchair. The two women were black as black could be—frightful black, Mister Mallard would have said—and so squeezed together that the younger woman was practically sitting on her mother's lap, and the baby, a boy, black as coal, sat on top of the two of them. If not for the arms on the chair, they might've fallen off onto the floor.

Charlie stopped in front of the strange arrangement of women and baby boy. He ducked his head. "My sincere condolences, Missus Legabee."

"Your daddy come?" said the widow.

"No, ma'am."

"He still havin' his problems?"

"Yessum," said Charlie. "Still havin' his problems."

"He like the talkin' skull," said the daughter. "Lots to say, but nothin' helpful comin' outta his mouth."

"You'll be buryin' him next," said the widow, which struck Cassie as truly improper, but Charlie just opened a hand toward Cassie.

"Here the young lady the Reverend Glade told you 'bout."

The two women eyed Cassie like predatory birds, their eyes black as ink, and the baby's somehow even blacker.

"You a pretty girl," said the widow. "You light-skinned too, like Ovid Beale said."

"Mister Beale told you 'bout me?" said Cassie. "Is he here?"

"He ain't here, but we talked to him," said the daughter.

The man who was a mule—or whatever they'd seen weeks ago in Mississippi—came back to Cassie as a bad feeling. "How—how can you talk to him?"

"Girl, ain't you heard of a telephone?" said the daughter. "He my daddy's nephew. Course we talk. He told us you was headed to Virginia with a crazy white girl claimin' to be your half sister. That true?"

Cassie nodded. The bad feeling might have been just too much pie in her stomach.

"Half sister," said the widow. "You daddy a white man?"

"Yessum."

"You almost light enough to pass," said the widow. "Tell me that ain't somethin' you long for."

"I ain't wishin' for something that ain't gone to happen."

"You a liar," said the widow.

"You meet Charlie Mallard's daddy?" asked the daughter. "You see how white that black man is? And you see how black he is underneath that pale skin? He a cursed man, 'cause if his skull woulda look different, he coulda walked on outta the South that he was born into, free as a bird. Coulda gone to some white man's school in the North, coulda got some good-payin' white man's job, but 'cause of the way he look underneath his skin, all he ever gone to be is a pink-eyed, white-lookin' Negro. You hear me?"

"Yessum," said Cassie.

"An' don't think he ain't bitter 'bout it," said the oil-black widow. "Don't think he ain't come to us asking for somethin' to change his state of affairs."

"An' don't think we ain't tried," said her daughter. "An' don't think we don't know what he likely told you 'bout us."

"He didn't say anything."

"You a liar," said the widow again. "But it don't matter, because even if we cain't do for him, I knows we kin do for you. We gone to gift you, little cinnamon-color gal. We gone to give you a gift like you ain't never got before, and we givin' it to you 'cause Ovid

Beale sent you this way and 'cause Mister Charlie done brought you to us."

"You don't have to give me anything," said Cassie.

"But we do," said the daughter, "an' you gone to take it. But first you gone to make a solemn pledge." She held up her right hand, and Cassie did too. "I pledge never to forgit the past," said the daughter. "I pledge to recollect my roots, no matter what my state of affairs."

Cassie repeated the words and was about to put her hand down, but the widow shook her head sharply, so she kept her hand up.

"And you further pledge never to say a word 'bout what you gone to find out in a minute."

"I pledge it," said Cassie.

"That's good," said the widow. "Now touch the baby. Go on," she said impatiently as Cassie hesitated. "Touch his head. Touch his hands."

Cassie put her fingers to the baby's warm forehead. His jet eyes seemed to soften, and he smiled at her. He stuck out his baby hands, and she put her fingers into his palms. His palms were the same black color as the rest of him, not pale, like every other colored person she'd known. He gurgled and squeezed her fingers with his damp baby hands. When he released her and she turned her hands over, there was some kind of sticky substance left behind.

Charlie, who'd been standing back this whole time, stepped forward. "Rub your hands together," he said in a soft and urgent tone.

Cassie did. The sticky stuff came off in a tarry black wad. Charlie took it from her fingers and turned her right hand so the knuckles were up. He rubbed the stuff across them.

"Look," he said.

Her skin was lighter where he'd rubbed, like he'd taken an eraser and wiped away a layer of her.

"God," she said.

He put the stuff into her palm and closed her fingers around it.

"Now git," said the daughter, "and 'member." She shook her coal-black finger in Cassie's face. "You don't show nobody, or that black gonna come right back."

Charlie pulled Cassie away, and the next thing she was aware of was trembling beside a punch bowl on one of the buffet tables, gripping the wad in her right hand. Charlie was next to her with a paper cup and a ladle. Cassie heard herself ask where the bathroom was, and he pointed to the left. She wobbled off until she found the door marked WOMEN.

She locked that door behind her and stared at herself in the mirror. She looked at the black wad of stuff in her hand. What was it exactly? It looked like tar, exactly like tar, and when she sniffed it, it had a faint tarry smell. She looked into the mirror again and touched the tar to her cheek. She took away the tar. The spot it had touched was ever so slightly lighter. She had the impression that if she started to scrub at herself, within an hour she would be as white as Judith, as white as some of the people out there at the wake, waiting to get behind the curtain, to leave their food at the candle-covered altar. Waiting to leave Porterville and their past behind.

CHAPTER ✦ ELEVEN

Cassie lay awake that night with Judith beside her, snoring peace-
fully, while the lump of tar, or whatever it was, stayed hot inside
Cassie's fist. *You don't tell nobody, or that black gonna come right
back.* At home, she would have shown it to Lil Ma, shown her
what it could do. And then what would have happened? Because
she had told, would Lil Ma's black come right back? Or only her
own? Was this piece of tar for her and her alone? If she found some
roundabout way to tell Lil Ma that Beanie Simms was right and
there was no need to have a light-skinned child now, how could
she help Lil Ma find this place, which seemed to be one place on
the map and somewhere else in reality? Cassie sat up in the bed.
Judith sighed in her sleep. Cassie put on one of the bathrobes
Mrs. Glade had left at the foot of the bed. She put it on over the
nightshirt she couldn't remember ever seeing before, over the smell
of scented soap from a bath she didn't recall taking. Cassie went
out of the bedroom, closed the door softly, and sat in the dark
hallway at the top of the stairs. A clock somewhere on the first
floor chimed two. She squeezed the tar in her hand until it oozed
between her fingers, black in the blackness, just texture and

warmth. Was it changing her now? Was it turning the back of her hand the same pale shade as the palm?

She needed light.

She went downstairs in the dark. On the first floor was a powder room with a toilet and a mirror over the sink. Cassie turned the electric light on with the switch. There was a rose in a little vase on one side of sink and a bar of scented soap on the other. Cassie recognized the way the soap smelled. She squinted in the light and checked her hands. The tar held the impression of the inside of her fist. The skin on the back of her hand still showed the light mark where Charlie had demonstrated what this gift could do. She peered at her face and found the pale streak she'd made herself. How hard would she have to scrub, how long would it take, to change herself completely? And what about her skull? Like Mister Mallard, would her bones give her away? She examined her features: her mother's eyes, Judith's mouth, and an unremarkable nose that looked nothing in particular like one race or another. She touched her hair with the hand not holding the tar. It was dry, flat, and neglected. It needed to be healed with oils and experienced hands. What would happen to her hair?

Someone turned on a light in the hallway, and a female voice said, "Cassie?"

It was the minister's wife, Mrs. Glade. It would be impolite to not answer. Cassie cracked the powder room door. Mrs. Glade came into view and smiled. Cassie pushed the hand with the tar into the pocket of the bathrobe.

"Can't you sleep?"

"Nome."

"Come on. I'll make you some warm milk."

In the kitchen, Cassie sat at the small table by the window. Mrs. Glade poured milk from a glass bottle into a pan on the stove and lit the gas burner. She adjusted the gas and came and sat down across from Cassie. "Reverend Glade and I were talking about you girls after you went to bed." Mrs. Glade was a chatty woman, Cassie now recalled. She didn't look a bit sleepy, and Cassie wondered if she'd been to bed at all. "Your friend—well, your sister—seems to have things all planned out for herself, but she didn't really have anything to say about your future. Have you thought about your future?"

"I want to get to New York with Judith."

"And do what when you get there?"

It was hard to think. Hadn't she and Judith discussed this? "If Judith can't get famous, I can find laundry work."

"It takes years and years to get famous," Mrs. Glade said, in a tone reserved for children—sleepy, uninformed children. "What're you going to do for years and years?"

"We've always been together one way or the other," said Cassie.

"Just because things have been one way for a long time, doesn't mean they have to stay that one way," said Mrs. Glade.

This conversation, Cassie finally realized, was about sending Judith off on her own to become a reddio star and never seeing her again. Because telling anyone about the tar—and maybe especially telling Judith—would make all that black come right back.

"For example," Mrs. Glade said, "have you thought about learning a trade besides the laundry? Or starting a business of your own? Or going to school?"

It was the middle of the night. What kind of questions were these to get asked in the middle of the night?

"Reverend Glade and I have friends in Boston we'd like you to meet. They grew up here, but they've moved on. We could send you up on the train. You'd be welcome at their house and in their community."

"You'd send me to Boston?"

"We'd be glad to pay for your ticket." Mrs. Glade got up and went over to the stove. The milk was steaming. She took a spoon from a drawer and lifted the skin that had formed. She lifted it like it was a thin wet napkin and shook it off into the trash.

"What about Judith?"

"What about Judith?"

"Well. She's my sister."

"Your half sister, isn't that right?" Mrs. Glade poured the milk into a pink coffee cup and brought it to the table. "No matter how you're related to her, she's really not your kin. Kin doesn't ask kin to be their servant while they seek fame and fortune."

"She never asked me to do that."

"Of course not," said Mrs. Glade. "But when she's audition-ing, what'll you be doing? Waiting in the wings with her hat and coat? When she has a performance, where will you be? Cleaning her apartment?" Mrs. Glade pushed the pink coffee cup of steam-ing milk at Cassie. "Would you do anything for her because she's your sister? Or is it that you haven't given any thought to what you could be doing instead?"

"You make her sound like a bad person."

"There's nothing bad about knowing what you want out of life," said Mrs. Glade. "It's the waste of an opportunity that's bad."

Mrs. Glade was a light-skinned woman. Her hair was straight and fine. She was lighter than what Cassie's grandmother referred to as *redbone*, lighter even than what she'd heard white folks refer to as *high yellow*. If Mrs. Glade herself had her own piece of tar, why wasn't she a white woman yet? Why was she still here? Why wasn't she in Boston with her friends and their *community*? What *opportunity* was she waiting for? Or was she like Beanie Simms—only the messenger?

Cassie gripped the sticky wad in her pocket. "You mean the—the tar."

"The what?"

"The tar. From the baby. That's what you mean about Boston and—community and opportunity."

Mrs. Glade smiled faintly. "You must've had a dream. I didn't realize I was upsetting you with all this talk. Drink your milk now and go back to bed. You've had a long day."

In the morning, the Reverend Glade let in Junior Mallard in his mechanic's coverall. Junior was explaining that the old junk car the girls had driven across three and a half states was no longer fixable. It was dead, deceased.

Judith had come downstairs in her nightgown and terry robe just before Junior knocked, and was standing in the kitchen doorway with a cup of tea when Junior broke the news. Cassie was at the top of the stairs, where she could see but not easily be seen.

"How kin it be daid?" said Judith from the kitchen door. "It bin sittin' inna woods for years. Some ign'rint redneck boys't cain't even read done made it run, an' you cain't—." She stopped herself. In the uncomfortable silence, the smell of pancakes, syrup, and bacon drifted up the stairs.

"Miss, you been runnin' it without a lick of oil," said Junior. "The engine got so hot it melted."

"Mistah Beale's nephew made it run. All he hadda do was put gas innit."

"Sorry, miss," said Junior. "There's nothing we can do."

"Hail," said Judith. Then, with a glance at the Reverend Glade: "'Scuse me." She looked up the stairs to see Cassie. Cassie watched the Reverend Glade put a comforting arm around Judith's shoulders and walk her back into the kitchen. He would be talking about putting her on the train to Virginia or New York, whichever she preferred. *But I ain't got that kinda money*, Judith would say. *Don't you worry about that*, the Reverend would say to her, and Cassie could almost hear him. *We'd be glad to pay for your ticket. You can leave today if you'd like.*

After breakfast Cassie and Judith sat together in their bedroom upstairs. Mrs. Glade had left a basket of clean, neatly folded clothes for them, all from church donations.

"For the needy," said Judith. "I ain't feelin' so needy no more, though. One day soon I might buy me a new dress." She held a light-blue frock up to her chest. "You like that?"

"It's okay."

"S'matter with you? These folks gonna pay t'put us onna train to New York or Virginia or ennywhere else we want to go. We kin git to Virginia with time to spare. These right Christian folks for sure—an' I never said that 'bout ennyone else, not even all them white church ladies with their tater salads and fried chickens—so why you so sad-lookin'?"

"I'm not sad."

Judith shook out a pink dress with dainty rosettes at the cuffs of the sleeves. "Now you know that'd look so pretty on you. Pink's your color."

Because it gave her cinnamon skin a rosy cast. Lil Ma had always said so. "Ain't there somethin plain in there?" said Cassie.

"How 'bout this ugly ol' apron dress? No, that's for some woman with big boozums. Why you want somethin plain? Oh well, here's a white dress with no ruffles or nuthin'."

It was a chalk-colored dress, short-sleeved, and would fall just below her knees. It would be a marker for her change. A yard-stick to measure her difference by. Cassie held it against her chest and felt a surge of hatred for it. It was a particular and familiar hate she'd last felt at Tabitha Bromley's estate sale, when a worth-less old white woman on a sagging old porch called Lil Ma a nigger because of a wringer. Cassie's grandmother had overseen the humiliation, to make sure it happened, because there would be no new wringer without it. Nothing so simple as paying. She'd hated Grandmother for knowing that so well. It was that exact hate she felt for this dress and for the people in this house. She understood why it was important to erase everything dark, but it had never been so clear to her as now. It had never been so apparently possible. She hated that too.

Judith paused her pawing through the basket of donated clothes. She was nearly to the bottom, where panties and brassieres were hidden underneath everything else. Judith looked at them doubtfully. "I kin see wearin' some other gal's dress, but I ain't sure 'bout their knickers."

"You gonna need a bra in New York City. And clean knickers."

"I s'pose." She picked out a bra with cups like soup bowls.

Cassie fished out a pair of pink panties. "These'll fit you." She tossed them into Judith's lap.

Judith squealed and pitched them back. "I ain't wearin somebody else's panties!"

"You'd wear 'em if they was mine."

"No, I wouldn't neither!"

"Yes, you would, I mean washed and all." She shook the panties for emphasis. "These is washed. They even smell good."

"I don't care." Judith threw herself back on the bed, rumpling the covers and scattering pillows. She covered her face with both hands. "I don't care. I ain't wearin' 'em!"

"Why?" said Cassie. "Because they come off some colored girl?"

Judith lay still with her hands over her eyes, breathing hard.

"Oh, that's just stupid," said Cassie. "That's stupid, and I don't even believe it."

Judith let her hands fall away from her face. "I said a bad thing this morning."

"Judith, a day don't pass when you don't swear. I know you cain't help yourself, not even in a minister's house."

"I don't mean the swearin'. I mean I said something rude to Mister Junior when he came in to say the car ain't never gonna run again. I said even redneck white boys could fix that car, and I was ready to say some more. An ever'body got real quiet. An then Reveren' Glade started talkin' to me 'bout leavin' on the nex' train."

"I heard you."

Judith blinked away tears. "I cain't stay 'cause I insulted them."

"You want to stay?"

"Ain't you stayin'?"

"Why you say that?"

"I kin see you like it here. They nice people. They like you."

Cassie put the panties down on the bed. The wad of tar was like a hot coal in the pocket of her bathrobe. "You goin' to New York City, Judith. You cain't stop now."

"I cain't see myself goin' without you."

"You got a callin', Judith. All I got is laundry. What'm I gonna do in New York sides be your maid?"

Judith pushed herself upright on the bed, flushed and serious. "You ain't never gonna be my maid. You my sister."

"I ain't really. If I was your white sister, it'd be different. Maybe we'd sing together."

"But you cain't sing. I mean you kin carry a tune and all." Judith picked at the clothes in the basket. "Is that what you want to do?"

"I ain't no singer."

Judith's face started to crumple. She moved closer on the bed. "What you want to do, Cassie?"

"I don't know."

Judith threw her arms around Cassie's neck, and Cassie felt hot tears on Judith's cheek. "You got to come as far's Virginia. Kin you come that far? Come back here after, but we got to do that together."

Cassie put her arms around Judith's shoulders. Judith started to sob.

"If I was your colored sister," Judith wept, "would you come to New York with me?"

"What you gonna do," said Cassie, "cover yourself with shoe-black and pass for a gospel singer?"

"You think that'd work?"

"No."

Judith sniffled and tried to laugh. "Will you come to Virginia?"

Cassie nodded. "I'll come to Virginia."

"And then we'll see?"

"And then we'll see."

Judith went to wash her face and Cassie went to wash hers, and when Cassie came back, Judith had fallen asleep curled up on the blue dress, which would have to be ironed now.

Cassie sat next to Judith. Judith didn't budge. "Judith?"

Judith sighed in her sleep. Her skin was so fair and fragile-looking after being washed, she looked almost bruised. Cassie wasn't sure she'd ever seen Judith this clean. Her hair was fluffy and made little curls around her ears. Even her ears were pinker, like someone had made her scrub them, front and back. Cassie imagined Judith covered with shoe-black. Seeing her that way wasn't very hard.

Cassie looked at her own lightened knuckles and at Judith's chapped red hands. She waited a long minute and took the tar out of her pocket. She held it so it was hidden in her fist. Was just taking it out with someone else in the room a form of "telling"? Judith was asleep. Cassie watched her knuckle, but the light streak didn't waver. She opened her fist to expose the tar to daylight. The light streak stayed. The tar was black with an oily sheen, but when she rubbed it with her fingers, it felt almost powdery. She picked it up with her thumb and forefinger.

"Judith?" she said.

Judith's eyes flickered under thin lids.

Cassie touched Judith's left hand with the tar, drawing it across the knuckles. There was no change. She did it again. Judith smiled in her sleep, which made her look like she was ten years old. Cassie wiped the tar across Judith pale skin a third time. No change at all. She put the tar in her pocket and got off the bed. She went out of the bedroom and downstairs to tell Mrs. Glade and the Reverend that they had both found dresses that they liked and that she would be leaving with Judith for Virginia on the next train.

When they asked if she would go on to Boston when she was finished with her business in Virginia, Cassie said yes.

CHAPTER ✦ TWELVE

The Reverend and Mrs. Glade dropped them off in front of the train station in the town of Parmetter, about twenty miles east of Porterville. It took two hours to drive there on unpaved roads, and Mrs. Glade kept making Cassie repeat their phone number so she could call if she had any problems on the way to Boston because there was no way to memorize the route back to Porterville and no one in Parmetter would know the way.

They reached the train station late in the afternoon. Reverend Glade gave Cassie the money for the train tickets. There was enough for her to buy a one-way ticket to Boston and about two-thirds as much for Judith, to get to Virginia, where Bill Forrest was, and then be on her way to New York. The station in New York where Judith would get off was called Grand Central, and it sounded so very grand to Cassie that it was hard to not want to go. How bad could it be, really, to be a maid in a place with a Grand Central Station? Would Boston have anything like that? None of the newspapers or magazine pages lining the walls at home in Heron-Neck had mentioned anything about Boston. She only knew that Mrs. Glade had told her that it was cold there in the winter and she would have to dress warm.

The Glades drove away, and Judith and Cassie stood on the wooden platform and waved. Each of them wore a secondhand dress and shoes with white ankle socks. Each had a purse and a small suitcase of secondhand clothes, including brassieres and underwear. Judith kept sticking her thumbs underneath the band of her brassiere through the bodice of her dress.

"This is the most uncomfortable thing I ever put on."

"The price o' fame," said Cassie.

"I'm hungry," Judith said. Mrs. Glade had given each of them a paper bag with peanut butter and jelly sandwiches wrapped in waxed paper, apples, and brownies for dessert. "Let's eat."

"It's only five in the afternoon," Cassie said.

"I'm gonna git me a Coke from that drugstore crost the street. You want one?"

"You know I don't like Coke."

"Then you git the train tickets."

"You the one gonna buy 'em."

"Why you think the Reverend Glade done give you the money? He think I'm liable to run right off with it." She pointed at the ticket booth, directly under the clock. "Jus' go on over there and tell 'im where we goin'."

It would have been so much easier for Judith to saunter up to the white man in the ticket booth. This was the real reason that Reverend Glade had given Cassie the money. It had nothing to do with trust. It had to do with the tar. She could almost taste the humiliation of being a colored girl asking for two train tickets.

Farther down the platform a group of colored women in church hats chatted with animated gestures around a heap of luggage. "You ain't gonna be the first colored t'buy a ticket today. You sure you don't want somethin' from the sodee fountain?"

"I'm sure."

Judith went across the street and disappeared into the drugstore.

Cassie wandered over to the ticket booth and examined the schedule pinned into its frame. The columns of numbers and places made no sense to her. She went to the ticket window and said, "Hello, suh." The stationmaster, reading the newspaper, ignored her from inside his little cage. There was no one else by the ticket window, and the platform was empty except for herself and the colored ladies down a ways. The stationmaster scowled at her from under bushy white eyebrows.

"You gettin' on a train?"

"Suh," she said, "you got a train goes to Grand Central Station in New York City?"

"Shore we do. Cost you fifty-three dollars."

"How long it take to git there?"

"Three days and two over-night, but see here," he said. "If you ain't takin' no train, you wastin' my time askin' 'bout it."

"No, suh," said Cassie. "I ain't mean to waste nobody's time. You mind if I ask you 'bout 'nother train?"

"Where to? The North Pole?"

"Oh no, suh, that be way too cold. But my daddy's in Virginia. You got a train goes to Virginia?"

"We got trains go all over Virginia. Different places got different fares. Where's your daddy?"

"Remington, Virginia, suh."

He consulted the papers on his desk. "That's thirteen dollars and fifty cents."

"What time it leave, suh?"

"That train come in one-half hour from now."

"When it git to Remington, suh?"

"Nine oh five tomorrow mornin'."

She took the money out of her secondhand purse and laid the bills on the counter. "Kin you give me two tickets to Remington, suh?"

He eyed her, her money. He looked like he wanted to know where she'd gotten so much. "Two tickets for the colored seats."

She had anticipated this but not in a way that kept her from saying so quickly, "Suh, the girl I's trav'lin' with is white."

"Two tickets then," he said and held them until she slid the cash under the bars in his window. He slid the tickets out but didn't let go as she put her fingers on them.

He said, "Where'd you get all that money, gal?"

She didn't take her eyes off the tickets. "Suh, ain't you heard of Miz Judith Forrest?"

"Cain't say I have."

"She a singin' star from Mississippi to South Carolina. She travel from church to church spreadin' the gospel word. I's surprised you ain't heard of her yet, but you will once she git on the reddio. Her voice so beautiful, it lift your soul right up."

"So what're you doing with her money?"

Cassie raised her eyes just a little, just enough to see the bottom of his white beard. "I's her maid, suh."

She felt him let the tickets go, and she scooped them up before he could change his mind, behind those white eyebrows and beard. "Thank you, suh," she said. "You lissen to the reddio, now. Miz Judith Forrest."

Judith came across the street with a bottle of Coke and a big paper cup of cold water. "They wanted t'charge me a penny for the cup. I had to tell 'em the cup ain't worth even half a penny." She sat on the edge of the platform and offered Cassie the water.

"You git the tickets?"

Cassie showed her.

"These to Remington."

"You kin git that New York ticket yourself."

"There enough money left?"

Cassie gave her the fare for the New York trip and took a long cold drink from the paper cup.

Judith opened the Coke and took a swig. She took the apple out of the dinner pail and took a bite out of it. She chewed while Cassie thought about introducing herself as *Miz Judith Forrest's maid* forever.

The train announced itself with a profound rumble that Cassie felt inside her chest before she saw it. She felt in her pocket for the tar. It would work, as long as she was willing to abandon everything. The train appeared from around a bend, enormous and black. Steam rushed out from under it in hot clouds. It rolled past them, heat billowing from its metal skin, wheels, and pistons, hotter than any part of the day. Passenger cars rattled past, each window a snapshot of the people inside.

Judith shouted over the noise, "We cain't sit together?"

"I don't imagine so."

"How'm I gonna know when to git off?"

"Nobody gonna let you ride for free. Someone'll tell you."

"You shore?"

"I'm sure."

Judith flung her arms around Cassie's neck and hung on like she was scared for the first time in her life. The train slowed and stopped, and Judith let go. She grabbed her suitcase and her dinner and ran to where a white conductor was helping white people down off the train. Judith pushed past them and clambered on. She turned once at the top of the stairs to wave and vanished inside. Cassie walked down the length of the train, looking for her through the windows but not seeing her. Toward the end of the train, she found a colored man in overalls tapping the wheels with a hammer.

"Excuse me," she said, "where's the colored car?"

"Down there. Number fourteen." He pointed to where the women in Sunday hats were getting on the very last car before the caboose. "You got a ticket, gal?"

She showed him, and he stuck his hammer in the loop of his overall and walked with her down to number fourteen. He helped her up on the wobbly wooden step and into the train car with a rough, strong hand. She found a seat by a window, back from where the Sunday hat ladies had grouped themselves, and watched the man in the coveralls as the train pulled away. He stood on the platform, hands on his hips as though the whole enterprise belonged to him.

Cassie put her palm against the glass and turned to watch him and Parmetter and everything south of it roll away, faster and faster still.

In the evening, the ladies took out a basket of fried chicken and biscuits and a carefully packed pitcher of iced tea. They didn't act like they'd noticed Cassie until she started eating her peanut butter and jelly sandwich, and then a lady in a white satin hat said to her, "Come over here and have some decent food."

They made room for her on the edge of one of the seats. These particular seats were arranged to face each other, as though the passengers were in a very small parlor. The ladies' knees practically touched each other, and the widest ladies squeezed the thinnest between them. They asked where she was going and where she was coming from and where her people were. She told them most of the truth and felt bad for not being entirely honest with them, as they were very generous with their food and their cold tea. She asked if any of them had ever been to Remington, and none of them had. They were all getting off in Maddox, South Carolina, for a wedding, and wasn't it ridiculous that this late train was the only one that stopped there and folks had to be bothered to pick them up at the station at ten in the evening. Cassie asked if any of them had ever been to Boston, and they laughed as though it was the funniest thing they'd heard all day.

"You got people in Boston?" said a lady in a blue hat, and Cassie said, "No, ma'am." And the lady said, "What're you gonna do in a place where you don't know nobody? Who gonna give you work?" and the other hat ladies *umm-hmmed* in agreement. "At least in the South ever'body related to ever'body else," she said. "People may not like it, but they cain't deny it. Up North, people from all over, don't know their own kin, wouldn't know a cousin or an uncle if they fell over 'em. You say your daddy in Remington?" Cassie nodded, and the lady in the white satin hat patted her hand. "Git him to show you round. You say you do laundry? Well ever'body got to git they draws washed, so you shouldn't have enny trouble findin' work."

One of the ladies, a thin one, said that even folks in Boston had to git they draws washed, but no one was listening to her, and the talk turned to the wedding and the cake and how the bride was too fat to ever look good in her mama's dress an' white sure wasn't the right color on her *ennyway*. Cassie sat with them until the train pulled into the Maddox station, well after ten. They wished her good luck and got off the train under yellow street lamps. Nice cars awaited them and drove them away into the darkness.

The lights stayed on in the train car all night but were only bright enough to show you the way to the toilet. Once the ladies left for the wedding, there were only two other people, a man and a woman at opposite ends of the car, both sleeping. Cassie was tired enough to sleep, but there was too much going on in her head.

Boston. Judith. New York. The tar. Boston. Judith. New York.
The tar.

The rhythm of the train on the rails started to sound like
the words in Cassie's mind. To make the beat stop, she opened
the bulky purse the Glades had given her and tried to organize the
few items in it. There was a compact with pinkish powder in
the puff but no mirror. She found a tube of used lipstick, which
made her think of Judith and the albino boy, and Judith bleeding
through her dress, standing in that creek in Alabama, wringing
out her dress and trying not to cry. There was a postcard in the
bottom of the purse. It was the one she'd written to Lil Ma before
they'd reached Enterprise but forgotten to send.

Dear Lil Ma and Grandmother,
   I am doing well. We have a car and people help us when
it doesn't run. Soon we will be in Enterprise in Alabama
where there is a monument to the Boll Weevil. I will write
more soon.
                                        Love, Cassie

She felt as though she'd written it years ago. What would she
say now?

Dear Lil Ma and Grandmother,
   I have the thing that will make me white.
                                        Love, Cassie

The tar in her pocket watched her thoughts. Writing a letter
might be all right, but mailing it would make the letter a lie.

Outside, South or North Carolina rushed by in the dark.
Cassie repeated the Glades' phone number under her breath. She
counted the money they had put into her secondhand purse, and

came up with fifty dollars. Cassie put everything back into the purse and snapped it shut. She looked out the window and noted with surprise that the trees were covered with blossoms, so thick and white they shone in the dark, lit by the passing train. To regular travelers this might not be remarkable, but only yesterday afternoon, in Porterville, the flowers had been frail and rotten, falling to the ground. Fresh white blossoms rushed past the train window, a second chance at the change of the season. Cassie leaned her cheek against the glass.

Boston. Judith. New York. The tar. Boston. Judith.

What would Judith do if Cassie abandoned her in Remington? Judith didn't need help finding Bill Forrest. She didn't need Cassie to become a big singin' star.

Boston. Judith. New York. The tar. Boston. Judith.

Judith would be all right without Cassie. Not happy. Furious when she had time to think about it. But unstoppable.

The sun was coming up, turning the blossoms, the sky, and the drab interior of the train different shades of pink. The iced tea changed from a pressure to a need. Cassie picked up her suitcase and her purse and went into the colored ladies' toilet, a seat with a hole and tracks rushing underneath it. There was a mirror but no washbasin. The mirror was opposite a shaded window. Faint daylight rippled through the shade as Cassie looked at her reflection. Mrs. Glade had brushed her dry hair out, oiled it, and braided it up behind her ears. It was soft and thick and looked better than it had since she'd left home. The tar in her dress pocket was a hot wad against her thigh. She took it out and touched her hair with it, lightly. She expected it to stick, a sticky joke on sticky hair, but where the tar touched, the texture changed. Kink became smooth. Black became brown. A strange feeling gripped her in the chest, like joy, or the kind of strangle she felt before breaking into sobs. She pulled out the pins and bands. She pulled her hair out of its careful braid. She wiped the tar all through until her hair became a white girl's hair. Not like Judith's, which was lank. The glossy kind, the kind white girls flipped over their shoulders and tied up in sprightly ponytails. It fell around her shoulders, loose and full. The tracks rattled past below the hole of the toilet. The hair lay around her cinnamon-colored face like a wig.

She tore the tar in half and scrubbed both sides of her face with it. Her hands shook as the cinnamon came off. She wound the tar into each ear, behind her ears, over the back of her neck. In the mirror, the hair framed her white face, her lean nose, her lips so similar to Judith's. The last thing that might speak for her, her skull, the shape of her bones, the skull underneath this skin, was mute.

Remington! Remington, Virginia!

She was sweating, and there were tears coming out of her eyes, which she was afraid would wash off the white and leave streaks showing the color still inside. She couldn't look at herself. She scrubbed her hands with the tar instead, back and front, and her arms up to her shoulders. The train slowed. She struggled out of the secondhand shoes and socks and wiped away color from her toes up to her underpants. She straightened up to see little tear-trails on her face. These she dabbed away with great care. Underneath, she was still white.

The train stopped. Outside the toilet door, people were getting off, thumping luggage. She pushed the window shade aside a finger's width to see the platform. She should get off. Her ticket was only good for this stop. She would have to get off without Judith seeing her, or all the black would come right back. She searched the platform frantically through the sliver of window. Where was Judith? Cassie saw only colored faces. Remington was the city rising beyond the platform—a traffic light, a brick bank, a wooden warehouse. New-looking cars waited at the traffic light. White people in the cars. Colored people crossing the street on foot.

Richmond! Richmond Special!

Richmond? How far was Richmond? Was Judith still on the train? What if she'd fallen asleep? Cassie turned from the window and saw herself in the mirror again, a panicked white girl. A white girl in the colored toilet. She made her face close, the way she made it close when white people looked at her. The expression looked different, but there wasn't time to figure out why.

Cassie put on her socks and shoes. She opened the toilet door an inch. The man and the woman who'd stayed in the car after the women had gotten off at Maddox were still in their seats. The man was sleeping. The woman was looking out the window. Cassie opened the door wider. No one stirred. She put her foot and one shoulder through the opening in the door. No one noticed. Her armpits were slick. She gripped the handle of her suitcase hard enough to feel her own short nails dig in her palm. She stepped out with her back to the woman looking out the window and the sleeping man. She made her legs move, her white legs, through the door, into the first of the cars for white passengers.

White people were getting on at the other end of the car, bustling around with children and luggage, hats, and lunch buckets. Colored porters helped them with their bags. Cassie sat in the first seat she came to, the seat against the back wall of the car. She slid over to the window farthest from the train platform. She would go to Richmond, wherever that was. She looked across the car at the crowded platform. Was Judith there? Cassie huddled down, with her suitcase and purse. There was room for three in her row, and she dreaded someone sitting next to her, but the front of the car filled up and everyone seemed to settle in, leaving the back half of the car mostly empty. The porters left. The conductor cried, *"Alll aboooard!"* The train lurched forward. Cassie looked over at the platform once more and this time saw Judith standing with her purse clutched to her chest, watching blankly as the train pulled away.

CHAPTER ✦ THIRTEEN

Cassie had never been around white people for such a long time without having to do something for them.

The women's toilet for the car was at the end of her unoccupied row. She could hear everything anyone said if they were standing there. It was strange to listen with no pressure to answer any demands. She looked the other way, out the window. The meadows, fields, and forests of Virginia sped past.

Mama! Look what I found!

Oh, where'd you pick up that nasty trash?

I found it on the railroad tracks. Look, it's a medal! I'm a soldier!

Get that filthy thing off that nice white shirt. It's just a dirty bit of tin. Here, give it to me. Give it to me 'fore I tan your hide! Now git in there and pull down your pants.

For a while no one came to use the toilet. Apart from the rhythmic chug of the train, Cassie heard disconnected threads from the conversations around her. Outside, a river ran invitingly, shaded by willows, maples, oaks. There were ducks on the water and neat little houses with colored folk on the porches and chickens pecking in the yards. The trees thickened, obscuring the river and any houses along its banks. Two women, older women, came to the toilet door.

> *I would never, ever say this to her face, but I have to wonder if all her health problems aren't God's way of sayin', You lived a wicked life, woman, and here's your reward. I mean, I would never say that, but I think you know what I mean.*
> *That time she had with Thomas.*
> *While she was married to Richard!*
> *But Richard was cheatin' on her.*
> *I'm sorry, but revenge-cheatin', or whatever you want to call it, ain't in the Bible, an' if it ain't in the Bible, God's got every right to give you bleedin' troubles in your womb and pains in your titties. Ain't it seem righteous to you?*

Cassie tried to imagine Mister Mallard, the albino man in Porterville, talking like this and couldn't. His bitterness was different. And the widow behind the curtain at the church in Porterville, her daughter in her lap, and the sticky black baby balanced on top of both of them? Would any of them say a thing like "God's got every right to give you bleedin' troubles in your womb and pains in your titties"? It was easy to imagine Mrs. Duckett, in the laundry, having a conversation with Lil Ma about God's revenge and "bleedin' troubles." Still, there was something in the way these voices spoke that made them different, as though they had a handle on something in particular that made their opinions, no matter how mean-spirited or common, more correct than if the same words came out of the mouth of a colored person.

The door at the far end of the car opened. The conductor came through saying, "Tickets, tickets, please." Cassie had seen him before, when he punched her ticket on the way out of Parmetter. He was an older white man with a short bristled beard and white hair under his conductor's cap. He arrived at her row.

"Ticket, miss."

Her old ticket was in her purse. The ticket didn't say COLORED on it. It didn't have to. She was afraid even to touch it, though, afraid whatever residue it carried would make him recognize her. She gripped her purse. Her fingers wanted to open the window next to her and leap free of the train, roll down the grassy embankment, and run away under the peach blossoms.

"Ain't you gotta ticket, miss?"

She shook her head.

"Where you gettin off, Richmond?"

She nodded at the purse in her hands.

"Four dollars and fifty cents," said the conductor. "You got that much in your purse?"

She looked hard at her fingers to see if there was any color left on them, but the tar had taken everything. Her hands were pale and lined with pale blue veins, which were so fascinating she just wanted to stare at them. She made herself open the purse and gather five bills in a sweaty crumple.

The conductor took the money and gave her change. He punched her new ticket. He went on through the door to the colored car. That was all.

Cassie shivered in her own chill. She repeated the Glades's phone number in her head. She understood now why they would have sent her to Boston. For the *Community*. For the *Opportunity*. The *Community* would never have let her travel alone like this, and the *Opportunity*, she was sure, would have shown her exactly how to smile at the conductor and hand over her money, cool as a cucumber, lily-white.

— ✦ —

Even the little towns around Richmond seemed bigger than Remington. They were so crowded together, she couldn't tell where the city itself began. There were traffic lights and junk yards and a big road with four lanes paralleling the tracks. The train rattled across switches and crossings. Cars drove as fast as or faster than the train; sometimes it looked like the car was still, and the trees behind it were moving. On one side of the tracks the houses were painted white, with flower gardens. On the other side were the Negro streets. Shoeshines, fruit stands, a laundry. A mule hitched to a cart. Children, barefoot in the dust, waving at the train. The train rumbled by in the midmorning, casting a shadow over all of them.

Last stop, last stop Richmond! Last stop, Richmond Special!

The train slowed to a crawl, and the passengers got up to collect their things. The train stopped. Some passengers hustled right off. Others, with children mostly, took longer. Cassie shuffled out behind the first group. At the door, a colored porter steadied a wooden stair while a second colored porter helped people off the train.

Cassie stepped forward, and the second porter caught her elbow to help her down. She gave him a nervous smile. He gave her the smile he saved for white folks.

"Help you with your bag, miss?"

"No, thank you," she said and knew immediately that *no thank you* meant something else coming out of this mouth; a curse, concealed in politeness. The wooden stair wobbled under her. The porter's hand on her arm was all that kept her from tumbling onto the brick platform.

"Steady there, miss," he said.

She didn't say anything at all, and that felt terrible too.

The beautiful shop windows of Richmond—jewelry and furniture, bakeries and dresses—were framed by blossoming trees and telephone poles complete with wires. It was lunchtime, and men either rushed past Cassie with a briefcase in one hand or sat, eating and drinking in restaurants. No one looked at her for more than a moment, which would have made her think that the tar had actually erased her if she hadn't seen her own white face in every display window she passed.

Her feet hurt in the secondhand shoes, and her mind was numb. What should she do now? In Remington, Judith was probably looking for work and a room. Perhaps, in Remington, Judith had found her father, confronted him with her state of progeny, and grabbed whatever money he still had right out of his pockets. Maybe she was already on her way to New York, leaving her past behind as well.

There were a few signs for jobs posted in the shop windows. SALESLADY WANTED. COUNTER HELP NEEDED. Nothing about laundry. Laundry jobs would be on the other side of the tracks, or in the backs of the stores, and for colored women. Cassie tried to imagine Judith, brash as usual, walking into a ladies' fine dress shop and offering her services as counter help. The ladies in the shop would laugh at her and yell at her to leave, because there was nothing more lowly than Judith, except for a colored girl. Even with white skin, Cassie understood that she had risen only a notch, and a shallow notch at that.

She repeated the Glades's phone number to herself. There were three choices. Go back to Porterville—if she could still find it. Go back to Remington and tell Judith about the tar. Or go on to

Boston, where she knew no one and would be depending entirely on strangers. If she went back to Remington, she might not have to say a word. The minute Judith laid eyes on her, the tar's effects would evaporate. Cassie would be the same as she was before, with only a sidestep in time.

She kept walking until late in the afternoon, when she found herself at the edge of a park. She took off her shoes and walked in the grass until she could see down a long hill to a river. Train tracks paralleled the river, just like back home, and she could see the station, perhaps two miles behind her, past a long, lazy oxbow. From the other direction, she heard music playing, and when she craned her neck, she could see a white tent rising behind blossoming trees. She smelled popcorn and roasting peanuts. She put the white ankle socks and flats back on her bare, dirty white feet. She tucked her suitcase under a low-hanging pine and covered it with needles, took a nickel out of her purse for ice cream, and walked down the grassy hill to see the circus.

Outside the big top, a man cranked an organ and a monkey danced, holding out his little red cap for pennies. The midway stretched to her right, crowded and noisy, smelling of fried meat, burned popcorn, sweat, and cigarettes. She heard a lion roar, looked for elephants but didn't see them. She wandered down the midway, surrounded by white people. Tall men in workmen's clothes smoked cigarettes, threw down the butts, and ground them into the dirt with their heels. Babies cried until they were red in the face. Little girls shrieked as little boys stamped on their new shoes. A white man said, "'Scuse me, miss," when he bumped into her. She didn't see a single colored person, not even hauling boxes behind the food stands. She passed the corn dogs and cotton candy. It was getting darker and cooler, and the lights inside

the little sheds made the food look unnatural. It was too chilly
for ice cream by the time she found where they were selling it, so
there was no line. The white girl behind the counter looked up
from a movie magazine, her lipstick-red lips pushed out in surprise.

"Choc'lit er 'nilla?" she said.

The prices were written out in pink chalk on a painted board.
Ten cents a scoop.

"We 'bout to close," said the girl. "I give you a scoop o' each
fer a nickel."

Cassie put her nickel, hot from being clenched in her hand, on
the counter. The white girl picked a pointed cone from a neat
stack and scooped the ice cream casually, expertly. She squashed
the glistening sphere of vanilla into the cone and the chocolate
on top of it. She wrapped the cone in a napkin and gave it to
Cassie.

"Already seen the show?" she said.

Cassie shook her head.

"Starts in 'bout five minutes," said the girl. "Gotta ticket?"

"No."

"You gonna miss it for sure if you doan go now," said the girl.
"You gotta dollar f'the ticket?"

"Yes," said Cassie.

"Well, look," said the girl. "I kin give you a ticket half-price.
Git you in f'shore, an' you ain't gotta stan' in line." She reached
for a napkin and wrote on it in the same pink chalk as the ice
cream prices.

Let this gal in sined Gloria

She held out the signed napkin to Cassie. "Fifty cent. Come
on, now. You know we gotta elephant an' a lion an' little dogs does
tricks."

Ice cream drips ran down to catch in the napkin around the cone. Cassie set her purse on the counter, dug in it for the right change, and gave that to Gloria. Gloria gave Cassie the napkin with a friendly smile.

"Enjoy the show," said Gloria.

Cassie turned back down the midway, which had emptied out. She licked the ice cream, which was good. When she gave Gloria's signed napkin to the man at the big top, he laughed hard and she knew she'd let herself be robbed. She gave him a dollar. He gave her a real ticket. She threw the remaining ice cream in the trash and went in to see the circus.

The circus had already started when she walked in, and all the bleacher seats in front were taken. Little dogs dressed as clowns raced in circles, jumping through hoops while trumpets played. Cassie climbed up to the top of the bleachers. A draft came in from outside, and the canvas smelled of mildew. Below and to her left was the flap in the tent where the animals and performers waited their turn. She didn't have a very good view of the ring, but she could see straight down to the women in glittering costumes sitting on the backs of dappled horses. A colored groom adjusted harnesses and handed up feathered headdresses. A white man in a dusty black jacket and a satin top hat sat on a bench smoking. A long whip was propped up beside him.

> *Laydeeez and Gentlemen!*
> *Children of allll ages!*

Drums rolled. Trumpets blared. The horses snorted, and their glittering passengers stood up on their backs, touching the lower bars of the bleachers for balance. The man in the top hat stamped out his cigarette, grabbed the long whip, and jogged out to the ring, waving to the crowd. The women on the horses followed, and the groom shoveled up horse manure. When most of it was cleared away, he pulled the tent flap wider for the elephant.

The elephant. It had been waiting just outside, visible, Cassie now realized, as a shadow against the canvas. It was enormous. She could have touched its back from where she was sitting. A woman rode the elephant, sitting astride just behind its ears. She wore a low-cut bathing suit made of bright red spangles and a headdress with scarlet feathers as long as Cassie was tall. The elephant smelled of hay and horse manure. The woman took a compact mirror out of her cleavage, checked herself, and dropped it back in. She saw Cassie staring.

"Well, honey," said the woman, "how do I look?"

"Fine," said Cassie breathlessly.

"You wanna pat the elephant?"

The way she said it, it sounded like another trick, but Cassie reached through the railing and brushed her fingers along the gray hide. It felt like the bark of a tree.

"Hey!" shouted the woman and Cassie jerked back, but the woman was looking down at the groom. "Get that horse shit off his feet! What the hell is wrong with you?" She straightened and pawed at her headdress. "Damn niggers," she said to Cassie.

Trumpets rang out. The elephant stepped forward, and the woman on top of him swept past in a flash of red.

Cassie glanced down at the groom. His face was hard to see. In the ring, the elephant strode around and stopped in the middle. The woman posed on his back, on his head. Trumpets tooted merrily. The elephant knelt in front of the man with the whip, and she stepped down. The man raised his whip. The elephant stood and raised one foot. With great drama, the woman lay down and put her head underneath. Drums rolled menacingly. The elephant lowered its foot until it was touching the woman's head, and the three of them held that pose while the audience gasped. Cassie looked down at the groom, watching, his arms crossed. She knew what he was thinking as clearly as he felt her gaze. He looked up, impenetrable. She looked away before he saw right through her.

She left before the lion and the clowns and the high trapeze act. They were lined up in that order outside the tent, and Cassie saw Gloria too. As a white girl, Cassie had the right to beat Gloria to a pulp to get her fifty cents back, but without the ice cream counter between them, Gloria looked spindly and underfed, and Cassie found herself feeling sorry for her the way she sometimes felt sorry for Judith. She kept going, away from the lights of the circus, back to the dense trees in the riverside park, up the hill until she found her suitcase. She took out Lil Ma's shoes and put them on and sat in the cool evening until it was completely dark. She put on one of the sweaters Mrs. Glade had given her and wrapped her legs in another and went to sleep with the suitcase as a pillow. When she dreamed, she saw Lil Ma sitting across a table from Grandmother. Lil Ma was as dark as ever, but Grandmother, dressed in red sequins and a fancy feathered hat, had turned as white as white could be.

In the morning Cassie straightened up as well as she could. The compact the Glades had put in her purse had no mirror; she could only guess at the state of her hair and her face. Her hands looked grimy, especially around the nails, and the fascinating blueness of the veins had turned to an unwashed bluish gray. Her clothes smelled of the damp ground. She needed to use a bathroom. She felt in the pocket of her dress for the tar. It was stuck there, not in any danger of falling out.

She changed back into the ankle socks and the flats that hurt her feet, put Lil Ma's shoes in her suitcase, and made her way out of the park.

She was terribly hungry. She turned down the first big street she came to. Shops were starting to open. She had fixed her hair as well as she could, but she wasn't used to this hair. It hung in tangled clumps and refused to obey her combing fingers. She found a bit of string in the bottom of the purse and tied it back. She felt sure her pale face looked puffy and dirty. For the first time since she and Judith had left Heron-Neck, Cassie felt a weepy desperation. She wiped her eyes, but that only made it worse. She stood where she was, eyes squeezed shut, clenching the suitcase in one hand, her purse in the other. People passed by. She felt them looking at her. A hand touched her arm, and she opened her eyes to see a well-dressed colored woman.

"You cain't be standin' round here with your suitcase and your cryin'. You scarin' away my bizniss."

Through the plate glass were dresses on hangers, scarves, handbags arranged prettily on shelves. There was a long counter lined with mirrors and fancy hats.

"This my shop," said the woman. "This our street and this our neighborhood. Y'hear? Now, you need some money?"

Cassie wiped her eyes. "Nome."

"You know where your side o' town is?"

"Nome."

The colored woman cocked her head. Other colored people had stopped to see what was going on. All were well dressed—the men in top hats with canes, the women in stylish dresses and beautiful shoes.

The woman pointed at the next intersection, where there was a traffic light. "Turn lef' at that light. That's Third. Walk all the way down the hill, an' you'll find a diner an' a flophouse. I 'spect they'll take care of you."

Big cars waited at the light, all driven by coloreds. At least one was driven by a colored chauffeur with colored passengers.

What *Community* was this? What *Opportunity* did these people have? Did the Reverend and Mrs. Glade know about them?

Did Mister Mallard know? She looked down at the mesmerizing blue veins in her own pale hands.

"Is you witless?" said the woman. "Dincha hear me?"

Cassie walked toward the traffic light. She turned the corner of Third and made her way down the hill past neat brick houses with roses in bloom, azaleas, apple blossoms, and tulips. Her own side of town was just ahead, past a used car lot and a vacant-looking warehouse. She could see the river. The railway station was visible past a jumble of industrial rooftops. Between her and the tracks were thrift stores and boardinghouses. She found a diner, called *Ida's*, where a white waitress served her without a second glance at the state of her hair and clothes, probably because the rest of the white people there looked just as shabby. She sat at a table by the window and ordered coffee, pancakes, hash browns, and sausage. The pancakes and hash browns were good, but the sausage wasn't cooked all the way through. She asked the waitress if she could borrow a pencil. The waitress said, "What fer?" and Cassie told her she needed to write a letter to her mother. The waitress looked around at the rest of the diner and said that since it wasn't crowded, all right, but if anyone came in and wanted Cassie's table, she would have to leave. She gave Cassie the pencil and asked what she was planning to write on. Cassie smoothed her unused napkin. The waitress said, "Wait a minnit," walked away, and came back with a clean sheet of paper. It had the diner's name and address at the top. "I should write my momma too," said the waitress.

Cassie wrote:

Dear Lil Ma,

The lead-pencil words lay on the crisp paper. The rest of the letter might as well be on the paper already. *I have found the thing that has made me white.* She could almost see the words. She erased *Lil Ma* and wrote *Dear Grandmother* instead.

Cassie folded the paper with trembling white fingers and put it in her purse without writing any more. She put the pencil in too, without thinking that it belonged to the waitress. She got up to pay at the register, and the waitress asked if she'd gotten her letter all written. Cassie nodded, and the waitress told her there was a post office down a couple of blocks by the train station. She gave Cassie her change, and Cassie remembered the pencil. She dug fruitlessly for it in the gritty bottom of her purse while the waitress watched her in such a way that Cassie was certain she had turned colored again before the woman's eyes. But the waitress took another pencil out of her apron and scribbled an address on the back of a used order slip. She pressed it into Cassie's pale palm.

"If you need somewheres to stay, you come over to my place. It's a hell of a lot safer'n some o' these damn flophouses, y'hear? An' I don't mean I'd charge you rent'r nothin'. You look like you could use a little help."

"Yessum," said Cassie. "Thank you, ma'am." Cassie walked out of the diner and turned left, down the hill. Judith, she thought, would have remarked upon the woman's kindness, but Cassie could only imagine how long it might be before the words *damn nigger* came out of that mouth. When she came to the train station, she wadded up the slip with the waitress's address and threw it in the trash. Then she sat on a bench in the shade, took the paper out of her purse, found the pencil, and finished writing to her grandmother.

I have made it to Richmond, Virginia. I have met some very nice people on the way. One of them gave me this. I think it is what you have been looking for. I have used it myself, but I think it will

still work for you. Scrub your hands and your face with it, and
you will see. You can't let anyone else know about it, not even Lil
Ma, or the black will come right back. You will have to leave
Heron-Neck forever if you decide to stay the way it changes you.

Cassie folded the paper in half, then in quarters. She took the
tar out of her pocket and squeezed it and pressed it until it was
absolutely flat, no bigger than a playing card. She folded it inside
the letter to Grandmother and checked her hands. Still white.
Would the tar work on Grandmother? Cassie had no doubt that
it would. Would Grandmother leave Lil Ma, vanish from Heron-
Neck, and make a new life for herself somewhere as a white
woman? Where would she go? What if she came to Richmond—
to the address on the diner's stationery—expecting to find Cassie
living her days and nights as a white girl? Cassie picked up her
suitcase and purse and went into the post office. She got an envelope and stamp from the postal clerk, addressed the envelope to
Grandmother at the Laundry on Negro Street, and sealed everything inside. Lil Ma would never see it or the tar.

There was one thing left to do before she got back on the train.
At the station, she found the phone inside a wooden booth.
She had never used a phone before, but Tabitha Bromley had
had one in her store, and Cassie had seen how other people did
it. The door folded closed, and there was a seat inside. The booth
was snug and almost soundproof, and far too small to fit the
suitcase. She left it where she could see it and sat for a while in
her terrible secondhand shoes. The white ankle socks were now
dirty and bunched. Her heels had blisters. She took the receiver
off the hook and waited for the operator to speak. She would give
her the number and tell the Glades she was sorry, but she was
going to stay a colored girl. She was going to go back to Judith,
but only until the business with Bill Forrest was settled. Then she

would come back to Richmond and find out how the colored
woman had gotten her own store and how it was that a colored
man chauffeured other colored men. She would ask the Glades if
they knew anything about the coloreds in Richmond.

"Operator," said the operator abruptly, in her ear. "What city,
please?"

Cassie told her.

"What number, please?"

Cassie told her.

For a moment there was silence. Then static, then a buzz.

"I'm connecting you now," said the operator, sounding far
away.

The buzz became intermittent. It went on for what seemed like
a long time.

"I can't hear anyone," said Cassie. "Are they there?"

"There's no answer, ma'am," said the operator. "You'll have to
try again later."

She hung up the receiver and leaned against the booth's
wooden wall. If the tar had still been in her pocket, would someone have answered the phone? She repeated the number in her
head, but this time wasn't sure she had it right. Or perhaps she'd
had it wrong the first time. She picked up the phone again and
waited.

A different woman's voice spoke in her ear. "Operator. What
city, please?"

Cassie told her.

"What number, please?"

Cassie told her.

"I'm connecting you now."

Another intermittent buzz, which Cassie guessed was the
sound of the phone ringing. It rang for a long time.

"There's no answer, ma'am," said the operator.

"Thank you," said Cassie.

She never tried to reach the Glades again.

Cassie bought her ticket to Remington at the Richmond station from a white man in the ticket booth. This one was younger than the man in Remington. He had a thick black mustache, but it didn't hide the look he gave her as she handed him the money for the ticket. It was the same look people gave to Judith—white people as well as colored people—which said, with languid movements of the eyebrows and corners of the mouth, that she was nothing, had never been more than nothing, and would never be more than nothing nohow. Cassie walked down the platform with her ticket, thinking that Judith could probably learn a lot from the Glades. With better clothes and a curl in her hair, Judith might be able to hoist herself up in the world. The Glades's *Opportunity* probably included makeup, heels, and a really good hat. Cassie tried to picture herself dressed just so, but in her mind's eye, it looked like a disguise, the same as this white skin.

She got on the train, avoiding the colored porters' helpful hands, and sat in the white car just in front of the colored car, in case something unexpected happened on her way south.

Cassie arrived in Remington at about four in the afternoon, almost exactly two days since she'd left Judith. To her surprise, Judith was still waiting on the platform, slumped beside her luggage in about the same spot Cassie had left her. She looked rumpled, like she'd been there the whole time. Cassie hunched down in the seat. She shouldn't have left without saying anything, but what else could she have done? To ask what Judith would have done in her shoes was pointless, but what really surprised Cassie was that

Judith had faltered. The girl with the bloody dress, the girl with the huge voice, the girl with the *plan* was still sitting out there, chin in her hands, bare dirty knees, and socks without shoes, like somebody's lost child.

The light dimmed inside the car, and Cassie caught a glimpse of her own pale reflection. What would happen now? Her cinnamon color remained on her body within the general outlines of a bathing suit. Her arms and legs and head stuck out of it. What if that was the way she stayed when Judith saw her? What if that was what the Glades and their community considered fair? Cassie dryly swallowed her doubts. The train shuddered to a stop. The conductor shouted "*Remington!*" She picked up her things and headed for the door.

Judith saw her the minute she stepped onto the platform and rushed over, leaving purse and suitcase in a sad little pile.

"What happened?" Judith demanded. "What happened? You fall 'sleep? You fergit to git off? I bin waitin' here forever."

Cassie looked down at her arms, as brown as ever, maybe turning the moment Judith laid eyes on her. The white people around her, who had been on the same car with her, who hadn't noticed her when she was white, took no notice now. Maybe the saddling gift of the tar was to encourage people to see what they expected to see, but she doubted it.

"Sorry," she said to Judith. "I fell asleep. I went all the way to Richmond, spent a night there, an' I had to pay to come back."

"I din't want you t'think I'd run off an' left you," said Judith, "so I stayed here till you came back."

"I'm real glad you did," said Cassie.

Judith squinted at her. "You miss me?"

"Maybe a little."

"For a while there, I was afraid you ain't never comin' back."

"It was only two days."

"Felt like longer."

"'Cause you was sittin' by the tracks the entire time."

"Where'd you sleep in Richmond?"

"Under a tree. Near a circus."

Judith's eyes lit up. "You go in?"

"I touched the elephant."

Judith looked impressed.

"The lady riding him called me names."

"For touchin' her elephant? That's jes' shameful."

"I thought so too."

CHAPTER ✦ FOURTEEN

Remington was smaller than Richmond and bigger than Enterprise. It lacked a dusty hardware store and a diner specializing in pie. No incongruous marble monuments stuck up out of its main street. But there were cars, bars, banks, and restaurants, tall brick buildings, and telephone poles. Drivers waited impatiently in the morning heat as people on foot made their way between traffic lights with speed and determination. The women—white and colored—wore heels and hats. The men wore ties and jackets. They all seemed to have business. Nobody took a second look at the girls from Heron-Neck.

"Did you eat?" said Judith.

"I had breakfast," said Cassie.

"Nice ol' granny lady gave me a sandwich this morning," said Judith. "Guess she thought I looked poor."

"You do look poor," said Cassie. Compared to the hats and heels and suit jackets, they looked like beggars.

"You don't look no richer." Judith smoothed her hair, uselessly. She straightened herself like a soldier, which made her look skinny as a stick. After her experience as a white girl, Cassie saw Judith's self-

importance as painfully revealing. Cassie knew just what was going
through her mind. *Progeny. Inheritance. New York City. Big reddio
star.* Cassie smiled, because it was good to be in familiar company.

"What's so funny?" said Judith.

"Nothin'. Let's find us a newspaper and see what the date is.
Then let's find your daddy."

Newspapers were easy to find. A colored boy was selling them on
the corner but refused to tell them even the date without a nickel
for the paper first. Judith, exasperated and tired, finally gave him
the nickel but didn't take the paper. The boy told them that it was
was Saturday, March nineteenth.

They were two days early for whatever was going to happen
with Bill Forrest, Eula Bonhomme-Forrest, and the riches left over
from the estate.

Up the hill from the train station, they found the Veranda
Hotel: a white four-story building with white columns across the
front, like an old plantation house. They stood across the street
from it, surveying the front and the people going in and out.

"It look kinda like Miz Tabitha's ol' place," said Judith.
"'Ceptin' not so run down. You think they coulda made a hotel
outta that ol' house?"

"Who'd come to Heron-Neck to stay inna hotel?"

Judith crossed her arms. "Still. Shame to let a nice ol' house
jus' fall to pieces."

"It was fulla ghosts," said Cassie.

Judith studied the hotel across the street. "You think this place
got ghosts?"

"It's got your daddy in it."

"*Our* daddy."

"Ain't that enough?" Now that they were so close, Cassie felt uncompelled to claim any part of Bill Forrest. "How much money you got, Judith?"

"Half the singin' money plus 'nuff to git to New York City."

"I got enough to get to Boston and a little more." Close to fifty dollars. A small fortune in her purse.

"Boston?" said Judith.

"I don't know yet." It was important to keep the money, not spend it on something frivolous that Judith might come up with. "Can you do maid work?"

"What," said Judith, "like makin' beds an' such?"

"Sweepin' and dustin' and cleanin' the toilet. Kin you do that?"

"I kin if you kin."

"Your daddy may not be here," said Cassie, because it had to be said.

Judith uncrossed her arms and picked up her suitcase. "He's here. I kin feel it."

"All right," said Cassie. "You go in front an' see if they need a maid. I'll go in back an' see if they need help in the laundry."

A narrow alley ran down the shady side of the hotel. Cassie found a service door at the very back of the building. The back of the hotel faced a parking lot, which opened onto the next street, where a movie theater took up a good portion of the block. Two stylized metal falcons faced each other from opposite sides of the marquis with polished monumentality. The marquis said:

OLDIES FESTIVAL!

IMITATION OF LIFE

CLAUDETTE COLBERT AND WARREN WILLIAM

Cassie'd never been to the movies, but the title struck her as obvious. Weren't they all an imitation of life? She wondered how much it cost to get in and if colored people were allowed.

She knocked at the service door. After a minute a middle-aged colored woman opened it, wiping her hands on a towel. Behind her was a huge, well-lit room with large tables stacked with folded towels and sheets. The colored woman looked Cassie over.

"Somethin' you need?"

"I'm lookin' for laundry work, ma'am," Cassie said. "I been working in the laundry since I could fold a hanky."

"You're not from around here."

"Nome. I'm from Mississippi."

The woman cocked her head at the cars in the parking lot and peered around the back of the building as though there might be accomplices out there looking for work. Birds sang in the warmth of the afternoon. Car doors slammed down by the movie house.

"Mississippi," said the woman.

"Yessum."

"That's where my daddy's from," said the woman. "You from Biloxi?"

"Heron-Neck. It's just a little town."

The woman looked around a bit longer. Finally, she said, "Let's see how you iron a shirt."

The woman's name was Eden Pomeroy, and she was in charge of the laundry. She was a big woman with a big bosom. When she put her hands on her hips, she looked even bigger, formidable. She put a basket of shirts on the table beside an ironing board. Cassie took the first one and spread it out. The shirt was linen, finely woven, and no doubt expensive. Cassie flicked water at the iron. Steam curled up.

Eden Pomeroy stood right next to her. "You do the yoke first."

"Yessum." She watched her own hands smoothing the white cloth, her cinnamon color compared to Eden Pomeroy's skillet black. She felt how hot and close this room would be, long before the end of the day. She leaned into the iron's breathless vapor. The fabric submitted, flat and crisp.

"Lemme see you do them buttons," said Eden Pomeroy.

Cassie touched the iron to the cloth between delicate bone buttons.

"Cuffs last."

"Yessum."

She did the sleeves and cuffs and put the shirt on a hanger. Eden Pomeroy ran her fingers over the creases approvingly.

"She *fast*," said someone from the other end of the room, and Cassie looked up to see two molasses-colored women, each with a cart of rumpled white towels.

"Hey," said one of them. "Your name Cassie? There a white girl upstairs lookin' for maid work sez she knows you."

Eden eyed Cassie, the same way she'd eyed the parking lot. "That true?"

Cassie wished she'd told Judith to wait half an hour before she decided to explode upon the scene. "Yessum."

"What's a colored girl from Mississippi and a white girl doing together?"

"We tryin' to get to New York City. We run out of money, so we stop to get some decent employment."

"What's in New York City?"

"Miz Judith gone be a big singin' star."

One of the molasses women laughed. "That girl? She way too homely to be on stage."

"She really amazin' when she sings," said Cassie. "She lifts up your soul." She meant it to sound sincere, but the words came out like something she'd said too many times already.

Eden Pomeroy gave an irritated snort and walked off in the direction the two molasses-women had come from, presumably to see what was really going on upstairs. The second she was out of sight, the two women descended on Cassie, demanding her name and introducing themselves as Bethesda and Iris. Both had the last name Meadows but insisted that they weren't related.

"You really think that white gal kin sing?" said Iris.

"She sing just like a bird."

Iris and Bethesda giggled.

"What kinda bird?" said Iris. "'Cause the only bird I could think she sound like was some kinda cacklin' hen."

Eden Pomeroy came back about twenty minutes later and pulled Cassie aside. "What's this white girl to you?"

"We known each other a long time. We from a real small town."

"You think she be good at maid work?"

"Oh, yessum," said Cassie.

"You sure? She cain't seem to stop talking 'bout herself."

"She jus' excited 'bout bein' this close to New York City."

Eden Pomeroy let out a breath, like she wanted to believe what Cassie was saying but was too suspicious at too deep a level to let herself do that. "The boss says all right, you hired. Two dollars a day."

"Yessum."

"You say anythin' else sides 'yessum'?"

Cassie looked back at the big room and at Iris and Bethesda, who were watching from a distance as though they could read lips. "You know anyplace got rooms for rent?"

"For who? You? Or you an' that white gal."

She wasn't sure what to say.

Eden Pomeroy studied her for a long, uncomfortable minute. "Damn," she said. "That girl's got your eyes. She got your mouth. You sisters?" She didn't wait for Cassie to answer. "You sisters. Does *she* know you sisters?"

"Ever'body in town knows."

"This world, this world." She angled her head at some point past the washing machines and dryers. "There's a storeroom where I stay in the winter when the weather's bad. There's a bed in there and a bathroom down the hall. You can have that."

"Both of us together?"

"Yes, gal, both of y'all together."

At six that evening, Cassie found Judith across the street from the hotel in her gray maid uniform, looking at the mannequins in the window of a fancy dress shop. Eden Pomeroy had given Cassie a uniform too, but it was such a depressing piece of clothing that Cassie had washed and ironed it and hung it so as to put off wearing it until the next day. On Judith, the gray drabness of the uniform made the dresses in the window seem even more exotic and out of reach. They were sleek and modern, close-fitting in shades of blue, each outfit with a matching but insubstantial hat.

"You sing like a chicken," Cassie said to her. "And you cain't afford none of those clothes."

"You got work?"

"I got work."

"I got work too. What they payin' you?"

Cassie showed her the two dollars she had earned for the day.

"Me too," said Judith. "Strange, though."

"What's strange?"

"I thought they'd pay you more'n me."

Cassie had been thinking just the opposite.

"'Cause you got experience." Judith turned to stare at the dresses again. "He ain't on the second floor."

"What?"

"Daddy. He ain't on the second floor. That's where they was

ABSALOM'S DAUGHTERS   205

showing me how they wants the beds made an' such. They showed me a buncha rooms. You know this a res'dential hotel? People live here. They got their pichers on the walls, little kids with toys all over. They got their dogs and cats! I din't see nuthin' of his."

"He's here. For sure?"

"He is," said Judith. "I asked."

"You tell 'em he your daddy?"

"I ain't a idjit," said Judith. "I asked about weren't there a big estate goin' up for auction 'cause of some rich man round here died."

"And?"

"Well, the girl who was showin' me round looked real surprised, like how'd I know 'bout that, but she said there's a big to-do, and it been in the papers how the Forrest fam'ly fightin' over who gits what. She said las' fall relatives was comin' into town from all over."

"Las' fall? They *all* still here?"

"I din't ask," said Judith. "The Forrest fam'ly. Never knew there was that many Forrests. It must be the same ever'where when it come to progeny, like Miz Tabitha back home. Ever'body want their share." She turned away from the window. "Let's go find 'im."

"Right now?"

"He's spendin' our inher'tince ever' passin' minnit," said Judith. "We got to get some 'fore it completely gone."

Since they couldn't search the hotel for Bill Forrest in their street clothes, they stopped in the laundry for Cassie's uniform. She took Judith to the storeroom Eden had shown her and changed there.

Judith surveyed the room. There was a bed covered with a clean throw and a mirror on the wall. A lightbulb hung from a cord in the middle of the ceiling, tented with parchment paper from the kitchen. The walls were thin enough to let in the heat and the rolling thrum of washers and dryers.

"We kin stay here?" said Judith. "Both of us together?"

"That's what she said."

"They gonna charge us?"

"I don't think so."

"I bet they do. You too innocent. People look at you and think, *Well, there's a ignorant Negro from somewheres south. I bet I can soak her.* You gotta learn to say, 'What's this gonna cost me?'"

Cassie wiped her forehead. She was hungry, and the heat in the laundry had left her with a layer of grit on her skin. What she really wanted was a decent dinner and a tub full of cool water, but Judith was in too much of a hurry.

Judith took a moment to pat at her hair in the mirror. "I'm ready," she said.

She already seemed to know the hidden passages for the service staff, and they went up the back stairs to the lobby. They stood by the service door for a moment, flanked by potted palms. In the lobby, framed by a pair of glass doors, a desk clerk with a pencil behind his ear handed out keys and mail from a bank of wooden pigeonholes. Outside, it was early evening. The streetlights had come on, casting a yellow glow over the Veranda's marble porch.

"You see 'im?" said Cassie.

"Nope," said Judith. "Maybe he in the salon."

Cassie followed Judith around the corner, where the marble floor of the lobby ended and the thick rugs of the salon began.

The salon was the biggest room Cassie had ever seen. Dark wooden beams in the high ceiling gave the room a gloomy graciousness. Windows stretched from floor to ceiling, draped with green velvet curtains. Sofas and soft chairs were arranged around little tables, where people read newspapers and smoked cigarettes. Two big chandeliers, each missing a noticeable number of lightbulbs, made the flocked green velvet wallpaper look faded and the leather furniture dull. Smoke caught in the lamplight, diffusing it into a layer of golden haze. The salon made Cassie think of the elephant in Richmond, big and old and a little dirtier than it ought to be.

Judith poked Cassie in the side. There was Bill Forrest, sitting, reading a newspaper. He, too, was smoking, a pipe, not a cigarette. Smoke curled over the top of the newspaper and made a little cloud.

"That's a new jacket," hissed Judith. "An' lookit them shoes. An' a *pipe*?" She let out a kind of growl. "Oh, I shore as hail hope he ain't spent my entire inher'tince already."

Bill Forrest shifted in the chair, crossing his legs, checking the clock. He folded the paper, tapped out his pipe, and glanced expectantly at the elevator at the far end of the salon. The elevator made a sharp *ding*, the doors opened, and a thin, elderly woman with a cane came out. She was dressed all in black, including a thin veil that covered her face, as though she were in mourning.

He stood up as she came across the room.

"Good evenin', Miz Eula," he said, so loudly that everyone looked up.

"That mus' be Eula Bonhomme," whispered Cassie. "The one who wrote to your momma."

Eula Bonhomme extended her gloved knuckles for Bill Forrest to kiss. "How are you this evening, suh?"

"Jus fine, ma'am, and you?"

"As well as can be expected." Her voice was faint and papery. She fanned herself feebly with her fingers. "My heavens, I feel I've had one foot in the grave all day."

"I kin gitcha glassa water," said Bill.

"No, no thank you. I've just come down to get my mail."

"You set down right there," said Bill. "I'll git it for you."

Eula Bonhomme lowered herself to the edge of a leather sofa, stiff as a dry branch. Bill Forrest strode across the salon, right past Cassie and Judith, heading for the lobby and the desk clerk. He passed close enough to leave a trail of aftershave. Cassie could have touched his sleeve. He looked neither left nor right. He shouldered through the guests waiting for the clerk and rapped on the front desk with his pipe.

"Miz Eula Bonhomme's mail," he said in a very loud voice. "Room 414."

The clerk checked the pigeonholes with the kind of indifference that made it seem like this happened every day.

"Nothin', suh."

"You certain?"

"Certain, suh."

Bill turned and marched back to Eula Bonhomme, and this time Cassie was sure he would see them. He didn't. He sat next to Miz Bonhomme and spoke in a low voice. She put her hand to her forehead as though she felt faint. He helped her to her feet and walked her to the elevator. They both got on, and the doors closed like a curtain. In a moment, the lights above the elevator door stopped at the fourth floor.

Judith turned to Cassie with her face an expression of pure disgust. "Oh, he's a rat, jus' like Momma said he was. Oh, he's jus' a *rat*."

They took the stairs with no clear idea of what to do when they found Miz Bonhomme's room, what they would say if Bill was there—or how to explain themselves if he wasn't.

They arrived panting on the fourth floor. Judith made a beeline to the linen closet and took out a stack of towels.

"You better put those back," said Cassie. "What if someone sees you takin' 'em?"

"This what a maid does inna hotel," said Judith. "You bring clean towels to each room, ever'day, and you takes th' old towels to the laundry whether they dirty or not."

"You mean we washin' *clean* towels?"

"That's what they tol' me this mornin. Come on."

Cassie followed her down the hall, watching the numbers on the doors, which were even on one side and odd on the other. Miz Bonhomme's room was on the right.

Judith pressed her ear to the door.

"What're you *doing*?" whispered Cassie.

"I just wanna know if he's in there." Judith listened another moment. "He ain't."

"Course he ain't. She's proper."

Judith put her hand on the doorknob, but Cassie caught her wrist. "What if this isn't a good idea? What if she think we're thieves?"

"We practically her relatives."

"We got nuthin' that says who we are."

"We got her letter."

"You got her letter?"

Judith took her hand off the doorknob. "Don't you?"

"I ain't seen it since we was at the Glades'."

Judith switched the towels to her other arm. "Was it in the car?"

"It don't matter where it *was* if we don't have it *now*."

"Well, we got the words in her letter anyway."

"She's old," said Cassie. "What if she can't remember what she wrote?"

"Well, we ain't lost nuthin' till she say *no*. An' even if she does, we ain't no worse off. Ain't that right?" She patted Cassie's cheek. "You got to have a little more conf'dence," and before Cassie could say anything else, she rapped on the door. "Maid with th' towels heah, ma'am!"

There was a rustling behind the door. It opened, and Eula Bonhomme peered out. She was even older so close. Her hair hung in a long braid, iron colored, with the unsilky look of a horse's mane. Her eyes were black, sharp over high cheekbones and a narrow, suspicious mouth.

"More towels already? Put them in the powder room."

Cassie followed Judith in. The room was spare and dim. The bed was neatly made. There was a kitchenette with a sink, a refrigerator, and a hotplate. Opposite the bed, ancient pictures of an ancient family hung behind the armchair where Miz Eula had been sitting, reading by lamplight. She eased herself back into the armchair while Judith puttered in the bathroom.

Cassie stood in the middle of the room, realizing that she had no duty to perform.

Miz Eula picked up a leather-bound book from a side table, opened to the middle, and marked the place with a piece of ribbon. "You're new," she said. "You both are."

"Yessum," said Cassie.

Judith emerged from the bathroom, and Miz Eula raised an eyebrow. "I didn't know Mrs. Pomeroy hired white girls for the laundry."

"We been doing laundry together since we was little," said Judith, stretching the truth yet again. "We sisters."

Miz Eula examined Judith. "Most young women in your position would have the sense to pass for white."

"Ma'am," said Judith, "I am white. Cassie an' me, we got diff'rent mommas but the same daddy."

Miz Eula smiled faintly. "I'm sure it's most interesting," she said, "and sadly, far too common, but you must have other things to do this evening besides explaining yourselves to me."

"Ma'am," said Cassie, because there was no stopping now, "our daddy's name is Bill Forrest."

Miz Eula put the book in her lap. "William Forrest."

"You wrote a letter to my momma," said Judith. "You said there was a inher'tince. You said I was *progeny*."

"I recall the letter." Miz Eula looked at Cassie, piercingly this time. "And what are you?"

"Ma'am, I reckon I'm progeny too."

"I reckon she is, ma'am," said Judith.

"And I 'reckon' she is, even without you saying so," said Miz Eula. She put the book on the small table beside her. "Are you supposed to be working right now?"

"We're off for the night, ma'am," said Cassie. "We saw you in the salon with Judith's—our daddy, I mean—and we thought we better come up and introduce ourselves."

"We 'fraid he's done gone an' spent all our inher'tince," said Judith. "Do you know if it's true?"

"Sit down," said Miz Eula. She pointed them to the foot of the bed and a threadbare quilt. "Let me tell you about your family."

CHAPTER ✦ FIFTEEN

Miz Eula Bonhomme rose from her chair, her brittle black clothing crackling around her. She opened the room's only closet and took out a large, stiff folder made of some animal's scaly hide. She untied the silky ribbons that held it shut and opened it on the bed. Inside were newspaper clippings and pages from old magazines, each separated from the other by a sheet of onionskin. All the paper except the onionskin had turned brown, giving the contents of the portfolio a layered look, fawn-colored ruffles alternating with white, like some old party dress, once flounced, now flat.

"What's important is the past," said Miz Eula. "Since William is father to you both, this portfolio contains his past, my past, and yours as well, your *begats* if you wish." She turned the layers of paper and onionskin to a yellowed page of poetry. "This, for example, was written by a great-great-great-aunt of yours, a southern woman who, while northern soldiers devastated the countryside around her, wrote poems to honor the Confederate dead. Did anyone in your family ever tell you about the ghosts?"

"My momma tol' me my great-grandmomma had to shoot her

husband with his own horse pistol," said Judith, "but she never said anything about no ghosts."

Miz Eula turned to Cassie. "What about you?"

"My grandmother told me I was named for my great-great-grandmother Cassandra. She said Judith and I were probably sisters and cousins both because our white great-great-great-grandfather and his white son had gone around sowing their wild oats."

Miz Eula turned over another layer to expose a second, smaller portfolio, this one made of fragile cardboard. "Let me show you the ghosts." She opened the smaller portfolio with even greater care. Inside were three silvery black rectangular glass plates, each wrapped in fine white cotton cloth. "These are called daguerreotypes," she said. As she unwrapped them, Miz Eula laid them on the faded quilt. The images were impossible to make out without better light, but Miz Eula spoke as if they were paintings in plain sight upon a wall. "The first one is William, my husband, your father's great-great-grandfather. Your father was named for him."

"You were married to our great-grandfather?" said Judith.

"Your *great*-great-great-grandfather," Miz Eula corrected. "My faithless William who came from poverty in the foothills of Virginia and built the mansion here in Remington starting from nothing but a swamp and a crew of wild slaves. His vision was to start his own dynasty. He is the thread that connects us. I am no actual blood relation to either of you. I am the abandoned wife, like Sarah in the Bible, who came from the desert to be the vessel for a great and noble line. But I became wrong." She touched her iron-colored hair self-consciously. "Too black, though you two are the only ones who know that, and I rely on your discretion. And then my William, no Abraham to be sure, chose his own Hagar— your great-great-great-grandmother, whose name was Helen."

She held the picture out to them, and Cassie took it carefully, turning it to the light. A man stood in front of a columned veranda, hands on his hips, hat cocked on his head. He looked for all the world like William Forrest—the current one. "This is our great-great-great-grandfather?" she said. "The one whose mansion's going to be auctioned off?"

"Him indeed," said Miz Eula. "And look here at the second ghost. My son, Charles. See how handsome he is, how finely he sits on his horse, how strong the line of his jaw, how white he is, just like his father. Yet this is the son William claimed was tainted with black blood and so disowned."

"He disowned his own son?" said Cassie.

"Not just his son," said Miz Eula. She picked up the third daguerreotype. "His grandson, too. Here is your discarded cousin. My only grandchild. Look how fair he is, how pure, and still ruined by the drop, the single drop of black blood." She took a ragged breath. "I gave William a *good* son. And he repudiated us, left *us* in wrack and ruin, forced us out as though *his son* was only a mule. He considered our marriage null, void, to mount a different mare more fitted for his *dynasty*. That's why I wrote the letter to your mother, Judith. So that her William, your father, doesn't abandon his family the way my William abandoned me." She turned to Cassie. "But you—*you* are most like my son. Too black to be bothered with. I had no idea you even existed." She stood by the bed straight as a rod. Tears came down her parchment cheeks.

Judith touched her arm. Miz Eula just stood there. "Go," she said. "Take the portfolio with you. Take everything, even the ghosts. They're yours now."

In the basement room beside the furnace, Cassie and Judith sat on the bed with the contents of the portfolio spread between them. It was warm and late, and they had undressed to their underwear.

Judith, cross-legged on the coverlet, smoothed a newspaper clip-
ping dated 1861.

"How old you think that ol' lady is?" said Judith. "An' she don't
look colored to me."

"Not as old as she thinks she is, and she's white enough to
pass." Cassie held one of the daguerreotypes at an angle to the
tented bulb. "I never seen a picture like this on glass. Look at this
man with his mustache and fine hat and short little horsewhip.
This her son, Charles. But it can't be. She can't be that old."

"Mistah Legabee was. Them Mallard boys said he was a hunnert and twenty-five."

Mister Legabee's widow had given Cassie the tar. "You believed
that?"

Judith came to peer over Cassie's shoulder at the black glass.
"His daddy left him, like my daddy left me—our daddy, and us.
He sure don't look poor, though. I mean he got some nice clothes
an' a pistol, an' this horse must be worth a bundle." Judith picked
up the next bit of shadowed glass and held it like a mirror to the
light. "This her grandson? He fair, sure enough." Judith put her
bit of black glass down and shuffled through the papers in the
portfolio. "Look a' this," she said. "It's one of them poems by
that southern lady aunt. Kin you read it?"

Cassie read aloud.

Then God bless him the soldier,
And God nerve him for the fight,
May he lend his arm new prowess
    To do battle for the right;
Let him feel that while he's dreaming
    In his fitful slumber bound,
That we're praying—God watch o'er him
    In his blanket on the ground.

Judith sat cross-legged on the bed. "She wrote this kinda thing with shootin' all round? I think I'd be tryna find a way outta there."

Cassie put the poem back on its bed of onionskin. What had she, Cassie, said when Judith told Miz Eula who they were? She had said, "Ma'am, I reckon I'm progeny too." And Judith had said, "I reckon she is, ma'am," and Miz Eula had said, "And I 'reckon' she is, even without you saying so." Cassie pressed her tongue against her teeth and to her surprise, tasted tar. That was why William had left Miz Eula and her son behind. He'd discovered the taint, the way the blood divided out into halves and halves and halves again, until it was down to one half a drop, and that was still too much. No matter how finely divided, it would never disappear. The taste of tar. Had always been there? Did Miz Eula have this taste in her mouth, too? Did Grandmother have it?

The contents of the portfolio lay spread out across the coverlet. Newspapers and photos and clippings from a hundred years ago that might as well have been pasted to the kitchen wall back home in Heron-Neck to keep the drafts from coming in.

My Dearest Sister, I am sorry to tell you that our father is dead.

What did any of this mean for her? Would she be wealthy from her part of the inheritance and live the rest of her life in ease? Not likely.

"What's important is the past," Miz Eula had said, and she was right to a point, but, Cassie thought, put a yam and a sweet potato in front of the old woman, and she would not know one from the other. Cassie looked up at the ceiling as if she could see through the layers of floors in the hotel, all the way up to the fourth, where Miz Eula wept over her family history. She pictured Miz Eula's hair, coarse as braided wire, wrapped up tight as a spring. And why? Yams from sweet potatoes. Without restraints, that hair would escape into its natural billow and reveal the drop of blood it came from.

Miz Eula and Grandmother would've had a lot to talk about. Both would've jumped at the chance to meet the widow Legabee's sticky grandbaby and erase themselves without a second thought.

"I'm tired," said Cassie. "We got to work in the mornin'."

"You sleep," said Judith. "I'm a keep lookin' at all this fam'ly history."

Except for William, though, Cassie thought, it was the colored side of the family Judith was looking at. The daguerreotypes, the poetry, the stories Miz Eula was so distraught about had nothing to do with Judith. They were Cassie's history. Cassie lay back on the bed, too warm. The dryers thrummed behind the walls. What if all she and Judith had in common was a father and a distant great-great-great-grandfather? It didn't really change anything. She thought back to the day she'd defied Lil Ma and helped Judith pull the wagons up the hill. That was the day her life had changed. That had put her on this track. Otherwise she would be back home now, struggling with Grandmother over the albino boy. Cassie turned over and hugged the pillow. She missed Lil Ma. The first thing she would do, when she was sure Grandmother had used the tar and was clear of town, would be to send the Boston money to Lil Ma and get her out of Heron-Neck for good.

CHAPTER ✦ SIXTEEN

In the morning somebody banged hard on the door, and a woman's shrill voice sawed into their sleep. *"Ain't you up yet? You hear me in there, Judith Forrest? It five thutty! You hear me, gal?"*

Cassie jerked awake, thinking she had somehow fallen asleep at Judith's house in Heron-Neck. Judith practically leaped out from under the sheets, shouting, "Yessum! Yessum!" She grabbed her wrinkled uniform dress from the foot of the bed, gave it a huge shake, as though that would take care of the wrinkles, and dragged it over her skinny shoulders. She raked her fingers through her hair, jumped into her shoes, slammed the door, and was gone.

Cassie sat up and rubbed her eyes. Eden Pomeroy had told her to be in the laundry room by six. She reached up to turn on the light and saw Miz Eula's newspaper clippings scattered on the floor. Judith might have left them in some kind of order, but the wind from her exit had blown them all over the place. Cassie gathered up the clippings, poems, papers and put them back between their onionskin layers and wrapped the daguerreotypes

in their swaddle. She put everything back into the ancient portfolio and slid it under the bed.

Eden Pomeroy and morning work were waiting for Cassie in
the laundry room. Three brittle black dresses in a heap. Black
underthings, including three pairs of silk stockings and a garter
belt so narrow, it would have fit a ten-year-old girl.

"You know anything 'bout this fabric?" said Eden Pomeroy.

Cassie rubbed the hem of one dress between her fingers.
"Taffeta?"

"And lace," said Eden Pomeroy. "This lady act like these dresses
her most prize possessions. She send 'em down here all at once
and 'spect to get 'em back the same day. I ain't got the hands t'do
it. So, you know anything 'bout taffeta?"

"You got to be gentle with it."

"Ain't no shortcuts with taffeta. And them stockings, them
dainties—"

"They ain't all that dainty if you ask me!" said Bethesda from
where she was ironing sheets. Iris was folding towels with mechan-
ical precision.

"Lawyers is comin' to see her tomorrow," Eden Pomeroy said
to Cassie. "She got to look right. You think you kin do this?"

"I kin," Cassie said.

The laundry sink, where the luckless were sent to wash by
hand, wasn't far from Bethesda's ironing and Iris's folding. Cassie
filled the sink with warm water and three or four shakes of Borax
powder. She sank the tired dresses into a pillow of suds and guided
them gently back and forth. "Why this ol' lady got to see lawyers? She a big criminal?"

Iris and Bethesda laughed in great snorts.

"She only about a hundred year old," said Iris, rapidly folding towel after towel.

"She been here for months," said Bethesda, "waitin' on the settlin' of the estate."

"The contestation of the will," said Iris.

"All I know," Bethesda said to Cassie, "is this old white fella useter live in a big ol' mansion out a ways from town, and he died las' fall, and suddenly, he got relatives crawlin' out the woodwork." She flicked a drop of water on the iron, and it sizzled. "He got cousins and uncles and nephews and nieces, first, second, third removes."

"There was some *philanderin'* in the fam'ly," said Iris, "if you know what I mean, but they blood jus' the same, and they think they owed some piece of the pie."

"This ol' lady," said Bethesda, "*claims* she some kinda in-law, but she so old she don't know what she is. She prob'ly don't even know *where* she is."

"Or *when* she is," said Iris.

"Ennyway," said Bethesda, "ever'body else got sick o waitin' for them lawyers to do their revisin', and they all left."

" 'Ceptin' that one fella." Iris put the towels to one side and began folding washcloths.

"William Forrest," said Bethesda. "He some long-lost somethin'-or-other, and he been hangin' on her since way back when."

"Since duck huntin' season," said Iris.

"Must be a nice mansion," said Cassie. She pressed the taffeta gently into the froth of bubbles.

"I ain't never seen it," said Bethesda. "I guess it musta been nice at one time. Ever'body talking 'bout Oriental rugs an' crystal chandeliers an' armoires an' fine china."

"It old too," said Iris, "been round since this town was jus' a sawmill. My great-granddaddy used tell us 'bout his uncle what was on that plantation, an' his uncle tol' him the place was fulla spooks and hoodoo."

"Full-blood African hoodoo," said Bethesda. "Folks still talk about the haints inna woods there." She put the iron down and said to Iris, "You know Myra, Doyle's girlfriend? She tol' me Doyle's boys snuck on down there to see if there was ennythin' left inna mansion. Somethin' started howlin' inside, an' they ran outta them woods like they pants on fire."

"You know, ain't nothin' livin' in that house, an' there ain't nothin' gonna howl in them woods 'cept mebbe a bobcat. Them two boys ain't got a brain between 'em!" Iris was done folding washcloths, stacks of gleaming white terrycloth, without a stain, a fray, or a loose thread. She reached for the pile of sheets but kept pressing her lips together like she was trying to hold on to her own next words as long as she could. Finally, she said, "That howlin', prob'ly Doyle ruttin' with his *other* girlfriend," and she and Bethesda burst into laughter.

That seemed to be all they had to say about Miz Eula, the mansion, and the will. Iris and Bethesda chattered on about Doyle and the woods and the likelihood of poisonous snakes. Their hands never stopped except when they came to some kind of stain or tear, and they had to comment on the hotel resident who had spilled coffee or grape juice or who had used a perfectly good towel to wipe up dog pee.

Cassie took her time with the dresses and the dainties. She ironed shirts. She folded linens. The dresses hung to dry. Eden Pomeroy brought sandwiches and coffee from the kitchen for lunch. She looked over Cassie's work and didn't say anything, which Cassie took as a good sign. The three black taffeta dresses had been hanging in the breeze of an open door all morning and would be completely dry in about an hour. Cassie could press them and have them ready to go by two. Shortly, the housekeeping staff would bring down the loads of laundry for the afternoon. In the meantime, Eden Pomeroy allowed her staff a break. Iris and Bethesda went outside to smoke cigarettes. Cassie went upstairs to find Judith.

Judith was making beds on the second floor. She looked as disheveled as she had when she'd run out of their room this morning, but the bed she was making was perfect. The pillows were fluffed like marshmallows, the sheets crisply turned, the blanket tucked immaculately at the corners. Judith tossed a white coverlet across the bed and made sure it was even on all sides.

"Where'd you learn to make a bed like that?" said Cassie, because surely it hadn't been back in Heron-Neck.

"From Miz Frances," said Judith, breathless. "She run the maids. An' she said she'd whup me no question less'n I did ever' bed on this floor jus' zactly right. Come on!" Judith rushed into the hall, where there was a cartful of fresh, precisely folded sheets, towels, and washcloths. Cassie followed Judith into the next room. The last had been spare and unremarkable. This one had a kitchenette, a sitting room, and three bedrooms, two apparently occupied by young children.

"Why they leave their damn toys all over?" Judith scooped up baby dolls and teddy bears and dumped them in a toy chest. Someone had spilled a bowl of cereal and milk right next to the bed. Judith didn't see it until she put her foot in the puddle. She let out a growl, kicked off the wet shoe.

"We gotta find our daddy," said Cassie.

"Oh, I found his room, but he ain't in it." Judith picked up the wet shoe and shook it. "There was letters with his name on 'em. Open letters on a table. From somebody-and-somebody, esquires."

"Lawyers." Cassie grabbed her hand. "Miz Eula's meetin' with lawyers tomorrow. There's something goin' on about the will."

"I'll show you the letters." Judith abandoned the spilled cereal, slipped into her wet shoe, and pulled Cassie out the door, leaving the unmade beds. Out in the hall, the elevator made a musical *ding*.

"*Hail*," Judith whispered with terrible despair, "what if it's Miz Frances?" But it was Miz Eula who emerged from the elevator, terribly thin, wrapped in a white bathrobe, her iron-gray hair loose in a frizzy billow. She looked both ways, as though crossing a dangerous street.

"I've been looking for you," she said when she saw them. She reached into the pocket of the robe and pulled out a crumpled page. "The auction's tomorrow, and first the lawyers are coming. You must come with me to the meeting to establish your claim."

Cassie took the letter and tried to read it, but the only thing she could really understand was that *issues* in the will were *unresolved* and that the auction was set for the next day at three in the afternoon.

"Without your claim, you get nothing," said Miz Eula. "Your father gets his share but not you."

"But we've come all this way," said Cassie.

"It wouldn't matter if you'd come from the moon," said Miz Eula.

"We're *progeny*," said Judith.

"I'll take you to the mansion," said Miz Eula.

That evening, though the weather was clear, Judith came into their storeroom with an umbrella and a flashlight. She leaned the umbrella against the bed, reached under the mattress, and pulled out the horse pistol. Cassie was almost glad to see it.

Judith dropped the gun and the flashlight into the umbrella, like it was a pocket. The umbrella bulged a little, but no one would have guessed what was inside.

There would be no point in Cassie asking about the gun. Judith wanted to take the gun because she had a gun to take.

"'Bandoned house," said Judith. "Might be haints."

"You ain't gone hit a haint with no bullet."

"No," said Judith, "but we'll be ready fer ennythin' more solid."

Judith gave Cassie the umbrella. Cassie hefted the awkward weight of it and hooked it over her arm. "Better not rain," Cassie said.

"It ain't gonna rain."

"Then we gone look stupid carryin' this umbrella. You put bullets in the gun?"

"Sure did." Judith smoothed her dress, the blue one the Glades had given her. "We gonna get our due," she said, so gravely that it surprised Cassie at how adult she sounded. "We not gonna be poor no more, wearin' these old hand-me-downs. We gonna have more than a penny to our names."

Cassie wanted to point out that not only did they each have far more than a penny; Judith had sung them up a notch from their poverty. The Glades had gifted them with cash. In Cassie's opinion, this adventure into the snake-filled woods that Bethesda and Iris had been talking about was almost unnecessary. The sole reason was to show Bill Forrest that he still owed his family, and while that was important, it might not be important enough to invade an old house filled with Miz Eula's ghosts. She didn't say any of that. Judith was set on this path, and it was time to follow.

Cassie hefted the umbrella. "You gone tell Miz Eula we gotta gun?"

"Now why would I tell her that?"

"So she don't bring her own."

"If she do have one, it's gotta be small. She don't have the strength to lift a cuppa coffee."

"Still," said Cassie, "I wouldn't want to be around if she start shootin'."

Judith went over to the door and opened it. "Me neither."

Miz Eula was waiting for them in her freshly pressed taffeta under the only light in the parking lot. It was late, and the sun had vanished behind the trees, leaving only the indigo bowl of the sky. She motioned them over with stick-figure gestures and pushed the car key into Judith's palm. Miz Eula sat in the passenger seat and insisted that Judith drive, which put Cassie in back with the umbrella, the gun, and flashlight. The car wasn't much newer than the one Cassie and Judith had driven from Mississippi to South Carolina, but it was cleaner.

"Which way?" said Judith.

"East," said Miz Eula. "Straight out of town. Follow the railroad."

There were few other cars and no trains either. The dark seemed pure and empty, quiet except for the sound of the car itself and the night calls of birds. Cassie rolled down the windows. The sweet evening fragrance of honeysuckle blew in.

"I'll show you where to stop," said Miz Eula. "But the drive is a shambles. We'll have to walk in."

"How long a walk?" said Cassie.

"A good half mile," said Miz Eula.

"Kin you walk that far, ma'am?" Judith.

"I assure you that I *can*."

They missed the entrance twice, not because it wasn't marked but because it was. A gas station had been built at the end of the mansion's drive; a business for however long, then abandoned. The gas pumps were gone. What remained were a concrete apron and a boxy building with plate-glass windows, all shattered.

The first time they passed the entrance, Miz Eula remarked that she didn't remember any buildings on this road. The second time Cassie held the flashlight as they passed and made Judith creep forward so the old woman could peer into the woods. After the second U-turn on the empty highway, Judith pulled in to the remains of the gas station and angled the car so the headlights shone into the trees.

"This has to be it," said Miz Eula.

"When was the last time you were here, ma'am?"

"It was winter," said Miz Eula "No. It was spring."

Judith turned off the engine, and Cassie helped Miz Eula out of the front seat. Cassie hooked the umbrella over her right arm.

"Will it rain?" Miz Eula said.

"You never know," said Cassie.

Judith pointed the flashlight into a darkness made more dense by thick brush. Crickets and frogs called from deep in the forest, and Cassie could smell the wet decay of a marsh. Miz Eula hung on to Cassie's left arm, getting her footing as they made their way from concrete into the tall weeds. She weighed hardly anything and smelled faintly of camphor. She was hot but dry, almost feverish through the black taffeta. The bones in her thin arm poked into Cassie's ribs.

The trees parted slightly, and Judith shone the flashlight over a rutted track where heavy rains had cut uneven channels into what had once been a drive wide enough for two carriages to pass side by side. The smell of swamp grew stronger.

"You sure you want to do this, ma'am?" said Cassie over the creak of insects.

Miz Eula gripped Cassie's arm even more tightly, teetering in her narrow black shoes.

Judith glanced back at Cassie. "You want me to take the umbrella?" meaning she wanted the gun, but Cassie wasn't ready for her to have it. There were too many imaginary things to shoot at just yet. The real things were ahead in the house, and there were only three bullets.

Miz Eula was breathing hard, but she didn't show any sign of stopping, not so long as the phantom house lay ahead. Cassie could feel that pull herself. She glanced at Judith, striding along, swinging the flashlight so that the beam rushed up into the dense branches and then down again, like she knew where she was going and didn't need the light anyway.

Miz Eula leaned more heavily on Cassie's arm. Up ahead, the roaming flashlight beam glinted off something that might have been a window. Cassie felt her heart jump.

"Hand over that umbrella," said Judith. "I think I see the house."

Miz Eula swayed in the dark, breathless and hot. "The house. *The house.*"

"Turn off that light," Cassie said.

Judith obeyed and took the umbrella, felt noisily around inside it, and gave it back, lighter. The three of them stood at the edge of the black canopy of trees, letting their eyes adjust to the depth of the night, and the size of the house, burdened by years and weather, its roofline sagging against the stars, its walls plastered with ancient advertisements for snuff and shoeshine, cigarettes and whiskey.

"It was a dry goods store," said Judith, sounding surprised. "Jus' like Tawney's back in Heron-Neck."

"Bigger than Tawney's," said Cassie.

The front stairs were still sheathed in marble and gleamed eerily in the shine from the stars, but the porch, *the gallery* as Grandmother would have called the ruined stoop that ran all the way around the first floor, was wooden and rotten.

"Watch where you put your feet," said Judith, flashlight still turned off. The horse pistol was a dull, iron shape in her hand, looking more like a club than a gun.

The three of them edged across the broken porch, making for the front door.

"It'll be locked," said Miz Eula. "You'll have to break in through the windows."

The windows were shuttered, but as the three of them came closer, they could see that at least one shutter had already been pried open. Judith put a tentative hand into the even deeper blackness that was the window.

"There ain't no glass," said Judith. "Someone's got here 'fore us."

"Go *in*," Miz Eula hissed.

"I ain't goin' in without no flashlight," said Judith. "They snakes in there. I know it." She groped at the window, then caught her breath like she'd heard something. The three of them froze, listening in the dark for a sound from the house, bounded by the calls of night birds, frogs, and crickets.

"He's *here*," whispered Miz Eula.

"*Who's* here?" Judith squinted at her in the dark.

"She's talkin' about the past," whispered Cassie.

"There is no past," moaned Miz Eula. "There's only *now*."

"What we're askin'," said Judith, "is if you think someone's in there right *now*."

Miz Eula trembled, hot as an ember.

Cassie heard Judith cock the horse pistol.

"Turn on the flashlight," said Cassie. "If anybody's inside, they're bound to've heard us."

Judith pointed the flashlight into the empty house. Cassie craned forward to see blank walls and a rotting floor. There was no furniture. No fixtures, no carpets or chandeliers. What was left of the wallpaper lay in heaps. The mantle from the fireplace was missing, with only a blank frame of bricks around a yawning hearth to show where it had been. There wasn't a single thing worth auctioning off. There was nothing left but crumbs.

"Did you ever live here, Miz Eula?" said Judith.

"Yes," whispered Miz Eula, "and then he banished me."

They climbed in through the glassless window. Judith went carefully ahead, checking the floor, toe-first, the pistol held out at arm's length as though it could sense intruders, aim on its own, and kill them before she had to think to pull the trigger.

"Can you see them here at Christmas?" whispered Miz Eula as they crept through what must once have been a grand sitting room. "Can you see my William, his new wife plump-cheeked and unmindful, his son and daughter, the mistletoe, the slaves, half sisters, half brothers to his legitimate heirs? The slaves, dressed for the occasion, laying the table in the next room. The slaves that were his own children." She shuddered as though she might shake apart and all that would hold her together would be the black taffeta. "We said good night to our wedding guests from those stairs."

Judith shone the flashlight along the tilting banister. "They don't look so safe. Ev'ry third step's missin'."

"Can't you feel the ghosts?" said Miz Eula in a whisper. "My son, my Charles, a brave young man."

Upstairs, something heavy fell and broke. Someone in the shadows near the top of the stairs let out a curse.

Judith aimed the gun and the flashlight up into the dark.

"It's him. It's *him*," gasped Miz Eula. "*William!*"

Judith began to shout. "You! You up there, you-all come on

out where I kin see you!" She shoved the flashlight at Cassie and held the horse pistol in both hands.

Cassie stuck the flashlight out, her hand shaking, the umbrella hanging like a flightless bat. Miz Eula quivered on Cassie's other arm. And whoever was upstairs shuffled into view.

"Don't shoot," said a man's voice, and in a moment, he appeared, heavyset, at the top of the stairs. His arms were loaded with all that he could carry. "Who the hail's down there? Don't shoot!"

"William!" cried Miz Eula.

"Eula?" said the man.

"Jesus Christ," said Judith, not lowering the gun. "Daddy?"

They heard him take a breath at the top of the stairs. "Judith?"

"You stay right there!" Judith shouted. "Momma was right when she tol' me you was nothin' but a rat!"

"Honey, din't Momma tell you I was comin' up here for her? For *us*? Din't she tell you I was comin home jus' soon's I could?"

"You lef' us for a *hoor*!" Judith said, as firmly as she could. "You lef' us with *nothing*!" And whether she meant to or not, she fired the primordial gun.

The noise was like a cannon. The bullet left a trail of sparks, which lit the room for an instant and left a choking stink. The bullet hit something with a terrible thump. Miz Eula screamed and collapsed into Cassie's arms. Cassie dropped the flashlight. The flashlight rolled over to a hole in the floor, dropped into it, and the whole place went dark. Bill Forrest let out a sound just loud enough to let everyone know that the bullet had missed him, and the house groaned. A chunk of the ceiling fell. Bill bolted invisibly down the stairs. The ransacked booty in his arms dropped away as he descended, crashing like pottery or rolling like coins.

"Dammit!" said Bill as he hit the main floor. He switched on his own flashlight and yanked the pistol away from Judith. "Your momma sent you with this?"

"I came on mah own!" Judith shouted. "I came to tell you I'm progeny too!"

More ceiling fell. Splinters and dust cascaded over them.

"Miz Eula?" Cassie crouched over the taffeta husk in her arms. "We got to leave!"

"What's she doin' here?" Bill demanded and shone his flashlight in the old woman's face. Miz Eula's eyelids fluttered. She looked pale as paper, limp, and bloodless. "Now looky, Judy, you done give her a heart attack!"

There was a quick movement to the left, and Bill swung his flashlight over to reveal a night watchman, who was small and old and clung to a baseball bat as though there were dangers in the old mansion no bullet could stop.

"Whoever y'all are," he said, brandishing the bat, "you're trespassin', robbin' hoodlums, just like the rest of 'em. The police are here. Y'all just stay right where you are."

Flashing red lights poured over them, flashed on the peeling walls, turned blinding white and then red again. Male voices came from another part of the house, speaking in commanding tones. Red light washed across Miz Eula's face, and she opened her eyes long enough to see Bill Forrest leaning over her.

"My William," she whispered, "I've found you."

There were two police cars outside the back of the house, where long ago the slaves would have come and gone. Now there were four policemen with guns. One grabbed Bill by the arm and yanked the still-smoking horse pistol away from him. They put him in handcuffs and shoved him into a police car. One of them crouched over Miz Eula.

"Call an ambulance!" the policeman shouted. He paid no

attention to Cassie because she was, of course, Miz Eula's maid
and a passive player, if a player at all.

"A little late for you to be wandering around in an old house,
ain't it, missy?" one of the policemen said to Judith. "And with
this old lady too. Ain't you see the NO TRESPASSIN' signs?"

With lights on, Cassie did see that this side of the mansion
was generously covered with NO TRESPASSING signs.

"We came in the other side," said Judith, without apology. "We
came to get my inher'tince."

"Your inheritance?" said one of the officers. "This place been
empty for years. Hardly anything worth taking. You could've
waited for the auction tomorrow instead of trying to vandalize
the place."

"*Vandalize*?" said Judith.

Cassie left it to Judith to tell either the infuriated truth or out-
rageous lies. She held Miz Eula's head in her lap. A floodlight
showed the back half of the property. The woods had been cleared
and replaced with a lawn, wide and neatly trimmed. A long, paved
driveway passed a sign that said MANSION MINIATURE GOLF. Just
down the hill from the sign lay a shadowed wonderland of wind-
mills, castles, elephants, and ogres. Just beyond that were tables
covered with white sheets, set up for the estate sale. The police
were right. What was left to auction off?

"Miz Eula," said Cassie. She took Miz Eula's hand, cool and
limp. "Can you see all that?"

When the ambulance arrived, a broad-shouldered white man
hurried over, pushed his fingers against Miz Eula's bird-neck, and
listened to her taffetaed chest. He straightened and told the policemen that she was dead.

CHAPTER SEVENTEEN

The night clerk wouldn't let them into the Veranda. He didn't believe Judith and Cassie were employees. It was two in the morning. Without their gray uniforms, they looked like vagabonds.

The desk clerk called the hotel manager at home. Fifteen minutes later, the manager arrived; his wife, her hair in curlers, waited in the idling car outside. The manager expressed terrible shock that Miz Eula had passed on and that Mr. Forrest was in lockup. Judith, dirty from poking around in the mansion, disheveled in her secondhand clothes, spoke out righteously and at length about her due as progeny and about how her father had robbed her *and* Miz Eula. She didn't mention Cassie. Cassie sat down in the nearest chair and waited to hear her own name come up. The clock edged closer to three. Finally, when Judith was red in the face and on the verge of genuine hysterics, the manager offered to put her in a room upstairs free of charge until the lawyers arrived in the morning.

"Now, who're you?" the manager said to Cassie.

"Oh," said Cassie. "I'm progeny too."

The manager let out a laugh that indicated he was glad

someone in the room was willing to acknowledge how ridiculous this business was, with this crazy dirt-poor white girl and her midnight rant about lost riches.

"It's true," said Cassie. "I'm her sister. And I want a room upstairs too."

The manager, his wife still waiting in the car, handed Cassie a key with a number on it. "It's on the fourth floor," he said. "Just keep quiet."

The room upstairs was clean and quiet. The bed was soft under crisp sheets. Cassie lay down on the softness, but she couldn't sleep. She was too angry at Judith to do anything but get up again and sit by the window, watching the lights run around and around on the movie marquis on the other side of the hotel's parking lot. At five o'clock, she straightened the bed she hadn't slept in, replaced the towel she'd used to dry her face, and took the dirty towel down to the laundry.

At about nine thirty Eden Pomeroy came over to where Cassie was ironing and told her that a couple of lawyers up in the salon were looking for her. Iris and Bethesda stopped midfold and midgossip. As far as Cassie could tell, no one knew that Bill Forrest had been arrested or knew what had happened to Miz Eula. Judith was no doubt still sound asleep, too sure of what was coming to her to get up and be a maid.

When Eden Pomeroy told Cassie about the lawyers, Iris made her eyes big and her mouth round. "Don't you go up there," Iris said. "Them'll send you t' *jail*."

"Don't be a fool," said Eden Pomeroy. "They ain't that kinda lawyers. They prob'ly think you know where that white girl's hidin'." Cassie seemed reluctant to leave, and Eden Pomeroy said, "Git up there, gal," the way someone would speak to a carthorse.

— ✦ —

There were two lawyers, both white men with cigars and ties. One was fat and wore glasses. The other was fatter. Judith was already with them, and so was Bill Forrest. Bill Forrest looked like a man who'd spent the night in jail. Judith had taken time to clean herself. She was wearing the second best of all her secondhand dresses. The dress was blue, and she had done her hair up in a bow, also blue. Cassie had never ever seen Judith's hair in a bow. The color of the ribbon matched the dress so perfectly, she suspected Judith had cut it out of the hem.

Judith motioned Cassie over. Despite the dress, the bow, and all, she looked furious and pale in contrast to last night when she'd been furious and red-faced. "Now we kin start," she said to the lawyers.

"Who the hail is *she*?" said Bill Forrest.

"She's your other chile." Judith actually shook with anger.

"I ain't never seen her before in my life!"

"What's your name, gal?" asked the fat lawyer, and Cassie told him.

"I don't see the connection," said the fatter lawyer. "What makes you think he's your father?"

"My mama told me," Cassie realized how thin that sounded. "Ever'body in town knows it."

"*I* knows it," said Judith, "and *he* knows it."

"You got documentation?" said the fat lawyer to Cassie. "We really can't do anything without documentation."

"You got a birth certificate?" asked the fatter lawyer.

"*I* ain't got no birth certificate," said Judith, "and he *married* my momma."

"Well then," said the fatter lawyer, "I see we're going to have a problem."

The lawyers began to talk to each other in what seemed to be a language not quite English. There were words Cassie recognized: *inheritance, birthright, descendants.* And those she didn't: *assertion, bequest, allegation.* And those she could guess at: *legacy, entitlement, testimonial.* But there was nothing she heard that translated into Judith's rendition of *progeny,* and as the conversation went on, Cassie could see Judith's fury fading into worried hope. After some time, the lawyers, their thick necks folding and unfolding, turned to Bill Forrest and to Judith.

"Concerning your claims to be heirs to the Forrest estate," said the fat lawyer.

Bill Forrest drew himself up, unshaven and unwashed. "Yes."

"Other than the late Eula Bonhomme, who seems to have been divorced from the original William Forrest, the Forrest line is too disparate for any single person to be considered an heir."

The fatter lawyer nodded as if any fool could understand. "There is no reason to postpone the sale of the estate. Whatever comes out will be split among the remaining claimants."

"Remaining claimants?" said Bill Forrest.

The fat lawyer took a pad of paper out of his briefcase and consulted it. "There are twenty-three that we know of."

"Twenty-*three*?"said Bill.

"Just because they aren't here doesn't mean they don't have a claim," said the fatter lawyer, speaking to Bill as though he were a child.

"But my *name* is Forrest!" said Bill.

"Of course it is," said the fat lawyer, "and once the estate is sold, you'll get your equal share of the proceeds, along with every other Forrest who's made a claim."

"Equal share," said Bill. "How much is that likely to be?"

The lawyers frowned as though they were silently debating the numbers.

"I would say no less than eighty-five dollars," said the fat lawyer.

"*Each?*" said Bill.

"Certainly no less," agreed the fatter lawyer. "After our fees, of course."

Eden Pomeroy let Cassie off for the rest of the day, and since Judith had been fired for not showing up for work that morning, Cassie and Judith went to the estate sale in Miz Eula's old car, which had been towed back from the mansion and slumped in its old space, leaking oil, drop by drop.

"Eighty-five dollars is a lot," said Judith as she drove the rattling old heap. "I guess I thought it would be thousands, though. Mebbe millions."

The breezy warmth of the afternoon blew in through the car, dispelling the smell of gasoline and oil. Since they didn't know how to get to the front of the mansion, they parked in the back by the gas station and walked in through the overgrown drive again. The walk seemed much shorter this time, and this time they didn't go through the house. They found a path along one side and made their way to the front.

Unlike Tawney's, hardly anyone had shown up, and those who had were clustered around the draped tables. All of them were white people, probably just curious about all those rumors about lost riches. Cassie and Judith wandered over to see what was left from the house. There were a few sconces, a couple of broken figurines, a set of jackknives, as though someone had been collecting them, and a satin-covered box filled with faded, stained silk handkerchiefs. The rest was rusted junk, barely enough to cover the three tables, and when the auctioneer started selling the lots, he sounded dispirited, as though this auction was hardly worth his while. Cassie and Judith looked for Bill Forrest and found him, keeping his distance on the far side of the tables.

"What you gonna do with your share?" said Judith.

"I ain't getting any money," said Cassie. "An' if I understood it right, you ain't getting any either."

Judith let out a long sigh. "If I still had that ol' gun, I could shoot my daddy and get my inher'tince direct from him."

"You'd be spending it in jail."

"Well," said Judith, "I 'spect eighty-five dollars might go a long way in jail."

Cassie rubbed her eyes. "Judith," she said.

"Hmm."

"You got enough money to get to New York, and you ain't got no job here."

"You know what I'm gonna do."

"You gone have to do it by yourself."

Judith looked away at the tables with their poor spread of goods. "I was real upset when they brought us back to the hotel last night," she said. "I know I din't mention you. I din't think they'd understand that an' ever'thin' else what was goin' on. I'm sorry for that."

"It's all right," said Cassie softly.

Judith looked down at her own feet. "You gonna stay here?"

"I guess I am," said Cassie. "When are you gone leave for New York?"

"I ain't got no place to sleep no more," said Judith. "So I guess I'll be takin' the train today." She squinted at her father, who was studiously ignoring them.

"You kin probably still sleep downstairs."

"It's all right," said Judith. She smoothed her blue dress and blue hair ribbon. "This what I bin' waitin' for. I may's well git started."

They left the mansion and its minigolf facade. A sign across the doors said CONDEMNED.

When they got back to the Veranda, they went in to get Judith's suitcase. In the dim, warm room, when everything was packed, they took each other's hands.

"Ain't you gone say good-bye to your daddy?" said Cassie.

"He doesn't care, and I've had just about enough of him."

"I guess I'll be washin' his towels."

"No," said Judith. "They gonna kick him out on account of not payin' his bill. Miz Frances tol' me." She squeezed Cassie's hands, hard. "I'll write to you."

"You can't write," said Cassie. "You can't read neither."

"Then you write to me," said Judith. Her hands, gripping Cassie's, were hot and sweaty. "I'll git someone to read it to me."

"I won't know where to write to," said Cassie. "Less'n you learn how to use the telephone and call me."

"Telephone?" Judith's nails pressed into Cassie's palms. "You think they got 'em in New York?"

"You don't have to go," said Cassie. "You could probably sing round here and get famous just like that."

"I know."

"I can't come with you," Cassie said and gently pulled her hands away. "I ain't gonna be your maid, an' I guess I can't really be your sister."

"I know." Judith picked up her suitcase. "I'm sorry I din't tell them police you was progeny too. I'll come back an' see you. In mah big ol' car with mah lil ol' dog."

"I'll be list'nin' to the reddio," said Cassie. "Every single day."

CHAPTER ✦ EIGHTEEN

With or without Judith, it fell to Cassie to clear out Miz Eula's
hotel room. Eden Pomeroy had guessed that Judith and Cassie were
sisters. To Eden, it was a family duty and entitled Cassie to whatever she found up there, a few old books and the faded quilt,
worn but neatly kept.

Cassie was putting everything into Miz Eula's suitcase when
she found the two thick envelopes on the nightstand by the bed.
One was addressed to Judith. One had Cassie's name on it. That
was the one she opened. Inside there was a roll of bills and a letter.
Cassie counted the money first. It was two hundred and fifty
dollars. Heart pounding, she put the money back in the envelope
and took out the letter, which was written in the same neat hand
as the one Judith had brought to the laundry months ago.

> *Dear Cassie,*
>
> *This money is your legacy. I know there will be nothing of
> value tonight at the manor, and that you'll get nothing from the
> estate sale tomorrow. You are an outcast like myself. This small
> sum cannot possibly compensate you for the troubles you have had*

in your life, but hopefully it will make some difference in your future.

Perhaps in some way we were sisters, like you and Judith, but regardless, you both are part of my family and I cannot let you go without knowing that you have a past and generations of relatives, all of whom were striving for the same kind of justice you and I (and Judith) deserve.

By the time you read this, I will be gone from the hotel and on my way home. I hope you will keep me in your thoughts.

Yours,

Eula Bonhomme-Forrest

Cassie picked up the other envelope, which had a similar size and heft. Miz Eula had left the same for Judith, most likely with a different note. Cassie read hers over again and this time put the money in her pocket. She put Judith's envelope in Miz Eula's suitcase and took the suitcase down to the room by the furnace. Then she sat on the edge of the bed with the lump of bills in her pocket, trying to think. She was as close to rich as she was ever going to get, and her mind spun with what to do with the money. It wasn't clothes and a car, like Judith would've wanted. Judith would probably have been jumping around the room, crowing with victory. For Cassie it was getting Lil Ma out of Mississippi.

Since there was no will, the funeral home cremated Miz Eula's body. The manager of the hotel offered Cassie the ashes in a cardboard box; she took them to the old mansion to scatter them.

Even from the golf-course side, which had been shored up and painted white, the condemned house was swaybacked and buckling. When the mansion was torn down, it would probably disperse as dust, not as beams, bricks, or shingles. From the front, where Cassie and Judith and Miz Eula had entered almost a week before, Cassie stepped out under the leafy branches of the ancient live oaks and picked her way through brambles and creeper, past what might have been a summer kitchen, and farther into woods to where the slaves had lived. Once, cabins had lined either side of the barely visible path; now no more than two bricks stood on top of each other. Back at the mansion, which showed as a shadow behind the trees, like the elephant shading a canvas flap, Cassie opened the box and gingerly scooped up a bit of the ash. She scattered it as far as it would go, which wasn't far. Her dress caught in the thorn bushes. More ash spilled as she pulled herself free. She apologized to the box. Judith would have looked at her like she was crazy, roaming around in a ghost-infested forest with yet another potential ghost right there in the box. Judith would have told her to *git the hail out*. This was life without Judith. Cassie took the rest of the ashes up the steps of the big crumbling house and set the box on the porch under the broken shutters, just to the side of the front door.

Birds trilled in the soft air. Wild flowers had grown up in the remains of the mansion's front lawn, and she picked a few, thinking she would leave them by the box, but the gray, vandalized face of the mansion was no place for flowers. Miz Eula had always worn black anyway.

Cassie used some of her money to move out of the Veranda and in with an old widow on the colored side of Remington. The widow, Mrs. Morgan, had one daughter, who lived in Baltimore, and Cassie rented her old room. Every night after Cassie got home from work, Mrs. Morgan made her sit down for a cup of hot tea and ginger cookies and told Cassie about how, after Mister Morgan had died, her daughter had insisted that she sell the house and move to Baltimore. "He built this house with his own hands!" Mrs. Morgan would say. Every night Cassie did her best to act appalled and to offer advice. She wrote a letter to Mrs. Morgan's daughter and after several weeks, received an envelope with ten dollars in it and a note about how awful Baltimore was this time of year. Mrs. Morgan had no relatives in town, but she showed the money to her elderly friends and told them that even though her daughter was rich now, there was no way she would ever abandon Mister Morgan's hand-built house. Her elderly friends visited regularly and fussed over Cassie as if she was somebody's long-lost child. It made Cassie unbearably homesick. It made her think about Heron-Neck and what life might have been like without the burden of Grandmother's designs.

Cassie started eating supper at the Veranda and coming home well after Mrs. Morgan went to bed. She found herself less homesick at the laundry and stayed longer hours than she might have; not just because of Mrs. Morgan's tirades, but because of Winston, one of the bellhops. Winston was cherry-black, as Lil Ma would have said, with eyes so warm they melted her insides.

Cassie started meeting Winston for breakfast. He was charming and handsome and eighteen years old. He told her about his life, growing up in Remington with his granny, his mama, and his six brothers and sisters. Cassie found herself envious of the idea of brothers and sisters and even more envious of the extended family of aunts, uncles, and cousins, all growing up in the same section of town. She told Winston about Grandmother and Lil Ma. There had been nothing else but laundry, and as for extended family, only Judith. She didn't mention Grandmother's grand

plan for lightening the family bit by bit, or the albino boy, and
certainly not Porterville, but she did tell him some of the adven-
tures she and Judith had had on the way from Heron-Neck, and
some of them, mostly the ones about Judith and her harebrained
schemes in pursuit of fame, were funny. Cassie and Winston
laughed together.

Later, Cassie felt guilty for laughing at Judith, and at the
widow's house, she turned on the radio very softly, right around
midnight, to pick up WINS. She tried to listen as often as she
could, straining to hear Judith's voice among the background
singers, but she was never sure she did. One night, though, it was
different.

. . . tonight we have a special hello from one sister to another—
you know who you are, gal!

The disc jockey played the song they'd heard at the Wivells'
coming from the albino boy's bedroom, and on the road to Porterville, the time they hadn't found the place. It was the energetic
colored version too, not the mediocre white rendition. Cassie
knew the song was sent from Judith, better than a postcard. It
gave her hope that Judith was on the right track and had at least
learned how to use a telephone, since that was the way you got
dedications onto Radio WINS.

The song ended, and the DJ played some ads. There was no
more message from Judith. Nothing like *I have become a big star
an' jus' you lissen.*

She introduced Winston to Radio WINS, and they would stay
up late together in the laundry room listening to radio and sometimes even dancing to the music. He was a good dancer, not the
same way as Judith was, but when he took her into his arms the
first time and spun her around, she thought she might pass out

with joy. For the first and only time, she felt sympathy for Grandmother for falling in love with a colored man and having a child
by him. Heat was what she felt right now.

Late in August, certain that by now Grandmother had discovered
the benefits of the tar and was long gone, Cassie wrote to Lil Ma.
She used the Veranda stationery, which was thick and cream-
colored, with a hand-drawn sketch of the hotel and its address
embossed at the upper left corner. It was beautiful paper, and she
wrote on it in her best hand.

> *Dear Lil Ma,*
>
>   *I am writing to tell you that I am well and in Virginia. Judith*
> *found her daddy. I don't know if he ran off with a hoor or not,*
> *but it turns out even though we have the same great-great-great*
> *granddaddy, there was no money for Judith or me in his estate.*
> *Bill Forrest got $85 as far as I know, and had to pay it all to*
> *the hotel where he was staying and where I am working.*
> *Otherwise the police would have took him to jail. I can send you*
> *money if you need it and you should come up here if you want,*
> *but I am not coming back to Mississippi.*
>
>   *I have had many adventures, but I miss you.*
>
>

Your daughter,
Cassie
>

Days passed. Two weeks passed. In the laundry, steam rose in
starchy puffs from the iron. Light filtered in from high, bright
windows. The air was warm but not oppressive. The smell of bleach
was a pleasant tang. A letter was imminent. Cassie could feel it.
But the first piece of mail she got at the Veranda was a postcard
from Judith.

Eden Pomeroy gave it to her with a *tsk*, like she'd already read it.

> *Dear Cassie,*
>
> *I have made it to New York City. I stayin' with Shelly, who sings in clubs. She has give me a nice dress. We gonna be famous. Lissen for us on the radio.*
>
>

Your friend,
Judith Forrest

It was written in a scrawl—presumably Shelly's—barely more literate than Judith's blocky signature at the bottom. The black-and-white picture on the other side was of the Statue of Liberty. Cassie read the postcard again. *Your friend*, not *Your sister*. That told her everything Judith hadn't told Shelly, and that Shelly was white. There was no return address.

"Girls all alone in the big city," Eden Pomeroy said and threw the whites in the washer.

For the next few nights, Cassie stayed up late, listening to Radio WINS with the sound turned low. None of the singers sounded remotely like Judith. Her worry over Judith clouded her sense of how soon Lil Ma's letter would arrive. When Eden Pomeroy handed her an envelope from Mississippi a few days later, Cassie found herself relieved that it wasn't from Judith, full of veiled, worrisome news. She expected Lil Ma to be far more straightforward.

> *Dear Cassie,*
>
> *I hope this letter finds you. Your Grandmother left six weeks ago on the train. She wouldn't tell me where she was going. She didn't even pack her things. She just took half of all the money we had and left. Perhaps she came to see you? I saw Judith's momma,*

and she was angry that Judith had run off to be rich just like her
daddy, and now she is afraid that Judith will not send back any
of the money. I told her what you said in your letter, but it made
her even angrier.

Mrs. Duckett is running the laundry now, and I have enough
money to come on the train. You do not need to send anything.
I will be there on October 13 at 9:15 in the morning. I miss you
very much.

Your mother,
Adelaine

Adelaine. Not *Lil Ma*. But not *Lainey* either.

Lil Ma sounded puzzled over Grandmother, as though she
might find her in Remington. Since she'd mailed the tar from
Richmond, Cassie had wondered if that was where Grandmother
might go first, expecting to find her granddaughter erased and
waiting. Cassie had pledged to herself never to set foot in Richmond again. She thought about Grandmother, but as time passed,
she found her presence less insistent, as though Grandmother were
physically moving farther from Richmond, Remington, and maybe
even Virginia. Cassie folded the letter and put it in her pocket.

Iris, ironing sheets, said, "That from your crazy singin' friend?"

"It's from my mama. She's coming to see me." It was just the
beginning of October. Lil Ma would be here in ten days.

"All the way from Mississippi?" said Bethesda, pressing down
on her iron. "Just in time to keep you from gittin' in trouble with
that Winston boy."

"She already in trouble with *him*," said Iris. "Her mama comin'
up for the *weddin*.'"

Cassie denied that, and they laughed.

— ✦ —

On the morning of the thirteenth, Cassie walked down to the station. She'd wanted Winston to come, but he couldn't get the time off, and as she waited for Lil Ma on the train platform, she thought it might be better if Lil Ma didn't meet him right away. Lil Ma hadn't approved of the albino boy in Heron-Neck, but Winston was dark. Very dark. Even if Lil Ma had signed herself *Adelaine*, it didn't mean Grandmother's shadow had vanished completely.

The autumn morning was warm. There were only a few people at the station. Half a dozen white men stood together at one end of the platform, smoking cigarettes and checking their watches. A colored woman and three little children waited at the far end with suitcases and a picnic basket. A white woman stood alone between the two groups, hatless, smoothing her hair against a nonexistent breeze.

Cassie made her way toward the end of the platform where the woman and her children were. She passed the spot where Judith had waited through Cassie's two days as a white girl. It made Cassie nervous to be anywhere near there. Someone at the station might have witnessed Cassie's transformation. Some porter, some conductor, some engineer, some stationmaster with a bristly white beard. The fear that a guest at the Veranda would recognize her was a nightmare that often woke her.

The white woman on the platform turned to watch Cassie. She was elderly, with bleached-looking hair and a lot of lipstick. Her cloth coat was too heavy for the mild autumn air, but she hunched into it like she was cold. There was no way to get to the far end of the platform without passing her, and Cassie looked at other things—the leaves on the ground, the benches, the cloudless sky—anything to keep from looking at this woman whose eyes she felt examining her from head to foot. For a terrible second Cassie thought it was the waitress from the diner in Richmond who had offered her a place to live—back when she was white. But this woman was too old. Against her will and after months of resolve, Cassie glanced into the woman's face for just a second. As their eyes met, the woman flinched as though she'd actually been struck. She clutched her coat and backed away, and in that moment, Cassie saw the kinky iron color her hair had once been, her dark complexion.

Everything on the platform seemed to freeze. At their end, the white men paused in their smoking. At the other, the colored woman frowned in their direction. The white woman's face took on a terrible expression. "Get away from me," she whispered in Grandmother's voice. With gummy slowness she took a step and another. She fled with tremendous effort, across the tracks and away from Remington, her feet seeming to stick each time they touched the ground.

Cassie stumbled to the nearest bench and sat, seized with fear that the tar could work in reverse, and that when she looked at her own hands again, all the whiteness she'd left in Richmond would come rushing back. She kept her eyes on the trees on the other side of the tracks. Had this woman—Grandmother?—been on her way to Boston to be absorbed into the Porterville *community*? Cassie dared to examine her own hands, her arms, her ankles. All still cinnamon.

In a while the train came, carrying Lil Ma in the car at the end, reserved for colored people. When she finally saw Lil Ma, all she could do was sob in Adelaine's arms.

Lil Ma loved Winston. He was charming and beautiful, and she told Cassie in girlish whispers what a catch he was. Mrs. Morgan fell ill and became very frail. Instead of looking for work, Lil Ma took care of her. She sent letters weekly to the widow's daughter in Baltimore, describing Mrs. Morgan's worsening condition. Often there was no reply.

In the kitchen one November evening, over tea and ginger cookies, Lil Ma said, "I'm worried about her. She's fading. Someone in her family should be with her." Mrs. Morgan was asleep in the next room. Lil Ma kept her voice low. "Her daughter said she was glad we were taking care of her. She said she would try to come at Christmas. She sent money in case we need a doctor." Lil Ma was quiet for a long while. "Children should come when their parents are in need."

The house was silent. The tea cooled.

Lil Ma said, "Cassie, do you know why your grandmother left?"

Cassie took a sip of too-hot tea and swallowed, too guilty to speak.

"Do you have any idea where she is?"

"Nome," said Cassie, "I don't."

Lil Ma put her hands around her teacup and said in a soft voice, "I can't even tell if she's alive anymore."

Winston proposed to Cassie at Thanksgiving, and their engagement was announced in the colored paper, the *Remington Opportunity*. Lil Ma cut out the announcement, and instead of sticking it on the wall, like in Heron-Neck, she put it in a nice frame. Mrs. Morgan died right after Christmas. Lil Ma sent the obituary to Mrs. Morgan's daughter, who had never come down from Baltimore. Mrs. Morgan's daughter gladly sold them the house. Cassie used some of Miz Eula's money, telling Lil Ma she'd been saving up. Miz Eula would have approved, she thought.

In January, Judith's second postcard came to the Veranda. This time the writing was even and crisp; an educated hand. Even Judith's signature looked neater.

> Dear Cassie,
>
> I am doing well. I am waiting tables. I am singing in church every Sunday. Jesus is my savior.
>
> God bless you.
> Judith Forrest

The picture on the other side was of Radio City Music Hall. There was no return address.

"Judith Forrest is singing for the Lord," said Lil Ma. "Maybe she's finally on the right track."

"At least she has a job," said Cassie. Iris and Bethesda had told her everything they knew about New York City. They had friends, uncles, and cousins of cousins who knew how terrible and dangerous big-city life was. Cassie did her best to sort the absurd from the likely, but the likely was pretty bad.

The picture of Radio City Music Hall was in color, decked out with Christmas lights arranged to resemble an immense tree and a line of huge candles. The candles were twice the size of the people standing below in the snow, waiting to get inside. The place would speak to Judith. Clearly anyone who sang in the Music Hall would end up on the Radio. She hoped they sang gospel in the Radio City.

One rainy Sunday when Winston had to work and Lil Ma was napping, Cassie wrote a letter to Judith. There was no address to send it to, but Cassie felt that if she ever found out where Judith was, a reply would have to be quick. Judith didn't seem to stay in one place for long.

Dear Judith,

    I am still working at the Veranda Hotel. My mother is here, too. I am engaged to Winston Childs, who is a bellboy. We plan to get married in March and start a family.

    I have gotten your postcards from New York City. Iris and Bethesda tell me how dangerous that place is, but I know you will make the best of what you find. I am listening to the radio as often as I can. I know I will hear you one day.

    Miz Eula left you an envelope with some money in it. I haven't opened it so I don't know how much, but when you have an address, please let me know so I can send you your part of our legacy.

She stopped. The hopeful words felt empty. Judith always acted like she enjoyed living by her wits, but she would almost certainly end up at the mercy of strangers with less talent and better lies. Cassie had pictured Judith homeless, dirty, frightened—at best, unhappily waiting tables—but always moving forward. She had never imagined Judith defeated, and she had no advice to offer. She wrote,

    If you ever get tired looking for fame and fortune, please come back to Remington. We will always have a place for you.

                              Your sister,

                              Cassie

On the first day of spring, Cassie and Winston got married in their own backyard. Friends from the hotel threw rice and peach petals. Their picture was in the *Opportunity*, and Lil Ma cut it out and framed it. Cassie became pregnant, and Lil Ma bought a dozen frames, anticipating baby pictures.

One of the upstairs rooms would be the nursery, but now it

was full of odds and ends from the late Mrs. Morgan. Before she got too big to do anything practical, Cassie set herself the task of cleaning out the room and making it suitable for a baby. Between winter clothes, old shoes, and a trunk of the widow's things, she found Miz Eula's portfolio, which she had brought from the hotel and forgotten about. When Cassie opened it, nothing had changed. The onionskin layers, the swaddled glass daguerreotypes, the ancient newspapers, and the yellowed pages of poetry. Cassie had seen Miz Eula's obituary in the newspaper. It had been short, noting that she had been a guest at the Veranda for some time, but made no mention of her age. Cassie had meant to cut it out, but hadn't, and now, seeing the bits of the past that Miz Eula had insisted on keeping with her, an obituary seemed out of place, like an end to something that could never completely end. *What's important is the past*, Miz Eula had said. Cassie took the daguerreotypes carefully from their wrapping, brought them downstairs, and put them in the frames Lil Ma had brought home for the baby.

They fit nicely, and in the glance of light from the kitchen window, the images there from a century ago reflected in black and white.

ACKNOWLEDGMENTS

This book could never have been written without the following authors: William Faulkner (especially for his novel *Absalom, Absalom!*), Zora Neale Hurston, James Weldon Johnson, W. E. B. DuBois, Charles W. Chestnutt, Laura C. Jarmon, Marc Fisher, Lorraine Johnson-Coleman, Dennis Danvers (for giving me *A Richmond Reader* on indefinite loan), Carol A. Kolmerten, Stephen M. Ross, Judith Bryant Wittenberg, Adam Braver, Edward P. Jones, Langston Hughes, Gloria Naylor, and last but not least, Toni Morrison and Alice McDermott.

People I can't thank enough for their help and support and numerous rereadings of the manuscript: Lisa Grubka, my fabulous agent, and Barbara Jones, my amazing editor and teacher.

Any acknowledgment would be incomplete without thanking Vicki Sipe for her love and patience when I needed a quiet house, and her willingness to read, read, read, and read again.

ABOUT THE AUTHOR

SUZANNE FELDMAN, a recipient of the *Missouri Review*'s Jeffrey E. Smith Editors' Prize and a finalist for the Bakeless Prize in fiction, holds an MA in fiction from Johns Hopkins University and a BFA in art from the Maryland Institute College of Art. She is the author of award-winning science fiction titles such as *Speaking Dreams* and *The Annunciate*, published under the pen name Severna Park. Her short fiction has appeared in *Narrative*, *The Missouri Review*, *Gargoyle*, and other literary journals. She lives in Frederick, Maryland.

Feldman, Suzanne, 1958-
Absalom's daughters